Stay Lucky

by
LETA BLAKE

An Original Publication from Leta Blake Books
Written and published by Leta Blake
Cover by Dar Albert
Formatted by BB eBooks

First Edition Copyright © 2018 by Lucky Honey Books
Second Edition Copyright © 2020 Leta Blake Books
Print Edition
All rights reserved.

First Print Edition, 2018
Second Print Edition, 2020
ISBN: 979-8-88841-013-4

Re-imagined Fairy Tales

Flight
Levity

Paranormal & Shifters

Angel Undone
Omega Mine

Horror

Raise Up Heart

Omegaverse

Heat of Love Series
Slow Heat
Alpha Heat
Slow Birth
Bitter Heat

For Sale Series
Heat for Sale

Coming of Age

'90s Coming of Age Series
Pictures of You
You Are Not Me

Audiobooks

Leta Blake at Audible

Discover more about the author online

Leta Blake
letablake.com

A second chance to build the family of their dreams…

Grant long ago gave up on a relationship with Leo. After all, even a successful doctor can't compete with a movie star. He never stood a chance.

But now, Leo's back with his adorable, genius daughter in tow. Did Leo come home looking for a fresh start?

Before the two of them can build a new family for themselves, they'll have to face health scares, the return of Leo's ex, and their own insecurities. Will the chemistry between them be enough to overcome the challenges?

Author Notes on the Second Edition: This book was originally drafted in early 2010 during a time when I was keen on working out particular themes in my writing: second chances, opposites attract, medical romance, and rudely honest heroes. I re-worked this novel for publication in 2018 under my pen name Halsey Harlow. In an effort to consolidate my books, I'm re-releasing all Halsey Harlow books as Leta Blake. Also, at the time of writing this book, my daughter was four years old. I modeled much of Lucky's behavior after her, including her obsession with Greek Myths. Some betas found the character of Lucky unbelievable for a five-year-old. Well, gosh, I always knew my daughter was unbelievable in every way! It's nice to have that confirmed.

For Luck

Warning: if you're employed in the medical field, some suspension of disbelief may be required.

Prologue

THE CICADAS RATTLED endlessly in the trees, filling the humid summer evening with sound. The chill of the soda bottle in his palm was the only relief from the sticky balm of the overheated summer as Grant relaxed back into the wooden lawn chair. He watched the blur of little Lucky's pale legs darting beneath her pale-yellow dress. Her brown hair trailed out behind her, as she skirted the edge of the glassy pond.

Holding one fist aloft, Lucky called out, "I have vanquished the foul Medusa! I, Perseus, shall save you now, oh, my darling Andromeda!"

"Are you certain the birth certificate wasn't forged?" Grant asked, sipping his beer and wiping the sweat from his upper lip. He ran a hand through his sweaty dark hair, and then over his equally dark chest hair, proudly shirtless and baking in the sun. His khaki shorts clung to his legs in the evening heat.

"Yes, I'm sure, jerk," Leo answered, twirling a piece of mint in his hand and sniffing it occasionally. He wore a white T-shirt and cut-off jean shorts. His wheat-colored hair swooped back from his forehead in a loose fall.

"She doesn't look or act like she's five, and this thing for Greek Myths is—"

"Precocious, I know." Gray eyes sparkling, Leo grinned at him.

Grant wrinkled his nose. "Ehhh, yeah, no, I was gonna go with weird."

"Her life's pretty out of control right now," Leo said. "The myths are messy, too, but they have their own kind of justice. Medusa's head turns the sea-monster to stone; Andromeda and Perseus are happy together."

"Zeus can't keep his pants on."

Leo laughed. "True. But I think she needs the myths right now."

"She needs *Sesame Street*."

Leo rolled his eyes adorably. "Come on, you love it."

Grant shrugged. He did. He loved taking Lucky around to the nurses' stations and watching all their faces go from delighted to confused in ten seconds flat. He loved the feel of her little hand in his and the way she smiled whenever she saw him. And he loved the most the way her father looked just a little healthier when Lucky was around.

It'd been ten months since he'd seen Leo for the second first time, and six months since he'd been able to do this like it was a regular thing, like it was part of his life that wasn't going to disappear. Six whole months of Lucky doing dot-to-dots at the table, calling out biology questions as they struck her, while Grant and Leo chopped up salad in the kitchen. Six whole months of the best days of his life.

"What's a brain eat, Dr. Grant?" Lucky had asked the prior Friday.

"Not junk food," Leo had said. "I can tell you that much."

Grant explained about glucose and Lucky had nodded along, saying, finally, "So, it does eat sugar. Jello has sugar."

"It's different," Leo hastened to clarify. "Tell her Grant."

Grant sighed. "My brain, which we all know is the greatest brain in the state, much less the room—"

"Why not say the whole country?" Leo smirked.

"I was attempting that modesty thing you're always telling me about."

"And failing."

"Because it's a lie! This proves my point! Modesty is just a lie designed to make others feel better about being losers."

Leo laughed and shook his head at Grant.

Clearing his throat, Grant had gone on, "So, Lucky, as I was saying, the greatest brain in the whole country loves to eat the sugar from Jello."

"Oh, Grant," Leo chided.

"Red Jello, especially. Either flavor, strawberry, cherry, I don't care, so long as it has those extra mind- and mood-altering substances in the dye. You know the dye made from smashed poisonous bugs and coal by-product? Yep, that's what my brain likes."

Leo had punched his arm, and it still made Grant happy to think of the smile that Leo had tried to hide under his mock anger.

That was three days ago, and now Lucky splashed in the edge of the water alongside the pond, slashing at the air, killing invisible monsters. Leo was probably right that it made her feel better to destroy something in her imagination when she couldn't kill the thing that terrified her the most in her actual life.

"What are you thinking about?" Leo said, tossing the mint at him. "You look unhappy."

"Tomorrow," Grant said. "Muresan is an arrogant idiot who barely scraped by with an A minus in his high school chemistry class, so why they let him anywhere near people's bodies with a scalpel, I don't know, and why you're going to let him touch you with it—"

"You looked up his high school records? Is that legal? How did you even manage that?"

"Your police chief Memaw shared my concerns," Grant said.

"Is it a good idea to undermine the patient's belief in his surgeon's competence like this?"

Grant opened and closed his mouth a few times before saying, "It's not too late to fly in someone better."

"Muresan's plenty good at this, Grant. He's done dozens of kidney transplants." Leo leaned over and rested his head on Grant's shoulder. "If we're going to worry about anything, we should worry about whether my sister is going to bail again. Mom says she's committed this time, but I don't know. It's a big thing, giving away a kidney. I'm sure she's scared."

"Oh, please. Last time I checked, you're raising her—" Grant barely stopped himself from saying bastard, just in case Lucky could hear him. "You're raising Lucky, and so I'd say she owes you. If her little feelings are in an uproar about having her side cut into and a pretty little scar left behind—"

"She's still my kid sister."

"Yeah, well, she's not a kid." Grant pointed at Lucky who was throwing sticks into the water. "That? That's a kid. And she needs you because her bratty mother hasn't done the right thing with her life even once since she was seventeen years old, so spare me your consideration for Hannah's feelings."

"Why, Dr. Anderson, who knew you were so opinionated?"

Grant said, "Everybody."

"I probably should be offended."

"Why?"

Leo rolled his eyes. "Whatever. I can't be bothered to explain it to you tonight. I'd rather think about other things. Like how nice it will be to feel better. I've been meaning to show you a thing or two," Leo said, wagging his brows suggestively.

"Yeah, right," Grant said. "Try the other way around."

"Like I said, it'll be nice."

"I don't always play nice."

"No joke." Leo laughed. "You're worse than a five-year-old when it comes to sharing, eating well, sleeping, and generally maintaining social decorum."

"I have to beat the competition," Grant said, nodding Lucky's way. "I can't let her win, can I? What kind of example would that set?"

"Somehow, I think you've got this all backward." Leo rested his head back against his chair and scooted down. "As much as I want to stay out here forever, watching Lucky, and making the day last, I'm getting tired."

Grant said nothing, the sweat on his body feeling suddenly cold. Tomorrow morning Dr. Ken Muresan would be cutting into Leo, taking the kidney they would harvest from Hannah in the adjoining operating room and putting it directly into Leo's right side, just above his non-functioning right kidney. Then they'd sew him up, leaving a fresh new scar on Leo's right side to match the one on his chest.

"I'm scared," Leo said.

"You'll be fine," Grant said.

"If something happens to me, I want you to know that Curtis is still legally her other parent. He's promised, though, to give up his rights and to allow my mother to adopt Lucky."

"Leo," Grant said, putting up a hand because he couldn't hear this. He couldn't think about this.

"Just listen, okay? And I've told my mom that I want you in her life. Okay? Promise me, if something happens to me, you'll be there for Lucky. No matter what."

Grant stared at Leo, and he felt like he could see Leo's brain, see the twisted, riveting gray matter that housed the person that Grant loved. "I give you my word."

Leo relaxed back into his seat again. "Thank you."

Grant stared at the side of Leo's face, the way his neck met with his jaw line, and the length of his lashes blinking slowly.

Lucky ran up to them, then, her hands covered in mud, and she held them out dramatically, saying, "Out, damn spot! Out, I say!"

Grant looked pointedly at Leo, who smiled and said, "Okay, so maybe weird."

Chapter One

Ten Months Earlier

GRANT WAS HAVING a terrible day. It'd started with a patient dying on the table. Unexpected damage that blocked the way to the tumor had resulted in one defining moment when Grant made a cut and a surprise bleeder spurted across the room.

It'd gone downhill from there, and the DNR made it final, even when Grant wasn't convinced it'd needed to be.

Then, inexplicably, his lunch had been stolen out of the freezer by some jackass. He wasn't even sure why, given that it was just a disgusting microwavable thing. *Then*, when he'd decided he'd just have to endure the dubious offerings of the hospital's cafeteria, he found it was closed for some kind of routine cleaning or maintenance. Grant didn't know which, and Grant didn't care.

He was hungry and angry as he stomped across the third floor's main lobby. And that's when he saw Leo Garner, *the* Leo Garner who'd dumped Grant in favor of his aspiring actor ex six years prior. He stood talking to a nurse, smiling, laughing, and gesticulating with his hands in a way that'd always made Grant's heart stop to take notice.

Why? *Why?*

And why now? After a day like today? Leo wasn't supposed to be here in Grant's hospital. He was supposed to be across the country with his now super-famous and super-hot boyfriend, Curtis Banks. What the hell? It wasn't even Christmas!

Without thinking twice, Grant turned on his heels and went to physician's locker room. He stripped out of his lab coat and scrubs, threw on his jeans and button-up shirt, and grabbed his bag. He was done with the day. Just done. He didn't care he that he had paperwork up to his ears, or that nurses would be left making frantic phone calls in confusion. Because for the first time in as many years as he'd worked at Appalachian Medical, Dr. Grant Anderson had decided enough was enough. A dead patient, no food, and an ex-boyfriend showing up in his hospital, on top of three weeks of keeping to a relentless pace in order to prove himself worthy of the recent promotion he'd been denied, had caught up to him. So, after telling the charge nurse he was leaving, he simply walked out and didn't look back.

Dramatic maybe, but he just knew if he didn't get away from Appalachian Medical right *now*, he was going to injure someone.

Possibly himself.

Back in his apartment, Grant popped open a beer and tore into his fast food burger. It tasted like sawdust. He stared at the blank television screen. Given the kind of day he was having, it didn't come as any surprise that there was nothing to watch. Even the cable company had apparently decided to pile on, presenting him with Pollyanna Lifetime Television bullshit or screaming politicians as his options, and the one soap opera he considered sinking into mind-numbing hell with currently featured a storyline with an idiot soap-opera-gay who couldn't choose between two equally ugly losers.

Grant threw the remote to the opposite side of the sofa. "Whatever. It's not like he'll get to sleep with either of them anyway. The American Family Association would burn the studio down."

He rubbed at his eyes and shook his head, trying to get a grip on the low, thrumming irritation that coursed through him.

His cell phone rang. Grant glanced at the caller ID and cursed. "Anderson," he said, holding the phone to his ear.

"Hey, partner," Dennis McGraw, his chief of staff, husband of his best friend, and his arch-nemesis extraordinaire, said cheerily. "Taking a mental health day?"

"My disappearance made the hospital message board so soon?" Grant asked, shaking his head in annoyance.

"Yep. Word is Dr. Anderson cracked up today. Finally. Money is exchanging hands all over the place. Apparently, there had been an ongoing pool over whether or not you were even human," Dennis said.

Grant rolled his eyes. "If you cut me, do I not bleed?"

"We weren't sure. Not that I condone that kind of thing. Hold on a second." Muffled, as though talking to someone beside him, he went on, "No, give me two twenties and two fives, and I'll give you three ones, and we're good. Huh? Sure. Okay, I'm back."

"Not that you condone that kind of thing," Grant repeated.

"So, you lost a patient today. Take a break. Work it out. We'll see you tomorrow."

Grant hung up on Dennis before anything else could be said.

It wasn't about the patient. Well, it was, but it was the cafeteria that had really been too much for him. It certainly wasn't seeing Leo that'd driven him out of the place. Sure, it was obnoxious running into his ex like that, but he'd endured the last four Christmas encounters just fine.

It wasn't as though he'd been in love with the guy. So far, his heart was pure in that regard. There'd never been any disturbing taint of unregulated affection. But, if he were honest with himself, which he was admittedly reluctant to be, with Leo it had been a very close thing.

If Curtis Banks had never returned to Blountville, North

Carolina, in order to beg Leo to leave for Los Angeles with him, using their history as high school sweethearts to persuade him, and promising Leo a bright future as the boyfriend of a brand-new TV star? Well, God only knew if Grant could have fallen down that terrifying rabbit hole known as love.

He shuddered.

Thankfully that hadn't happened. Truth be told, Grant didn't want to even think about where he could have ended up. He'd never been a fan of heartbreak. He didn't find it romantic, or charming, or sexy. He preferred clean relationships of casual friendship and good sex, uncomplicated by that painful affection he'd nearly had a taste of, and then so luckily been denied.

So, no, Leo was *not* the reason he'd left the hospital. It was a cumulative effect of unwelcome things. Grant turned the television back on and clicked through the channels again. Once again, there was nothing good on. He paused on the soap opera and rolled his eyes, groaning when the soap-opera-gay kissed one of the guys pining after him, while the other watched from around the corner with a broken-hearted face.

"Loser," Grant muttered, putting the empty beer bottle on the coffee table and leaning back in hopes of falling asleep. "I'd never be a loser like that."

The melodramatic swells of the soap-opera's love theme followed him into his dreams.

Chapter Two

A COUPLE OF days later, Grant's life had slowed down from the jam-packed insanity of making up for all of the things he'd walked out on after he'd found the cafeteria closed. Dennis McGraw, in all his blue-eyed, blond handsomeness, cornered Grant in the hallway, though, and congratulated him for taking time for self-care after his loss on Monday.

"It's always hard when we lose a patient, and I'm glad you did the right thing by giving yourself a break."

Grant stared at him, saying sarcastically, "Thanks for your permission, *friend*."

Dennis narrowed his eyes, sensing the challenge. "Alec sends his love." It was his way of reminding Grant of one important reason why they shouldn't fight.

"Of course he does."

Dennis sighed. "Do you have to be this way? I know you think I'm not good enough for him, but Alec is happy."

"There's happy and then there's *happy*."

"Let's not get into this again."

"You started it."

Just then some nurses came by and they both went their separate ways. They'd agreed that fighting in front of the staff over every ridiculous thing might cause a drop in morale, and while Grant didn't care about morale, so long as patients weren't dying and people were getting well, Dennis had convinced him with some not too disputable statistics that the two were related.

And it wasn't that Dennis wasn't good enough for Alec, it was that he *really* wasn't good enough for Alec. He'd started their relationship while still married to a woman, and then dragged the divorce out for over a year, torturing Alec's heart along the way. How was Grant supposed to forgive that, just because Dennis had chosen Alec in the end and then married him? Being best man had been one of the hardest things he'd ever done, but he'd at least managed to keep his mouth shut when the minister asked if anyone knew of any reason the couple shouldn't be joined together.

Plus, Dennis had stolen the chief of staff position from him. He'd had it in the bag until Dennis threw his name in the hat. Or so he liked to believe. Alec said he was delusional, but Grant knew he was leadership material.

Shoving those thoughts aside, Grant resolved to be nicer to Dennis the next time he saw him, for the staff's sake, and for Alec's. Maybe he'd even manage a semi-genuine smile. That'd make Alec happy at least. And, weirdly, Grant liked to make Alec happy. Their friendship was one of the only important relationships in his life.

The day passed quite nicely after that. Grant's patients weren't too weepy and their families weren't too pushy, for a change. The nurses skedaddled as soon as they saw him coming, just the way he liked. And the cafeteria was serving three-cheese lasagna, which was his absolute favorite, even if they were a little skimpy on the sauce at times.

He was still rolling the flavor around in his mouth, cheerfully enjoying the heavy, fatty feeling in his tummy, when he walked around the corner to see Leo Garner standing at the nurses' station again, laughing and smiling.

Just what the hell was he doing here? Didn't he have a life? In *California*? Last time Grant checked, that had been the case.

"Grant!" Leo called out as Grant tried to pass the station with his face buried in a chart, hoping to avoid any kind of interaction.

Grant stopped, turned slowly, and said, "Dr. Anderson to you, Leo. And what an unpleasant surprise to see you here on this fine autumn day. To what do we owe the honor?"

The nurse looked down at her forms uncomfortably, and Leo laughed. "You don't change at all, do you, *Dr. Anderson*? You're just as charming as ever." Leo smiled like he was happy to see Grant and tilted his head in a way that Grant was reluctant to admit was attractive.

"I have no idea what you mean."

"I just mean it's good to see you." Leo's smile turned sweet, which made Grant's chest feel tight. "Seriously," Leo went on, touching his arm, fingers gripping Grant's white lab coat. "You're looking great. How's life treating you?"

Grant's eyes narrowed. "It's treating me the way it always treats me. Like a busy surgeon. Now, if you'll excuse me, I need to go *be* a surgeon." Grant tapped his watch. "Time's a wastin'."

Leo's gray eyes twinkled with amusement as Grant stalked quickly away.

His heart hammering and sweat popping out on his forehead, Grant hoped that whatever was bringing Leo to the hospital would end soon, so that Grant could go back to his happy little bubble of work, more work, beer, occasional hookups, and more work.

Leo Garner had a very unpleasant record of messing up Grant's well-ordered life. And in that regard, Grant didn't want to see history repeat itself.

Chapter Three

"I HEARD LEO Garner is back in town," Alec said over the rim of his wineglass, his kohl-lined eyes all-knowing and wide.

Grant still wasn't sure how his best friend in Blountville had turned out to be the town's most flamboyant queer, but the fact remained that he was.

Still, Alec was worth all the double-takes and outright stares when they went out on the town together. His honesty, loyalty, and determination to be Grant's friend, even when Grant wasn't very nice to him, were priceless. Plus, he was pretty, and sweet, and deserved only good things for having endured growing up so incredibly, obviously gay in conservative Blountville, North Carolina.

Alec leaned closer, shrinking the distance between them on Grant's comfortable leather sofa. The spaghetti Alec had whipped up like a magic man when he first arrived was now balanced on their knees in large, half-full bowls. "Leo Garner," Alec repeated with a raised brow. "Back. In. Town."

"And?" Grant said, putting as much disdain into the word as possible. He shoved a bunch of spaghetti into his mouth, slurping up the noodles, hoping that being gross would distract Alec from this line of questioning.

"Well, aren't you even curious about *why*?" Alec asked. His lashes blinked long and slow, revealing the glitter eye shadow he insisted on wearing basically everywhere.

Grant rolled his eyes.

As a matter of fact, after seeing Leo at the hospital again on Saturday, he had indeed been very curious about why. So he'd checked the patient rosters looking for one of Leo's relatives, assuming that someone in the extended clan must be pretty sick for Leo to have come all the way from Los Angeles to visit them.

But what he'd found was something else entirely.

In fact, what he'd uncovered had now relentlessly occupied his thoughts for days. Beer didn't fix it, the hand job from the Grindr hookup a few towns over didn't fix it, and the two surgeries he'd been lead on since he'd found out the truth hadn't driven it from his mind.

The facts were: Leo had undergone a heart replacement three years earlier in Los Angeles due to massive damage from myocarditis, and he now suffered from transplant-related kidney failure. Dialysis. Three times a week. Indefinitely. And Leo couldn't be added to the transplant list due to the prior heart transplant making him a bad risk. Grant had looked that up as well. It was a rough situation.

Why he was in Blountville instead of Los Angeles dealing with it was beyond Grant's understanding, though. That was a mystery he had as yet to unravel. Alec probably knew the answer to it because he was a notorious gossip who knew everything about everyone, plus he bought every single gossip rag with their hometown superstar, Curtis Banks, on the cover. But if Grant asked Alec, then he'd have to admit to caring one way or another about Leo Garner. And he wasn't about to do that.

Grant cleared his throat. "I don't know why you think I'd be curious about him."

"He's sick," Alec said, keeping his tone gentle and watching Grant's reaction closely.

Grant forced his face into a stony blankness, and then decided even that might be too revealing, so he stuck out his lower lip and tried to play it off. "Too bad, so sad."

"Don't be a jerk," Alec said, putting his wineglass down and shifting his unfinished spaghetti to the coffee table. "I know you care about him."

"*Cared* about him," Grant clarified. "Past tense."

"Right," Alec said, raising a brow. "And that would explain why your face twitches every time someone says his name, and why his annual Christmas visits are near the top of your rather long list of why you hate the season."

Grant gaped at him.

Alec shook a finger at him. "Yes, I saw that list, idiot. You tacked it up over your toilet last year. I suppose it was to remind yourself every time you took a leak? Though, really, I can't see how you'd forget to be a Grinch. You're practically a professional at it."

"That was private."

"I take pisses here, you realize. And I can read, you know."

"Congratulations, you made it past first grade." Grant shoved more food in, hoping they could move past this topic but blanking on any other to distract Alec with and secretly curious as hell about why Leo wasn't in Los Angeles for treatment. Lord knows California's options for hospitals and treatment were far superior to Blountsville's tiny little regional facility, especially with the Leo's super-rich, super-famous actor-boyfriend's money to back him up.

Alec sighed. "Grant, he's quite sick. I think you should, you know, admit that you care and see if you can help him."

"I'm a cardiothoracic surgeon. He's in renal failure. It's not possible for me to help him."

Alec smirked. "You already knew all of this, didn't you? Oh, I get it. You don't *care*, but you spent hours researching and investigating what's going on with him, I bet." Alec sipped his wine with a gleeful grin. "I see how it is."

Grant stood up, grimacing. He collected Alec's plate from the coffee table and headed toward the kitchen. His open-plan apartment was sparsely decorated with furniture he'd collected since graduating from med school, and Alec was always on him about leveling it up. He didn't see a reason for that, though. Who would it be for? He didn't bring men home to fuck, and he didn't exactly need to impress himself, now did he?

Dinner with Alec was something he'd looked forward to all week. He missed his best friend now that Alec was so busy making a life with Dennis. Grant had been happy to think they'd spend a few hours alone together tonight. But now, Grant thought maybe he'd just tell him to go home. This line of discussion was ruining his appetite and his fun.

"Oh, come on, Grant!" Alec exclaimed following behind him with his wine firmly clutched in one hand. "Don't you even want to know the rest?"

"No," he said, taking Alec's wineglass from him and draining it himself in one large gulp. He slammed the empty glass down on the kitchen counter. "I don't."

"Leo's done with Curtis. Totally and completely done. I have it on very good authority," Alec said, crossing his arms over his chest and staring at him with happy, shining eyes. "Don't you get it? This is your chance, Grant!"

"My chance? For *what*?"

"Happiness!"

"Are you insane? How on earth is this *anyone's* chance for happiness? He's incredibly sick, he's an emotional screw-up, and—"

"And you're a prize?"

"Thanks, Alec. I was going to say, he's sick *and* on the rebound. So, frankly, I don't have any desire to be his trampoline again, *even if I wanted to*, which I don't, because I am quite happy on my own, thank you very much. I enjoy my job, my solitude, and I enjoy *not* dealing with indecisive, dramatic, heart-breaking queens."

Alec groaned and threw his head back. "Yes, fine. Tell yourself all of these pretty lies about how your true love is *surgery*, like you've got a scalpel fetish, and I'll say liar, liar pants on fire."

"Mature."

"Truth," Alec answered, grabbing another wineglass from Grant's cupboard and filling it from the open wine bottle on the counter.

Grant rinsed the dishes off in the sink, before turning around to shake a fork in Alec's direction. "And don't think I don't see just what you did here."

"What?"

"Coming over like we're going to hang out just to two of us when you really just wanted to poke at me with this past weakness I briefly indulged in, pushing my buttons."

"Did it push your buttons?" Alec sounded happy about that.

"Plus, you left Mina with Dennis, even though you knew I'd rather see that cute munchkin face of hers than have this ridiculous conversation about Leo Garner."

"Mina is Dennis's daughter! He deserves alone time with her, too." Alec seemed on the edge of laughing, his mouth trembling at the edges with suppressed glee. "Look, all I'm saying is that you loved Leo and—"

"I did not!" Grant flushed hot, and he didn't know if it was with anger or humiliation. "I should have guessed when you showed up alone that you had something up your sleeve, but little could I have imagined this particular come-to-Jesus spiel about love, or whatever the hell this is. But, if I'd known, I would have shoved you back out the door the minute you came in."

"Good thing that I waited until after dinner then."

"It's not too late."

Alec raised his glass. "I've had far too much wine for you to kick me out with a good conscience now."

Grant turned around, dropping the dishtowel on the counter. "Leo Garner isn't the end-all and be-all of men for me, understand? There are plenty of gay men in this state, Alec. Hell, in this *town*, even."

Alec hooted at that ridiculous exaggeration.

"Why are you trying to force the recently returned, emotional cluster-fuck, probably-dying Leo Garner on me?"

"Force is a strong word, but as for the why? It's because I saw what he did to you," Alec said, tenderly. "I saw how he affected you. He changed you, Grant. He made you *better*."

"No! He made me *worse*." Leo had made Grant care and that had made him vulnerable in a way he'd never experienced before. It'd been the worst experience of his life. "And if you saw so much, then maybe you also saw how he chose his ex-boyfriend and took off across the country with *him*. I'm not going to play second choice *six years later* for what amounts to a pretty piece of ass."

"Call it what you will." Alec raised his brow and took a sip of wine. "I'll call it what it *is*."

"And just what is that?"

"Love. True Love."

Grant scoffed. "Alec, you are insane. This is not *The English Patient*. I am not *pining*. I don't pine. I've absolutely moved on, and I'm sure that Leo has too."

Alec laughed lightly. "You've never even seen that movie, have you?"

"I thought it was a book."

"It *is*, but, whatever, Grant. You're right, this isn't *The Eng-*

lish Patient."

"Well, I'm glad you're seeing logic for once and—"

"Because that story ended painfully. This one will end in the triumph of the human heart! Just you wait and see!"

Grant picked up his phone and chose the unfortunately familiar name.

"Are you calling Leo?" Alec asked eagerly, as though Grant was actually the easily-influenced fool he believed him to be.

"Come get your husband," Grant said when Dennis picked up. "He's drunk." He disconnected the call, taking Alec by the arm, removing the glass of wine from his hand, and dragging him toward the door.

"You wouldn't!" Alec said. "It's only 40 degrees outside, and I didn't bring a coat!"

"Here," Grant said, thrusting one of his toward him. "I'll throw in a cap, even." He pulled a green knit beanie over Alec's perfectly spritzed hair, leaving him looking surprised and a mess.

"Grant," he said, struggling a little as Grant pulled open the front door of his apartment and shoved him out onto the open-air walk-up. "Grant!"

"A few minutes in the brisk night air will do you good. Sober you right up," Grant said, slamming the door in Alec's face.

"Don't think I'll forget this, Grant!" Alec yelled through the door. "Don't think that I don't know what this means! It means I'm right! It means you're a goner! L-O-V-E! Love! I'm telling you!"

Grant leaned his forehead against the door and exhaled sharply.

"Triumph!" Alec yelled. "Of the human heart!"

Grant banged his head against the door in protest, and then slid in a heap to the floor. Outside, Alec sang the "kissing in a tree" song and other childish anthems of love.

Grant buried his face in his knees, breathing in and out slowly as the minutes dragged on. He knew when Dennis arrived because Alec yelled, "Darling! Guess who's a total asshole when he's in love?"

One thing was for sure: Grant needed to get a better best friend.

<h1 style="text-align:center">Chapter Four</h1>

A S LUCK WOULD have it—if Grant believed in luck, which given how his life had gone since basically birth, he *didn't*—Leo was at the hospital the next day, walking through the halls with a nurse, looking tired and ill.

Grant stared after him until the nurse led Leo between double doors into the dialysis room. An urge to follow rose up in him, and he shoved it aside. Leo Garner didn't need him. He had plenty of friends and family in Blountville. Besides, he was probably busy making new friends right this second with the nurses and the other dialysis patients. It took, after all, three to four long hours, three days a week to purge his blood of toxins. It sucked a lot of time out of a person's schedule to have a failing body. And Leo was probably knee deep in 'making the best of it.' That seemed like something he'd try to do.

Grant shook his head.

As the doors swung shut behind Leo and the nurse, the weird breathless feeling passed. Grant decided that it was entirely reasonable to chalk it up to gas from the chili he'd eaten from the cafeteria for lunch. Truly, it was delicious, but the beans could make anyone a walking gas leak. Frowning, he blamed Alec for planting a seed that would allow him to think for even a moment that the feeling could be due to anything else.

He went back to his patient chart, trying to figure out what the words were saying, but instead he started thinking about this one guy back in medical school, a Dr. Wallace, who'd been a kidney guy, one of the best. He wondered if the idiot Dr. Muresan, the fool in charge of the renal unit at Appalachian Medical, would be willing to consult with Wallace on Leo's case.

Grant had just made an about-face, prepared to go speak to Muresan himself, or possibly sneak another look at Leo's chart, when Carrie Jones, the best nurse around in Grant's opinion, nearly slammed into him, holding the hand of a little girl with messy, long brown hair and hazel eyes.

"Sorry, Dr. Anderson," Carrie said, pushing a stray bit of hair back into her ponytail.

"Just watch where you're going," Grant said, irritably, taking his frustrations out on the wrong person, as he was far too prone to do.

"No, you watch," said the kid, lifting a defiant chin.

Grant stared down at her.

Carrie said, "Oh, ho, ho, now. That wasn't very polite. I bet your dad wouldn't like that *at all*."

The girl sniffed haughtily. "I'm just saying, *he* ran into *us*, so he should watch."

Grant frowned at her.

She glared at Grant.

"You shouldn't act like a brat," Grant said. "It's not going to get you far in life."

"I guess you would know," she replied. It was surreal to hear such a well-timed and biting comment coming from her tiny, cute face. Grant liked children usually, but this one struck him as strangely precocious in a way that hit a little too close to home and brought back his own painful childhood memories.

"Lucky, don't be rude, sweetheart!" Carrie scolded.

"He was rude first."

The kid's name was Lucky? What asshole would do that to an innocent child? Grant felt sorry for her then, but she just stared at him without any regret.

"You're right," Grant said. "I was rude first. And I apologize."

Carrie looked shocked.

Lucky lifted her chin and said with great magnanimity, "Apology accepted."

"Come on, now. Let's get you down to peds. Sorry, Dr. Anderson," Carrie said as she pulled the little girl down the hall.

Grant watched after them, wondering what illness the child was in the hospital for. She looked healthy enough to him. He felt guilty for having called her a brat, especially if she was sick. The kids in peds were heroic and entitled to have their moody, bad days. He'd have to seek her out later to apologize again, and maybe give her a teddy bear from the gift shop.

He turned down the hallway with the best vending machine. It had the marshmallow gooey nugget things he liked. They would settle his mind like meditation did for the New Age wannabes he saw too many of at the gym. And, thanks to Leo Garner popping up all the time, his mind certainly needed help getting settled more and more these days.

• • •

IN GRANT'S OPINION, any successful surgery lasting over eight hours deserved a reward—and not just more marshmallow thingies from the vending machine, but a decent meal at a fancy restaurant and a nice drink or two.

Little Apron was quiet on a Tuesday night, and Grant sat alone at a table in the corner, staring into space, going over in his mind the crucial moments of the surgery: the thrill of discovering the exact positions of the masses behind the patient's esophagus and right lung, the way the layers had folded back under his scalpel like warm butter, and the triumphant moments of cleanly removing the masses after so many hours and so much effort. It'd been a good day.

Grant startled out of his memory as someone sat down beside him at his table. "Uh, no, I don't want any company," he bit out, annoyed. Then he glanced over and grit his teeth together to keep from screaming in frustration.

Leo smiled. "Me, either."

Grant glared at him. "Then why are you sitting here?"

"To avoid—"

At that moment, Leo's grandmother, Marie Garner, swept into the room, looked around, and made a beeline for Leo. Her little beehive hairdo and tanned cheeks were stretched into a wide, toothy grin. She wore her sheriff's uniform, but her gun wasn't in the holster at her side. Maybe she was off-duty. The fact that Blountville had a lady sheriff had come as a surprise to Grant when he first found out. He'd pegged the place as Bible Belt enough to want women in the kitchen, not on a crime scene— not that there was a ton of crime in Blountville—but apparently the town had a progressive underbelly at times.

"Look, do me a favor and go along with this," Leo whispered urgently.

Grant snorted. "Why should I—"

"Please," Leo begged. His gray eyes went super wide and so, so pretty that Grant felt a coil of heat in his abdomen.

But he couldn't give that much thought because Marie was upon them then. "Sugar-butt, I thought that was you. I was just on my way out the door when I saw you come in. Having dinner with Dr. Anderson?"

"No," Grant said.

"Yes," Leo answered.

"I see," Marie said, narrowing her eyes. "Dr. Anderson here has quite the reputation in town."

"For?" Grant asked.

"Memaw," Leo warned.

"For loose morals and being rude. I know you dated my grandson once before, but I'd urge you to reconsider taking up the habit again."

"I don't intend to."

Leo rolled his eyes, stood up, and kissed his grandmother's cheek, and she hugged him fondly. "Memaw, how are you?"

Grant remembered when he'd first accepted the position at Appalachian Medical, he'd found the names North Carolinian people called their grandparents sometimes weird, but after all these years, he was used to it.

"Well, I'm fine, sugar-butt. The question is, *how are you?*" She turned her attention away from Grant and focused on her grandson. "Your mother said there was an incident yesterday at the farm, and I've been worried sick ever since."

"The farm" was a little bit of land up in the mountains that Leo's family had passed down for several generations now. It had a barn, a small house, and a pond, but not much else. They didn't plant anything or even keep any animals. Grant had only been to it once before things had ended with Leo six years ago.

Leo waved his hand, shaking his head. "Ah, it was nothing, Memaw. I'm hale and hardy. Like a horse."

"Right, of course. That's why you need dialysis three times a week and all of those ridiculous medicines. Your mother showed them to me. Bottles and bottles of them." Marie leaned closer to him, her face drawn and tired. "It hurt me to see them all. When do they think you'll be better? Is there a new kidney in the works for you, or what now? And how can Memaw help? Should I make a few phone calls—?"

"No!" Leo interrupted. "No, Memaw. Thank you. My doctors are optimistic, and I'm sure I'll be fine."

Grant raised a brow. That was a lie, and he knew it.

"And, don't get involved, please. Mom's still trying to get in touch with Hannah. You know how touchy Jenn can be. I don't want anyone or anything to run her off before we get a chance to speak."

"What about your cousin, Felice? Or little Blaine? Have they been tested?"

"Blaine's just a kid, Memaw. And we did test Felice, just to see, but she's still too young."

"She's a match, though?" Marie said, looking thoughtful. No, *scheming*. Grant could nearly see her crime-solving skills engaging, looking for the solution.

"Yeah, Felice is a match, but, legally, she's too young, Memaw. She told me, though, that if I still need a kidney when she's eighteen, then her extra one is all mine."

"Cute kid, that one!" Marie smiled, but it didn't erase her worry. "Has her priorities straight. Not like your sister." Marie rolled her eyes. "Hannah, it's like she didn't get even an ounce of Meryl and Chuck's steadfastness in her genes. She's all unpredictable, unaccountable, and uncontrollable. Heck, she's a piece of work."

"She'll come through for me, Memaw," Leo said. "If she's even a match."

"Oh, I'll bet she's a match all right," Marie said knowingly. "Someone in this massive family of ours has to be." Marie's eyes narrowed, and she snapped her fingers rapidly before tugging her cell phone out of her pocket. "You know, I just recalled. I have something out in the squad car for you." She slanted a knowing gaze at Grant. "And if Dr. Anderson here makes any moves on your virtue while I'm gone, sugar-butt, don't stress yourself. I can take him."

Grant lifted the edges of his lips in a sarcastic smile as Marie walked away. "What's her problem with me?"

Leo sat down at the table again. "She's just overprotective of me right now. And she remembers some of your choice rude comments during that family dinner you came to with me that one time."

"The pie *was* mushy. I wasn't trying to be rude."

"Oh, Grant, you're such a handsome asshole," Leo said softly.

"Honest and asshole aren't the same things."

"True. And I admit I've always liked that about you."

"Whatever. Apparently your Memaw doesn't."

"She doesn't like the idea of me being with anyone, frankly. She loves me and accepts me, but I secretly think she believes my health issues are a punishment from God for my sexuality."

Grant stared bug-eyed at him. "You think that and you still love her?"

"People aren't perfect, Grant. And she'd do just about anything for me. Plus, she's never said anything of the sort. I just suspect it."

"Wow."

"Anyway, thanks," Leo said, looking at Grant from under his lashes.

"For what? Sitting here? No problem. I had nothing better to do tonight anyway. But now I'd like to finish up my dinner. Alone. So I can get home and catch up on *Wheel of Fortune.*"

Leo placed his hand on Grant's for a moment. It seemed to tingle where it touched Grant's skin and he frowned down at it, confused. Leo pulled away after a moment, and Grant couldn't help but feel disappointed.

"Thanks for…well, let's put it this way. If I were alone, she would have grilled me like a crime suspect. Questions about *everything,* and I didn't want to answer the personal stuff. Not tonight, anyway."

"Well, it looks like you're not past the danger yet, because here she comes again, and here I go." Grant threw his napkin down and started to stand up.

"Grant, stay. Please. Just a few minutes. Then she'll be gone, and we can—Memaw, you're back."

Grant sat back down, curiosity about the large, yellow envelope in Marie's hand winning out over his desire to make a big show about how much he did *not* care about Leo Garner or his business.

"I almost forgot, sugar-butt, but your attorney—though I can hardly believe it given Doug's track record in life—dropped some paperwork by my office for you this afternoon. He said you knew about it. Said you'd pick it up today, actually."

Leo swallowed hard and took the yellow envelope from Marie's hand. "Thanks, Memaw. I've been waiting for these. I meant to swing by earlier, but time got away from me."

"I figured. I planned to drop 'em by tonight. Are they what I think they are?" she asked.

"Yes."

"Well, he took his sweet ass time getting it back to you. How long does a signature take? I think he made it good and clear how little he truly loves—"

"Thanks again, Memaw," Leo said, standing up, kissing her cheek, and then turning her toward the door. "Sorry to be rude, but I'm catching up on old times with Grant, here. So, you know…"

Marie looked skeptical, but she bussed Leo's cheek again, and then straightened her uniform after they hugged. "Well, bring that daughter of yours over to see me tomorrow and all will be forgiven. I'll leave you with Dr. Anderson." She leaned down to Leo's ear and whispered, "Are you sure you don't need rescuing, sugar-butt? Everyone in town knows the man is a player who's after only one thing."

"I can hear you," Grant said.

"Of course you can," Marie said. "It was intended as a warning. My grandson is in delicate health, and I am the law around these parts, so make of that what you will."

"Memaw," Leo said, rolling his eyes and flushing. "Back off, all right? He's no threat to me."

"Whatever you say, sugar-butt," Marie said and then turned back to Grant. "It would be in your best interest, Dr. Anderson, not to upset him or strain him in any way, do you understand? Or your little seduction here could end with him flopping around like a fish on the floor."

"Memaw," Leo warned again.

Grant stared at her with an open mouth, not sure what to make of these accusations. He wanted to defend himself by pointing out that, hey, Leo had crashed his dinner party for one and was currently upsetting *him* for another, but he couldn't seem to get his tongue to cooperate.

"His heart, you get it?" She narrowed her gray eyes at him. "It's not up to the task."

"*Memaw*," Leo said, standing up and taking her by the elbow. "This is entirely inappropriate and not your business. Thanks for coming back with the papers. I'll see you later."

Marie shot Grant another warning glare, tapped her hip where her gun usually rested, and then finally left. Leo watched her go as he made exaggerated shooing motions with his hands.

"God, it's exhausting," Leo said, sitting down once more, elbows on the table and chin in one hand. "Everyone is so overprotective and nosy. I forgot what it was like living here, with everyone all up in your business. Los Angeles was nice like that. I don't think my neighbors there even knew my name."

"Which I'm sure you hated," Grant said.

Leo wrinkled his nose in that ridiculously endearing way that Grant wanted to hate. "Yeah. I kind of did." He raised his hand and asked the passing waiter for water.

Grant watched as Leo drank nearly half of the glass in one long swallow. "Shouldn't you be watching that?" Grant asked.

"Oh," Leo said, looking guilty. "Yeah." He pushed the water glass away. "That's about twice the amount I have at any one time now. Don't want to pressure my kidneys. It'd be nice to be able to eat and drink like a normal person again. Ah, well. If wishes were changes." Leo's eyes went distant. "Lots of things would be different."

Grant could only assume that Leo was talking about Curtis Banks, and he wondered, briefly, what the hell had happened there. But he didn't dwell on it, because Marie had said something else that'd caught his attention. Something he didn't quite believe he'd heard correctly.

"So, did I hear your grandmother right? You took the ultimate leap of faith and reproduced?" He wondered what a child of Leo's would look like. Would she have her father's dimpled chin? Or was she adopted?

"Yeah. Kind of," Leo said, distracted, looking at the envelope in his hands, turning it over and over, as though he could read the contents via x-ray vision. "Lucky."

Grant snorted. "Yeah right, you're lucky."

"No, she is," Leo said, his voice still distant.

"Wait. Your kid's name is Lucky?" Grant shook his head in disbelief. "Well, I'll be damned. So, you're telling me the little girl I met with Carrie at the hospital? The one who told me off for being rude? That was *your* kid?"

That got Leo's attention, and he broke into a smile. "Oh, you've met her, huh? I didn't realize." He leaned closer, invading Grant's space like he always had, and said, in a conspiratorial way,

"Yeah, she's a feisty one. Like her mom. But hopefully better. She will be if I have anything to do with it."

"And who the hell is her mom?" Grant asked. The way Leo spoke of her made it seem as though Grant should know.

"Oh, really? You hadn't heard? I'm sure it was the talk of Blountville at the time. And Curtis and I sold rights to her baby pictures to several more reputable gossip magazines and sites, along with an edited version of her story."

"Gossip isn't really my thing, Leo, in magazines or otherwise," Grant said. Though, he supposed that was exactly what he was engaging in at the moment, and he definitely heard plenty of it spilling from Alec's lips whenever they got together. "Besides, there's so much going on behind the scenes of this town that I can't keep up. And celebrity gossip is always the same: boring."

"How could you miss it, though? The magazines are all right there in the checkout line at the stores."

"Grocery to Go app," Grant said, sniffing. "I click the buttons. They deliver. But it doesn't matter. I'm sure whoever your baby mama is, she wasn't a top story for long."

"Hannah – my sister, Hannah – is Lucky's mother."

Now that Leo mentioned it, Grant did remember overhearing some nurses talking about Hannah Garner and saying something about her having a baby. He hadn't really meant to listen but whispers about the Garners always seemed to sink in and stick in his brain meats. It was annoying that Leo was probably the reason for that.

"Oh, that's right. So you're raising your sister's 'accident'."

Leo's smile faltered. "Charming as ever, I see."

Grant grimaced. He didn't mean to be such an asshole, but he didn't like to mince words either. "Listen, I didn't ask you to sit down, so if my company isn't to your liking, then go right ahead and—"

"Oh, come on. Lighten up," Leo said, smiling again. The shine in his gray eyes did weird things to Grant's insides. "Yes, I'm raising my sister's child. I've adopted her, actually. Well, Curtis and I did, and so, well…she's my child now. And these forms," Leo said tapping the envelope, "they give me full physical custody of her since Curtis is still in LA and traveling constantly with filming. We aren't together anymore."

"What's wrong with her?" Grant asked, dismissing any discussion of the annoying Curtis Banks out of hand.

"Who? Hannah? She's just a mess. It happens that way sometimes in a family," Leo said, looking uncomfortable.

"No, what's wrong with Lucky. Why is she in the hospital?" It seemed extraordinarily bad luck to have survived a heart transplant only to end up with a child in the hospital at the same time that Leo's kidneys had completely failed.

"I don't know what you're talking about."

"Carrie—a nurse—was taking her to peds," Grant said. "I assumed?"

Leo chuckled. "Oh, no. Thank God. I mean, knock on wood, right? But, no, sometimes things are just too crazy, and I can't find anyone to watch Lucky, so she has to come to the hospital with me. You know, during my dialysis. It gets boring for her. So, Carrie—we went to high school together—takes her down to peds to play with the healthier kids, or the toys, or something. I don't know. Lucky doesn't tell me much about it. She doesn't like to talk about the hospital."

"Peds is no place for a kid," Grant said.

Leo lifted his brows. "Um, it's *pediatrics*."

"It's for sick kids," Grant said. "There's a difference. And you should know that."

Leo paled, and Grant felt oddly guilty, which was idiotic, because Leo was the one who wasn't thinking things through here.

"Yeah, I see what you mean."

"The very existence of sick kids is the cruelest thing on this brutally cruel earth. No one should have to witness that, unless it's your calling or your own damn kid. Your daughter doesn't need to see that crap. Or hear about it. Hell, I'm an adult and I don't want to hear about it."

"Yeah," Leo murmured. "I guess you're right."

"Of course I'm right. Oh, and teach her some manners. She's quite rude."

Leo looked momentarily offended, and then he laughed. "Hello, pot meet kettle. But, point taken. I've heard her say some things lately that make me think I may have made a mistake moving her across the country." Leo's gray eyes darkened. "But I tried it every way I could think of, and, in the end, I didn't see what choice I had."

"I see," Grant said.

But he didn't see. In fact, he absolutely didn't understand a lot of things. Like why Leo's smile and laugh made his fingers tingle, his chest ache, and his head a little light. He was pissed off that he had these irrational reactions to a person who didn't have the sense to choose him six years ago and probably didn't have the sense to make a good choice now, either.

Not that Grant wasn't grateful for Leo's idiocy, because he was! He'd come awfully close to losing a lot more than a chunk of his pride, and God only knew where he'd be today if things had gone differently. He rubbed his chest where his heart beat vulnerably.

As for tonight, he'd had enough.

"Well," Grant said. "Since I was kind enough to endure your little performance for Memaw, I guess the least I can do is leave you with the bill."

"Oh, I don't know, I'm not the boyfriend of a rich superstar anymore." Leo leaned close again, tapping the table with his forefinger. "I'll have them start a tab for you. They can send you a bill in the mail."

Grant rolled his eyes. He threw some cash on the table, like characters did in the movies when they didn't give a damn. Grant hoped Leo got the same message. "Wish I could say it's been a pleasure."

He wanted to slap himself immediately. Couldn't he have come up with something more biting to say than that?

"Sure, see you around, Grant," Leo said.

"Hopefully not, Leo," Grant said and felt a weird combination of rage and pleasure at Leo's blinding grin.

"I kind of like it when you talk to me like that, you know," Leo called after him. Grant didn't look back, but he still heard Leo say, "It's cute in a way, romantic even, how much you want to dislike me."

Grant kept walking, feeling Leo's eyes on his back, feeling Leo's presence in the restaurant as the door closed behind him, and feeling Leo in the building as he walked away.

It didn't ease.

That night, in his bed, Grant could feel Leo's presence in Blountville, could feel him pushing at the edges of Grant's consciousness, taking hold, and making him pay attention. Grant punched at his pillow and growled.

Leo Garner was quite possibly the worst thing that had ever happened to him. He made everything difficult. Ruined it all. First, he'd screwed up a simple celebration of Grant's victory in the OR, and now he was messing with his sleep.

It was like Leo made everything feel…unlucky.

• • •

"So, RUMOR HAS it you were on a date with Leo Garner yesterday," Alec said before Grant had grabbed his much needed first cup of coffee for the day. Alec wore a shimmery blue sweater and a pair of silver pants. Where he found his clothes, Grant would never know.

"Hear no evil, speak no evil." Grant handed money to the idiot behind the counter at Starbucks, some guy who always made him think of Billy Idol because of his short, bleached blond hair and his nose rings. He'd worked there for a couple of years now, but Grant didn't know his name. He didn't care so long as he gave him his mocha latte with an extra shot.

"Well?" Alec nudged him, batting his glittery lashes at him with a knowing grin.

Grant groaned. "I wasn't on a *date* with Leo Garner. I was *ambushed* by Leo Garner, which seems to be his M.O. by the way. And I was forced to endure crap remarks from Sheriff Memaw—and you know what, Alec? No. We are not having this conversation."

He grabbed the takeout cup out of Billy Idol's hand and turned away from the counter, exiting out onto the sidewalk with Alec at his heels. "Because whatever you think is happening isn't happening, won't be happening, will *never* happen, and I just want for one minute, just *one minute*, to enjoy my coffee without thinking about or talking about Leo fucking Garner."

Alec's brows were up in his carefully coiffed hairline, and he looked amused, which was bad. Amused meant that he didn't believe him. Amused meant that he was going to say something in return, and Grant didn't want to hear it.

Grant hustled down the sidewalk in the direction of his car, hoping to jump into it before Alec could catch up to him.

"Oh, please, Grant," Alec said, grabbing him by the elbow and swinging him around. "Who's been interrupting your daily coffee with Leo Garner conversations? Could it be that maybe, just maybe, *you* are the one having trouble not thinking about Leo?"

"Could it be that you have brain damage?" Grant asked. "You tell me."

"You can't stop thinking about him, and it's making you a dick. Like I said the other night—love. True love."

"Leo Garner is annoying, indecisive, opportunistic, and—"

"Gee, Grant, why not tell the entire town what you really think of me," Leo said, having appeared on the sidewalk just behind Alec. Beside him was Leo's old friend, and new local lawyer, Doug Silver.

Grant felt the world drop a little from under his feet, leaving him weightless, overly hot, and strangely sick.

"That's not," Grant started. "I mean, I didn't—"

"Know I was here," Leo finished for him.

"Yeah."

Leo's brows scrunched in that adorable fretful look that Grant had nearly forgotten about, and which he wanted to smooth away. He flushed hotly, embarrassed, and wished he could turn back time. Was there a class he could take to teach himself to not be such a jerk? If so, sign him up.

Leo said softly, "I bet you feel kind of like an asshole now."

Grant swallowed hard. "Yeah."

"Apologies are always accepted by Garners. So, hey, it's all good." Leo smiled charmingly, his rosy skin indicating he'd recently undergone dialysis. "Besides, the fact that you actually feel bad about it means that you have *feelings* deep down in your mean little heart. Who'd have thunk?"

"Not me," Doug said, patting Leo's shoulder. He carried a to-go bag from the doughnut shop next door. "See you later, Leo," he said as he backed down the sidewalk toward his shiny Audi. "I'll take care of everything. Have a good day, Alec. And you, too, Dr. Anderson."

Leo grinned at him and gave him a thumbs-up.

"Well, *I* knew Grant had feelings," Alec said, waving bye to Doug and smiling sweetly at Leo. "But it's a secret, so, you know, shhh."

Leo sighed and stuck his hands in his pocket. "Grant, c'mon. Can't we call everything bygones and be done with all the anger? I'd like to be friends."

Grant glanced at Alec, who gazed at him with gleaming, meaningful eyes. He looked up at the sky. Fluffy happy clouds moved slowly across it, cheerful and betraying. "Sure, I suppose we'll be running into each other a lot, so we may as well make the best of it."

"I'm good at that." Leo smiled.

"Yeah, well, I'm not." Grant's gut squirmed, exposed in the light of that smile. "Expect imperfection."

"I can teach you," Leo said.

Was he being coy? Flirting? Grant's groin tingled in response.

Leo went on, "It's easy enough to make the best of things. I'll give you an example." He nodded toward the Starbucks. "I'll go in there and place my order. He'll bring me the wrong thing. I don't know why, but he always does. I'll take two sips of it, and I'll think, 'It's a good thing I'm not supposed to be drinking this anyway, because it tastes awful.' Then I'll throw it away, leaving my kidney that much happier for it."

"Was 'find the silver lining' part of your post-surgical therapy following your heart transplant in LA?" Grant asked, curious while simultaneously skeptical of the entire line of thinking.

"Um, *rude*," Leo said, shooting Alec a 'can you believe him?' glance. "Discussing my health issues in public like that. And, no. I never actually attended post-surgical therapy. I'm kind of rogue that way."

"Ah-huh," Grant said. "And, sorry. I shouldn't have said that."

"This is so sweet, guys," Alec said, grinning. "Now you can be friends again, and hang out, and Dennis and I will have you both over for dinner, and, Leo, you can bring your daughter to play with Dennis's little one Mina, she'd love that, and we can go on vacations together, and—"

"Alec," Grant said. "We've called a détente, not a marriage."

"Lucky and I would love to have dinner sometime," Leo said to Alec, ignoring Grant. Then he grinned, and Grant's chest cracked open all hot and messy with some sort of unwanted feeling. "Invite Grant too. It would be fun."

"Don't *encourage* him."

"Go to work," Alec said to Grant, looping his arm through Leo's and smiling widely. "Leo and I have plans to make."

Grant sputtered, stared at them a moment, and then turned to go. He couldn't make sense of their idiocy, either one of them. Alec wasn't even being subtle in his matchmaking, and Leo wasn't batting an eye. It was ridiculous. Grant hated living in a small town. He hated Blountville. He hated Leo for making him almost wish that he could have dinner with him at Alec and Dennis's house.

"Where is Lucky, anyway?" Alec asked, as the two of them walked toward the entrance of the Starbucks.

"With my mom," Leo said, sounding tired. "I needed a break."

"Bye," Alec called to Grant over his shoulder, sticking out his tongue.

Grant waggled his fingers at him and then shot him the bird when he looked away.

"Well, of course you did. We all do," Grant heard Alec saying as the door closed behind him.

Grant stared at the closed door, feeling like a bigger asshole than usual. They hadn't even invited him to join them. But how could he blame them? Especially after his behavior today. He turned and walked toward his car slowly.

Why did he feel so disappointed about that?

Chapter Five

Present

MERYL GARNER, LEO'S country-as-they-come mother, was driving Grant crazy, hovering around Leo's hospital bed, tucking him in, moving his pillows around, and fussing up a southern-accented storm. It was all Grant could do not to tell her to get out of Leo's room because she was making Leo anxious. Hell, she was making *him* anxious.

"Mom," Leo said, grabbing her hand and looking up at her with his big, gray eyes that always made Grant's knees go weak.

They apparently also made Meryl melt into a pile of motherly goo, because she stroked back Leo's hair and said, "Yes, baby?" Her sandy-brown hair was cut in the gender-neutral short style oddly common in her generation, and she wore a Vandy sweatshirt over a pair of clean jeans.

"Could you leave me and Grant alone? I just need a minute with him."

Meryl looked at Grant like she was measuring him up. She turned her attention back to Leo, smoothed his hair back again, and kissed his forehead. "Sure, honey. I'll be right next door, checking on Hannah."

"And call to check on Lucky for me?" Leo asked. "Tell her everything's fine, okay? I'm sure Dad's got it under control, but she's probably nervous."

"Are you sure you don't you want to talk to her again? There's still time."

Leo shook his head. "I said what I needed to say to her this morning. If I say much more, it'll just scare her. Just call and ask about what she ate for breakfast, something normal, okay?"

Meryl sighed and took Leo's hand and pressed it to her heart. "Baby, you're just so good. Do you know that?"

Leo smiled and looked a little embarrassed. He laughed under his breath. "I don't know about that. Go check on Hannah, too, Mom. She probably needs the pep-talk more than I do right now."

Grant had busied himself with Leo's chart, but he put it back in the slot by the door as soon as Meryl left.

"Yes, good idea sending her to make sure the kidney hasn't bolted again," Grant said once the door had closed. "Can't be too careful there. We should have had Sheriff Memaw put a guard on her."

"Grant," Leo scolded. "C'mon, Hannah's doing me a gigantic favor."

"Yes, yes, I've heard that before." Grant waved the subject off. "She's a true philanthropist."

"*Grant*," Leo said again.

He sat down on the bed next to Leo and took hold of Leo's hands, holding them tightly as he asked, "How are you?"

"I'm ready. I'm a little nervous, but mostly, I'm just ready to feel like a million bucks again."

"Good," Grant said. "Keep thinking just like that."

"How about you? How are *you* doing?"

"I'm going to scrub in," Grant said, making the announcement he'd been skating around for days. He expected Leo wouldn't like the idea, but he was prepared to convince him if necessary.

"Excuse me?" Leo said. "Did you just say you were going to scrub in? To what? My surgery?"

"Yes," Grant said, keeping his voice calm and even. "I'm going to observe the procedure."

"Grant, you don't have to—" Leo began.

"Leo," Grant interrupted, and he leaned close, his voice low and intimate. "When someone you love needs something, you'll go to any length to get it for them, won't you? I know that to be true better than almost anyone."

Leo said, "Yes, but, you know I—"

"This is what *I* need Leo. This is what I need to do—not for you, for me. Because…" Grant took a breath, closed his eyes to steady himself, and then looked at Leo again. "I don't think I can handle being on the outside of that room, knowing what's going on behind the doors, knowing that…" Grant resisted the urge to disparage Muresan again. "That a surgeon is cutting you. I have to be there for that. I need you to let me. Otherwise, I feel like I'm coming out of my skin."

Leo stared at him, his mouth slightly open, and his eyes huge.

Grant gripped his hands tighter, and whispered, "Can you give this to me, Leo?"

"I don't know. Isn't it partly up to Dr. Muresan?" He trailed off, and then he said, "But, even so, I mean, you know what it's like. It can't be pretty, all the guts and blood. I don't know if I want you to see me that way."

"I do. I want to see that, Leo," Grant leaned even closer, his voice a near whisper. "There's nothing about you I wouldn't want to see. If Muresan gets to see the inside of you, then I want to see it, too. Why should he be more intimate with your body than I am?"

Leo shook his head, laughing softly. "You are a very sick man."

Grant cupped Leo's face.

Leo turned his face into Grant's palm, and then looked at

Grant out of the side of his eyes, gazing at him for a long moment before he said, "If you can get Muresan to agree, then it's okay with me."

"Muresan? Please," Grant scoffed. "What's he going to say? No?"

•   •   •

"UH, NO," DENNIS said as Grant tried to follow Muresan and his surgical team into the scrub room. "Just what do you think you're doing, Grant?"

"Scrubbing in." Grant pulled his arm out of Dennis's grip.

"The hell you are, my friend." Dennis blocked Grant's way. "This is absolutely out of the question, and if you care at all about Leo, you'll let his surgeon do his job."

A bolt jolted Grant's body and he said quietly, "You don't understand. They're cutting him. He's so fragile, with his heart and… Look, Dennis, you'd want the same if it were Alec, wouldn't you? And Leo expects me to be there for him."

Dennis looked disgustingly empathetic and Grant's fingers curled into fists. Dennis glanced around, confirmed that some nurses were watching avidly, and then jerked Grant closer, whispering, "You will be there for him. Just not in *there*, okay? What would you accomplish by staring holes into Muresan, making him nervous enough to endanger Leo's life? You'll make him screw the whole thing up."

"That's not—"

"So, you'll be up *there*," Dennis said, pointing toward the stairs leading into an observation room. "And I'll be there, too." Dennis put his hand on Grant's shoulder and squeezed reassuringly. "Just you and me, buddy."

Grant's hands flexed in and out of a fist. His breath felt like it was being dragged in through layers of cotton. "I promised him."

"Come on," Dennis said, guiding Grant toward the stairs leading up to the observation room. "Stay focused, Grant. Don't argue. Leo is going to expect you to pay attention to his surgery, not spend a bunch of time flirt-fighting with me."

Grant's fingers were completely numb, and his heart pounded so hard that he could feel it in his throat. The strange prickling feeling along his hairline turned out to be sweat when he swiped at it with his hand. He'd never felt like this before. He'd attended gobs of surgeries, performed two hundred and eighteen of them himself, but he'd never felt like he was going to be sick before one. God, what had happened to him? He pressed his forehead to the observation glass and took deep breaths.

"There you go, buddy," Dennis said. "Good long breaths in and out. That's good."

"Stop talking now," Grant said.

Dennis sighed. "Should I call Alec?"

"For what? Is he a surgeon? Can he promise me that everything is going to be fine? No. I'll just say something to make him cry."

Dennis sighed and sat down in a metal folding chair positioned directly in front of the observation room window. "They'll bring Leo in any minute."

"He'll wonder where I am," Grant said.

"Muresan will tell him. I have a feeling that Leo will know exactly why the decision was made, Grant. And I'm also sure that he'll know that you'd rather be down there with him."

"You make a lot of assumptions for someone who doesn't know crap about the situation."

"Are you always such a jerk when you're scared?" Dennis asked.

"I'm always a jerk," Grant said. "Remember?"

"Well, maybe you're always scared, then," Dennis said. "That would probably explain a lot."

"Keep your psychoanalysis to yourself," Grant muttered, watching as they wheeled Leo's gurney into the room.

He saw Muresan lean over and say something to Leo, and Leo's head pivoted toward the observation room. Grant could make out a small smile. Then they put the balloon over Leo's face. Grant counted down from ten in his head, and when he reached seven he saw the nurse's nod.

"He's under," Grant murmured.

"Relax," Dennis said. "He's going to be fine."

Chapter Six

Nine Months Ago

HALLOWEEN WAS NOT one of Grant's favorite holidays. Well, not since he was a kid and he could go door to door, staring at people menacingly until they gave him chocolate.

With the orange and black streamers festooning the hospital hallways, he decided to try the menacing glare on some nurses who were hording the chocolate kisses for the patients' families. It didn't work.

His glare just made them cry. Well, one of them cried, and the one who didn't put her arm around her friend and dragged her away from him, assuring the sobber that Dr. McGraw would never let Dr. Anderson fire her over some candy.

And yet *they did not give him candy.*

Grant wasn't sure how it had all gone so wrong.

"Why do you always make Sadie cry?" a small voice said.

Grant turned around to find Leo's kid, Lucky, sitting alone in a waiting area chair with a pile of chocolates and an iPad.

"She has faulty tear ducts," Grant replied. "They leak with very little provocation."

Lucky put out her hand, a silver-wrapped Hershey's kiss in the middle of her palm. "Here."

Grant took it from her, unwrapping it and popping it into his mouth. "Who said I always make her cry, anyway?"

"She did. When she saw you coming, she said, 'Oh, no, it's him. He always makes me cry.' And then she covered her mouth like this," Lucky demonstrated. "I don't think she's very smart. She let me have ten of these. My dad only lets me have two."

"Aren't you supposed to be…" He couldn't really tell how old she was, so maybe she wasn't in school yet? She looked to be about four but her mouth made her seem much older. Maybe she was small for her age. "Isn't there someone watching you?" Grant didn't think a hospital corridor was the right place for a child, no matter how old.

"Carrie was watching me, but she had to go do something for Mr. Baumgartner, and she said she'd be right back. Then Sadie said she'd watch me. But I guess she forgot."

"Don't you have a hundred relatives in this town? No one could watch you for a few hours?"

"Nope," Lucky said in her high-pitched voice, popping another chocolate into her mouth and chewing it messily. She held one out to him, this time with orange foil.

Grant let the chocolate melt on his tongue. He studied the girl: cut-off jean shorts, T-shirt with a cartoon monster on it, and a braid that had obviously started out well enough but had come partially undone through the day. She was clean, but there was something earthy about her, like she was a carrot grown in a garden, with a bit of wholesome dirt left in the crevices, even after a good scrubbing.

Lucky jabbed at her iPad and Grant looked over to see what she was doing. It was a numbers game of some kind with brightly animated characters and a lot of pinging sounds. Lucky sighed and poked at the screen, making the right choice every time.

"Fun game," Grant said.

Lucky shrugged. "I know all the answers."

"I noticed."

He noticed other things, too, like the way Lucky swung her feet slowly in a rocking rhythm, as though she was soothing herself, and the way that she looked so out of place in the hallway of Appalachian Medical, like that little carrot from the garden was placed on a shiny, industrial plate. Incongruous—that was the word he was looking for, and he muttered it under his breath.

And yet, despite the film of the country glossing her, Lucky was obviously very smart. Her fingers touched the right answer almost as soon as the screen announced the question. She was also clearly bored.

"Can I see it?" Grant asked.

"I guess," Lucky said, handing the iPad over to him.

Grant closed the app and opened another. He showed her the screen again. "Ever played chess?"

"No," Lucky said, handing him another chocolate and opening one for herself. Her hands were messy, but Grant didn't care. She looked up with bright hazel eyes and said, "Is it hard?"

"Sometimes," Grant answered. "Wanna learn?"

Her face took on an immediate joyful interest that Grant could barely remember experiencing. Lucky's interest was pure, and his desire to teach her to play surprisingly strong. He had some time between rounds, and when Carrie arrived looking terrified and shocked, Grant waved her aside, intent on demonstrating to Lucky the art of sound opening moves.

Chapter Seven

A FEW DAYS later Grant turned around in the middle of the corridor to try and escape Leo, who was heading right toward him.

Leo's presence in the hospital three days a week was starting to wear him down. No matter how hard he tried to avoid the guy, Grant always ran into Leo, who inevitably tried to chat. Or he found himself sitting across from Leo in the cafeteria while Leo ate his incredibly bland, renal-failure diet and talked about whatever came to his pretty little head like Grant wanted to hear it.

And what was worse, Grant did want to hear it.

He even found himself *hoping* that Leo would be in the cafeteria and was annoyed by his own disappointment on the four days a week Leo wasn't there.

It was becoming harder and harder to not feel things for Leo, and when Leo smiled at him, Grant's dick took notice. The formerly palpable attraction between them hadn't faded with time, and the fact that Grant found the pre-dialysis rings under Leo's eyes sexy clued him in to his dire need to go to Asheville, find a hookup, and get laid.

Today, Grant had patients he needed to get to, though, and he had no desire to linger in the hallway and let Leo flirt with him. Well, perhaps the desire was there, but the time was not, and so he turned on his heel without looking back.

"Wait up," Leo called out.

Grant sighed, rolling his eyes so hard that his entire head followed.

Leo's smile was bright, and Grant narrowed his gaze against the light of it. "So, Lucky told me some doctor that makes nurses cry has been teaching her chess."

"Strange," Grant said. "Sounds creepy. You might want to report that to security."

"C'mon, Grant. I know it was you."

Grant shrugged. "And? Should I not converse with small children left *alone* in the hallways of my hospital, which is, as I'm sure you're aware, against regulation, and—"

"Grant, *shut up*," Leo said, exaggerating the words like a petulant child. "I wanted to thank you. I couldn't believe Carrie left her alone. Anything could have happened to her."

"Yeah, well, you were lucky that it was just me who convinced her to share her chocolates. Don't leave her alone in my hospital again."

Leo glanced down at his shoes, his eyelashes shimmering on his pinked-up cheeks, and then back to Grant. Clearly, he was freshly dialyzed. "I won't. I'll make sure of it."

"Good," Grant said and tried to move on.

"Hold on," Leo said, grabbing Grant's elbow. "Could you just wait a minute? I wanted to ask if you'd like to come out to the farm this weekend? We're having a Halloween party for the kids. Bobbing for apples. Apple pie. Costumes if you want. Hay rides. And a big potluck dinner. Alec will be there with Dennis and Mina—"

Grant put his hand up. "You had me at pie."

Leo grinned. "Glad to see your appetite still drives you to do things that would otherwise make you uncomfortable."

"Believe me, my *appetites* have gotten me into plenty of trouble over the years." Grant thought Leo might be the ultimate example of this. He'd wanted the man in his bed so badly six years ago that he'd let himself get too close emotionally, but Leo had wanted to take things slow. They'd never gone beyond first base and yet somehow Leo had gotten under Grant's skin permanently. The unscratched itch. "My stomach, though, has yet to do me wrong."

Leo's eyes glowed with seductive warmth, and Grant's gut curled with a returned heat. Leo licked his lips, saying, "Hopefully, it won't steer you wrong this time, either."

"Let's hope not," Grant agreed, and then he broke away, his mind on anything but the patient he was headed to see.

Chapter Eight

AS GRANT PULLED up the gravel drive toward the small barn, the half-dozen kids running around dressed up in costumes and fueled by too much candy made him doubt the directives issued by his stomach. Though the wariness provoked by the children's antics was nothing compared to that brought on by the adults wearing idiotic outfits and clearly fueled by too much beer.

Grant nearly backed down the drive, but Alec spotted him and came toward the car with a brilliant grin on his glitter-covered face. So Grant didn't see how he could get out of it now. Besides, there would be pie. Leo had said so.

"Hey, stranger," Alec said wrapping his arm through Grant's, the giant fairy wings on his back flapping behind them both. He tugged Grant toward the knot of people outside the barn. "I've missed you! Why don't you answer my calls?"

"I've been busy," Grant said. "Some of us have actual jobs."

The excuse was only partially true. He did have several new patients, two with demanding diagnoses that required close monitoring in hopes of finding the perfect window of opportunity to go into surgery. But the other reason he'd avoided Alec's calls was because Dennis had told him all about Alec and Mina's recent play dates with Leo and Lucky. And maybe Grant had been a little jealous.

"I know I'm fortunate to spend my days being the stay-at-home daddy to my stepdaughter, but, believe me, it's a job," Alec sniffed. "One I'm not sure you could handle."

"Well, her mother certainly couldn't."

"Shh, don't diss Pamela. She had a hard time when Dennis left her for me. She didn't even know he was bisexual. It was traumatic for her."

"But it was her choice to leave Mina."

Alec sighed. "Let's not argue. It's a party! And, c'mon, you haven't been too busy for my calls. You're just jealous that I've been spending so much time with Leo and Lucky and you're not."

"Whatever."

"Why don't you come over to our place next Friday night for dinner?"

"Let me guess, it'll be a surprise double date with Leo?"

Alec grinned. "You really think I'm going to try to set you up with him? After everything that happened before and all your weirdness since he came back to town?"

"Well, aren't you?"

"Of course!" Alec replied, his eyes were almost as blue as the sky, just a little darker.

Grant rolled his eyes.

"But, hey, it looks like I don't have to," Alec said, indicating the barn, the white clapboard house, and the small field of running children. "You're here all on your own. Seems like your heart is making choices that your brain is still denying."

"Who gave you moron flakes for breakfast?"

Alec shoved him, his fairy wings flapping against Grant's back.

"Hey, Grant! You came!" Leo called, stepping from the darkness of the barn with a smile on his face that made Alec's look dim.

Grant cleared his throat, trying to ignore the rushing pleasure that suffused him. He especially didn't want Alec to see that he was *affected*.

Leo was dressed as a farmer—overalls, a straw hat, and big, brown farm boots. He held a water bottle in his hand and indicated a row of coolers lined up against the barn. "Beer, water, wine, cola, whatever you want is here."

"I'll be right back," Alec said, darting into the barn, making a show of looking around for someone. Grant figured it was probably supposed to be Dennis or Mina.

"Beer's fine," Grant said, and Leo reached down to grab one, handing it over. Leo's fingers were cold and wet from the melted ice in the cooler as they grazed Grant's. His eyes, though, were challenging and hot. A flirt, a tease.

Grant twisted off the cap, lifted the beer in a toast to Leo, and took a swallow. It was a local brew. Nice, not cheap at all, and Grant was surprised, though he guessed he shouldn't be, that Leo would have it out for a Halloween party. He took another swallow in appreciation of the caramel, woody taste.

"Good?" Leo asked.

"Wouldn't you like to know?" Grant said, unable to keep the innuendo out of his voice.

"Oh," Leo laughed gently, "more than you can imagine. I'd *love* to know. The beer and maybe the other thing, too. But especially the beer."

Grant had a strange moment of wishing he'd chosen water, or a cola, anything except this thing that made Leo long for what he couldn't have. The idea of Leo yearning created an urge in Grant that he didn't understand, a throb of want down in his gut, a restless need to make it better for him.

Grant cleared his throat. "So, where's the food?"

Leo laughed. "It's around. There's a lot of it." Leo's eye caught something over Grant's shoulder. "Oh, hey, sorry. My dad needs me. I'll see you in a while? You won't leave without telling me, will you?"

"Yeah, no. I can't really make that promise."

Leo laughed again and clasped Grant's shoulder in a friendly way, before heading off to join his father in studying a cart of hay that was hitched to a tractor. Chuck Garner was a wide, tall man with gray-gold hair and a sun-lined face. As Grant watched, he and Leo seemed to debate whether or not there was enough straw for the hayride.

There were too many people at the farm. People that Grant knew and a few that he even—well, 'liked' was a strong word, one he usually reserved for Alec. But there were a few that didn't bug him so much.

Like his fellow apartment dwellers, Jill and Tom Weinstein, both of whom liked to chat with him across the balconies while watering their plants. He raised his beer to them in acknowledgement, relieved when they didn't wave him over to talk.

He figured it was only a matter of time, though, before someone did, and he wanted to be mostly through a plate of food by then. He wasn't fond of socializing with Blountville's natives on the best of days, but, at the moment, he knew he was in dire peril of being roped into a long and boring conversation it would be difficult to escape. So he planned to find the promised food as quickly as possible, eat it, and skedaddle while the skedaddling was good.

Someone small bumped against him, and Grant looked down, narrowly avoiding spilling beer on his favorite small child—a distinction earned simply by the fact that Alec was her stepfather. There was something to be said for shared affections.

"Uncle Grant," Mina said from underneath her pirate patch, which seemed to be made from a glitter-covered orange peel. "Watch this!" And she struck the air mightily with a plastic rapier. "Don't I look awesome?"

Since the only answer Grant could imagine giving to that question was "No, you look ridiculous; don't your fathers love you at all?" Grant said nothing.

But Mina didn't mind, at least not from what Grant could tell, since she ran off hollering at the top of her voice and chasing what looked like a red-haired, blue-eyed, little-girl-shaped Harry Potter.

Grant grabbed another beer from the cooler, tucked it under his arm for later, and continued looking for the promised pie. The sooner he got it in his tummy, the sooner he could leave this place. "Come on, pie. Where have they hidden you?"

"There's gonna be apple pie after the fireworks," Lucky said from down around his elbow.

Grant stared at her massive headpiece of plastic snakes, noticing her gray, baggy, barely-held-together dress made from a dyed sheet and giant safety pins, and the green fingernails on her small hand that grasped one tiny can of cola.

"That late, huh?" Grant said.

"Yeah, it's tradition," she said. Her young tongue mangled the word, but Grant still knew what she meant. "Fireworks, then pie, then hay ride, and then everyone goes home."

"I thought maybe your father had lied to me about the pie."

"No. Daddy doesn't lie," Lucky said, but it was slow, like she was holding something back.

Grant wondered why she wasn't being entirely honest. "Spill it," Grant said.

Lucky looked up at him in confusion, but then twisted her wrist, dumping her soft drink on the ground.

Grant laughed, bringing his hand down on Lucky's shoulder to shake her a little.

She grinned up at him and said, "Now what?" Curiosity lit her face, like she was anxiously awaiting the next step in whatever game Grant was playing.

"Now you tell me where the food is and I eat as much as I can without exploding."

Lucky looked down at her spilled cola and shrugged. "But why spill it, though?"

"Get me some food, kiddo, and I'll explain it to you."

Lucky took his hand and led him to a table behind the barn that was the answer to all of Grant's prayers, the very substance of his dreams. There on the long table were hot dogs, hamburgers, casseroles that were cheesy and hot, and others that were cold and filled with marshmallows. There were cookies, and sweet potatoes, and deviled eggs. There was a ham salad that made Grant's mouth water just looking at it, and there were three cakes, and two pans of brownies, and a selection of potato salads to choose from. Grant didn't know where to start.

Lucky lingered by his side as he filled his plate and then followed him to a shady place under a tree.

"Your family has this party every year?" Grant asked, suddenly a little put out that the Garners had never invited him before. It seemed the entire town was in attendance. He could have been feasting annually for the last six years.

"Yeah," Lucky said. "But I've only been here one time before for Halloween. In California we just walked up and down the street for trick-or-treat. I put the candy in my pillowcase."

She sounded unable to reconcile some bundle of emotions running through her, probably about California, and leaving her other father, and moving here. Grant changed the subject in hopes that she wouldn't try to *talk* about those feelings.

"When I said spill it, I wanted you to tell me who it is that lies to you," Grant said, biting into the hot dog he'd slathered with chili and relish. He chewed as the realization hit him that the topic he'd chosen would probably be laced with *feelings* too, and he hoped she didn't cry. He'd feel like a jerk if that happened, and God knows he sure as hell wouldn't know what to do.

Lucky pushed a plastic snake out of her eye. "He only lies on accident."

"Who? Leo?"

Lucky said, "No. Daddy doesn't lie. Sometimes he's wrong, but he never lies. Papa, though, he promises things." Lucky shrugged. "Lies are sometimes by accident. Papa doesn't mean to lie to me. That's what Daddy says, and Daddy says the truth."

Grant said nothing.

"Dr. Grant," Lucky said, calling him the name he'd suggested during their chess instruction. "I'm gonna go now. Will you be okay?"

Grant chuckled at her sincere concern and then waved her off. He knew where the food was, and she'd told him something of interest to mull over for a while as he worked through his plate. Her job here was done as far as he was concerned.

Lucky ran away, chasing after Mina, a plastic snake dropping from her head to the ground. It was promptly picked up by another child who ran after a small girl shaking it at her and screaming. Grant was grateful for the beer taking the edge off things, and he opened a second one, settling in beneath the tree.

"That's a lot of food," Alec said.

Grant shaded his eyes, trying to see Alec as more than a dark shadow outlined by the bright autumn sun behind him. His fairy wings moved in the breeze and the sun set off the glitter he'd sprayed into his hair, too.

"Good food," Grant said, stuffing another forkful into his mouth.

"Oh, wow, and you actually have something nice to say," Alec said, shifting a little so that the light wasn't stabbing Grant right in the eye.

"They do this every year, did you know?" Grant said. "And they've never invited me before."

"Gee, I wonder why." Alec sat down next to Grant, his smile warm, and the scent of his aftershave familiar and friendly. "I have to leave in a few minutes to go with Dennis to have a phone call with Pamela. She wants to talk to us about something serious. I don't know. Something that might impact Mina, we think."

Grant frowned. "You don't think she wants custody again, do you?"

"No," Alec said, his brows creasing in worry. "I think she might be ready to renounce her parental rights and allow me to adopt her."

"Seriously?"

"She's been in Belgium for almost a year now. She's dating that man who has three daughters. I kind of think she's ready to erase what she and Dennis shared."

"But she can't erase Mina!"

"She can try." Alec's shoulders hunched, making his fairy wings flop sadly. "It's better if Mina stays here and has fun at the party. Leo has already said she can spend the night."

"That's great." Grant frowned and gazed toward the farmhouse. "So Leo's living out here?"

"Yeah, just him and Lucky. His folks still live in the house in town. Anyway, I didn't want to leave without saying goodbye."

"Good luck with it," Grant said, his mind supplying him with images from the inside of the farmhouse from the only time he'd come up here with Leo. It wasn't a posh place, but it was cozy inside. A good place for a kid like Lucky.

"Will you watch Mina for us? Be extra eyes on her until the party ends?"

Grant glanced out to the pasture where Mina, Lucky, and the other kids were playing with hula hoops and eating ice cream cones simultaneously. All of them were sticky messes that could morph into e. coli vectors at any moment.

"This is a ploy to get me to stay here longer, isn't it? So I'll talk more with Leo."

"And is it working?" Leo himself asked, suddenly crouching down beside him on the grass.

"You have got to stop sneaking up on me," Grant grumbled.

"I walked over here in plain sight."

"No, you approached from behind the tree. I don't have eyes in the back of my head."

Leo laughed. The sound of it was full of a kind of happiness that seemed all encompassing, like anyone could reach out and have some of it if they wanted. When he stopped, he said, "I hope you take Alec up on watching Mina for him, because I'd really like you to stay."

"There!" Alec said and slapped Grant's thigh. "It's a plan. Now, if either of you need anything, I'll have my cell phone. And Dennis will have his. Obviously."

Alec jumped up and was gone before Grant could even finish swallowing the deviled egg he'd stuffed in his mouth. He watched him go, the fairy wings flapping as he walked, and then Dennis stepped up to join him, kissing his forehead and smiling down at him before waving goodbye to Mina.

"Listen," Grant began, and then he didn't know what to say. He pinched the bridge of his nose and looked around. "This isn't exactly my kind of thing."

"No, of course not," Leo said.

"Now this food, though?"

"It's good, isn't it?" Again there was that longing in Leo's voice.

"Where's your plate?" Grant asked.

Leo shrugged. "If I can score a new kidney, I'll be able to eat a plate like that, too. Though, if you're not careful, Grant, we may have to roll you out of here."

"I wouldn't care," Grant said.

And he wouldn't because he would be full, delightfully completely full, and he wouldn't need to eat a Michelina's frozen dinner tonight. Plus, if he managed to get some leftovers to take home, he wouldn't have to eat one tomorrow night either.

"Whoever made this thing with the beans and the tomatoes and the maple syrup needs to be given an award," Grant went on.

"Oh, really? That would be me."

"You made this?"

Leo nodded, and Grant had to hold back from grabbing Leo's head and kissing him. The man was gorgeous and could cook and made Grant *want*. But he'd learned his lesson the first time, hadn't he? Leo was dangerous.

"So, what's my reward?" Leo asked, and he gave Grant a look so flirtatious that it almost made Grant hard.

"Congratulations, you won the honor of getting me another beer," Grant replied, forcing himself to look out to the pasture where Mina was sticking her head into a half-barrel, coming up with an apple hanging off her front teeth.

Leo grinned and laughed. "You can be such a jerk."

"You like it," Grant said.

Leo stood up and said as he walked away, "I never said I didn't. I'll send Lucky over with another beer."

Afternoon passed into evening as Grant gorged on food. He fended off townspeople commenting on his stomach as the bottomless pit, and he endured Mina sitting on his lap through the godawful sing-along portion of the evening. He covered Mina's ears while they told ghost stories, though. The poor kid was terrified and whimpered in fear while burying her head into his chest and just holding on.

The fireworks were small things, nothing elaborate or huge, and Grant stuck around telling himself that he'd just wait to make sure no one blew their hand off or blinded themselves. The fact that he'd lingered all day had nothing at all to do with watching Leo or studying the way Leo's hair glowed in the fading autumn sunlight.

God, it had nothing to do with that.

It also didn't have to do with the curiously comforting scent of bonfire smoke and burning hay that covered Leo's clothes, and which Grant could smell whenever Leo came back to sit beside him. It definitely had nothing to do with the lust that curled in Grant's stomach whenever Leo brought over another beer and ran his cold fingers over Grant's hand in the exchange.

Grant groaned. It had everything to do with all of those things.

"Hey," Leo said, having somehow escaped Grant's sight again and snuck up to where Grant sat with his back to the oak tree. Leo crouched beside him. "Did you get enough pie?"

"A man can never have enough pie," Grant said.

Leo lifted a brow. "I am so tempted to make a 'that's what my cousin says' joke, but I won't."

"Your cousin?"

"He's straight. Well, the three older ones are. The littlest one is still just a kid, so who knows?"

"Ah," Grant said. "You have too many relatives. A whole mess of them. That can't be sanitary."

Leo laughed and said nothing for a few moments, then he murmured sweetly, "Thanks for coming out here today. You seemed to have a good time."

"Don't fool yourself," Grant said. "But it was good pie."

"My Papaw's recipe," Leo said, his voice fond and soft. "He died a few years ago."

"I remember," Grant said.

Leo had been in town for the funeral and had stuck around for a few, long, annoying days, during which Grant saw him in Starbucks or Little Apron, and, as always, Leo's presence had been impossible to ignore.

"I'm really glad you came," Leo said, picking up a small stick and twiddling it between his thumb and forefinger. Then he sat down all the way, crossing his legs and resting his back against the tree, his shoulder pressing against Grant's.

"I'm glad I ate the food," Grant said.

"You're not gonna give me even a little bit, are you?" Leo asked, gray eyes and gentle smile making Grant's chest feel tight. "I mean, would it hurt you to say that you're glad you came, too?"

The beers must have loosened his tongue, because he said, "It might. It might be the magic spell that undoes all that's good in my life and leaves me broken beyond repair."

"You don't believe in magic," Leo chided.

"Nope. Or luck," Grant replied.

"You love your life here in Blountville, though, don't you?" Leo's voice was soft, respectful, but somehow affectionate, too.

A roman candle shot into the night sky; the light left a red trail and then disappeared into nothing. Kids spelled out words with sparklers and their delighted shrieks of laughter filled the air when a bottle rocket screamed its way up into the dark and exploded in a burst of color overhead.

"It ain't bad," Grant said.

Leo settled in beside him, his legs sprawled open, his arm against Grant's, and his hair smelling of some kind of mint shampoo and the smoke from the bonfire. Grant glanced over at him, watching his face light up with the next firework.

Leo caught his eye and his smile grew wider.

Grant was acutely aware of Leo's thigh pressing against his, but he didn't move away. He knew he should leave. Knew that Leo's fingers inched slowly toward Grant's hand, and that he didn't plan to do anything to stop their fingers from intertwining.

Leo breathed, "Nope, it ain't bad at all."

Grant was a goner, just like Alec had said, and he couldn't even begin to explain just why.

And while the pie and the food had been good, he suspected that it hadn't been *that* good. Not good enough to make up for all that was going to happen now, anyway. That was for certain.

Grant had managed to avoid falling down that rabbit hole called love the first time around, but this time he wasn't going to be so lucky. He'd already slipped, and there was no use in grasping at air on the way down.

So he grasped Leo's hand instead.

Chapter Nine

Eight Months Ago

IT HAD BEEN a month since the Halloween party, and Grant was still trying to come to terms with the fact that he was currently behaving in a way that was suspiciously similar to dating Leo Garner.

There'd been the 'double date' at Alec and Dennis's house. And there'd been a few Saturday lunch dates at a local deli. Lucky would pop French fries in her mouth and suck down a shake, while she and Grant played chess on the iPad, and Grant and Leo talked.

And once there'd been a night out at Little Apron, sitting at a table alone together, eating a nice meal. Then, when a small jazz band started playing, and folks started dancing, Leo had suggested joining them. Grant, to his own surprise, had accepted. It'd felt good holding Leo on the dance floor, and the curious eyes on them had only made it better. Having Leo's body against his for everyone in Blountville to see counted as a very big win.

In addition, Grant went out to the farm sometimes, and Leo and Lucky gave him lots of food to eat. Other nights Leo, either alone, or with Lucky, came over to the apartment and they ordered in a dinner, and occasionally they walked over to the park and sat on a bench while Lucky ran around and played.

During all this, Leo's health seemed to hold steady enough, but Grant couldn't forget the transplanted heart in his chest or the non-functioning kidneys in his back. It made every day that

Leo lived and laughed a little bit sweeter, and a little bit scarier, too.

Lastly, Grant had actually given Leo his cell phone number. What's more, he *picked up the phone* when Leo called, and he never failed to reply to a text from him either.

Amazingly, despite the red flags and danger signals sent up by his heart, Grant liked dating Leo Garner. The time they spent together had a certain rhythm and peace to it that Grant appreciated in his otherwise hectic life.

All the animosity and bitterness seemed to have bled out of him as he'd held Leo's hand under the tree on Halloween. Life was confusing. People made mistakes. Leo had made choices that didn't have a happy ending, but there was no reason why there couldn't be a new happy ending now. Well, no reason except for Leo's fragile health.

All in all, he was so satisfied with his new Leo-involved life that Grant heard the nurses whisper about how weirdly happy he appeared lately, and it seemed to unnerve them in ways that made Grant smirk with delight.

But it was true. He *was* happy.

He wanted to keep on dating Leo, spending time with him, and watching Leo be effortlessly amazing. Leo was such a strong man, going through so much, but always with an amazing attitude and a smile for everyone—even Grant. Not to mention, always doing his best to be a good father. Grant found little not to admire in the man, though he did wonder sometimes where Leo got his money. Perhaps from a settlement with Curtis, who, as everyone knew, was bringing in millions ever since he starred in a big superhero blockbuster two years prior.

But Curtis Banks wasn't something he and Leo discussed.

They talked about a lot of things, but they didn't talk about the past, and they didn't talk about the future, and they didn't kiss. And, frankly, if Grant was going to keep dating Leo Garner, something had to give on *that* front, because he was having the kind of dreams he hadn't had since he was fourteen years old.

Now seemed like a good time to bring it up. Sure, the movie they'd watched had been pretty stupid, but Leo's warm body tucked in next to him on the old, soft sofa in Grant's apartment had more than made up for the inanity as far as Grant was concerned. Plus, Lucky was hanging out with her grandparents, which opened up all kinds of possibilities, as far as Grant was concerned.

So when the credits flickered onto the screen, Grant's heart skipped a beat as he tried to think of how to broach the topic of physical intimacy.

Leo sat up, stretched his arms, and picked up his cell phone, checking for texts. He used his thumbs to press in a reply to whatever he found there. "It's from Dad. He says Lucky's welcome to spend the night with them. She'll love that. Dad'll make her pancakes in the morning."

"Pancakes?" Grant asked. He liked pancakes. In fact, it'd been a long time since he'd had homemade pancakes. He couldn't even remember the last time, actually. Maybe never.

Leo smirked. "Yeah, pancakes. Why? Want to go spend the night with my folks, so you can have some, too?"

"Well, if that offer's on the table..."

"Let's leave my folks to Lucky," Leo said. "You don't cook much, do you?"

"I leave that to Alec. He feeds me."

"Alec's a good friend." Leo smiled warmly at Grant and then bent close to nuzzle his cheek. The closest thing to a kiss they'd had yet. Grant's heart beat faster. Leo went on, "I could come back in the morning and make pancakes for you, though, if you want. I could even teach you how. It could be fun."

"In that case, why leave?"

Leo's lips curved into a radiant smile, and he flushed, glancing up at Grant and then back down again. "It's a little soon for that, don't you think?"

"Is it?" Grant asked.

A month of whatever this was, and it was too soon? How long did it take to court Leo Garner?

"You haven't even kissed me," Leo said. "So, yeah, I'd say it's a little soon."

"I could remedy that."

"Maybe you should," Leo whispered huskily.

Grant leaned forward, and just as their lips were about to touch, Leo's phone rang. "Tell whoever that is to—"

Leo flushed even more and fought a grin before picking up the phone.

"Hey, baby," Leo said. "Did Grandpa tuck you in yet? You've got Sammy Spider? Yeah…uh-huh? Oh, I used to love that one, too. I called her Freckles. No, she's a stuffed mare, not a donkey, silly. Okay, well, I love you, too. Sleep tight. Bye."

As soon as Leo hung up, Grant took Leo's phone and tossed it onto the coffee table. Then he leaned over and brushed his lips against Leo's, the rush of heat in his stomach pulling him in.

Leo's hands slid into Grant's hair, and the kiss was amazing, hot, and sweet. When Leo pulled away, wiping his mouth with the back of his hand, he laughed in a stunned amazement. "Uh, this is a little fast."

"Do you want to stop?" Grant asked.

Leo shook his head, breathing heavily but scooting away from Grant. His expression bordered on panicked, as though trying to get away from temptation, or fearing that Grant might drag him into a kiss again.

"Are you okay?" Grant asked. "We can stop."

"I don't know. I don't want to stop, but…it's a lot of things. Like, I've only been with Curtis. Ridiculous, huh? A gay man with only one prior partner? At my age?"

"Not ridiculous."

"And, God, it's just a lot of things, actually." Leo rubbed his hands over his face. "Not you, though. No, you're great. That kiss was great. And I—I sound like some silly uptight old biddy when I try to explain this, but I want to be careful. I want to be *sure*, you know? And conscious of the example that I set for Lucky."

Grant stared at Leo, affection welling in him along with frustratingly true admiration for Leo's old-fashioned earnestness.

Leo's face changed from hot-embarrassed to hot-something else, though. His expression was tender, fragile even, and he looked at Grant with so much vulnerability in his gray eyes. "Understand?"

"I do," Grant said, but he didn't move. He didn't pull away from Leo, just continued to sit there and look at him. "But why don't you tell me more about it?"

Leo's expression was one of relief mixed with a strange shame, and then he said, "Some if it's because of my sister, you know?"

Grant shook his head but kept his face neutral. He didn't know, but he'd like to. He wanted to know everything about Leo.

"Hannah never thought about how things affected me or my family. She was always a mess. Still is. And she's Lucky's biological mother, though, honestly, Lucky seems nothing like her. Thank God."

"You aren't like your sister."

"I know. But, regardless, I don't want to make things messy in my life, and then expect Lucky to just, you know, *deal* with it. It isn't fair to do that to a kid."

"No," Grant said. "It's not."

"And Curtis and I have already made things messy enough for her. And I feel like, if I'm going to put her in that position where she has to deal with me being invested that way in a lover, then…" Leo's voice was so quiet, so soft and intimate that Grant had to lean in a little closer. "Then I really need to know who I'm with. I need to know you, Grant."

Grant turned that over in his mind. He took a long, slow breath, ran his hand over his hair, and said, "All right. How do we do that?"

Leo smiled.

"C'mon, school me," Grant said, feeling warm and loose, almost like he'd been drinking, but all he'd had was the cola and some buttered popcorn.

It was Leo sitting there next to him, looking like warm vanilla, and somehow Grant was willing to open up a little, to stop resisting and just go with the flow. "How do we do this so Lucky isn't at risk?"

"We talk a lot more. About real things, not just the superficial, easy stuff," Leo said. "You know, you ask me things, and I ask you things, and we have a conversation."

"I'm capable of that."

"Good to know. Let's test that theory." Leo paused.

Grant shrugged and said, "Go on. Hit me."

"Okay, tell me about your first love. You know all about mine—hell half the world knows about mine now that he's in all those stupid gossip magazines. But when it comes to you, I feel like I'm missing out."

Grant shrugged. His mind supplied him with flashes of Leo's tear-stained face telling him it was over six years ago. "Off the top of my head, I can't say that I can think of anyone I'd call a 'first love'."

"Oh, c'mon," Leo said. "Surely there was someone. A crush?

A friendly acquaintance?"

Grant reached out for his cola as he said, "I dated this guy in college for a while. He thought I was going to be a successful surgeon bringing in big bucks, and I thought he had big hands. I think that was about the extent of the intimacy in our relationship."

Leo's brows crinkled. "That's it? That's…well, I'm sorry to say, but that's pathetic."

"It was a very *deep*, meaningful relationship. In bed."

"Oh, I'm sure," Leo said. "It was probably wrought with *intensity* and *feeling*, too."

"Exploding with it," Grant agreed, laughing softly.

Leo sighed, shifted a little, and his expression couldn't contain his disappointment.

Grant swallowed hard and then relented. "Okay. I was sixteen. He was nineteen and we were in the same grade at school. This was not because of my incredible genius, which tells you all you need to know about his intelligence. We were in the same class because he wasn't the brightest bulb on the Christmas tree."

"Yeah, so you like 'em stupid?" Leo asked. "Should I be insulted?"

"No, I like 'em pretty," Grant said as he settled back, gazing up at the ceiling, remembering the way Steven's hair had fallen over his face in soft curls that should have been trimmed back. But Steven's mother was dead, and his father never seemed to give a damn, so long as Steven wasn't in the way of his alcoholic stupors. At least, that's what Steven had said as Grant worked out the math problems for him and Steven copied the right answers into his notebook in his own handwriting.

"The neighborhood where we lived in Cincinnati was divided. The middle-class kids lived at the top of the hill, and Steven and I lived at the bottom. I don't know why he talked to me at the bus stop, but he didn't let the other kids pick on me, and I did his math homework in return. I remember he smelled like peanut butter all the time, and I thought I'd die of joy if I could ever get him to kiss me."

Leo's eyes shone bright with interest. "And did he? Kiss you? Ever?"

"No," Grant said, shaking his head. "He was put in a foster home before the year was out and I never saw him again."

Leo's sad, soft noise made Grant remember the way one of the other boys had shoved him, spit on his books, and said, "Steven's gone. He won't protect you now."

Grant had bent over then, crying out in pain, but it'd barely had anything to do with Michael Kurzac's swift kick to his shins, and a lot more to do with knowing he'd never see Steven again.

"I barely knew him, but, you know how it is. Somehow I'd imbued the idea of him with everything that was good, if stupid, in the world. I suppose, if I had to say that anyone was my first—crush, I guess—maybe it was him."

"What was his name?" Leo asked.

Grant paused, feeling strangely like he was handing something valuable to Leo, some kind of control that he hadn't intended to give up. "Steven. Steven Hamilton."

Leo smiled. "That's nice. Thank you."

Grant snorted, rolling his eyes. "Whatever. It was what it was."

"So…you've really never been in love?"

Grant remembered two fevered kisses from six years ago, Leo's hands in his hair, and a walk under the stars on Leo's farm. He remembered the sensation of falling every time he got close to Leo, the anger that he'd tried to horde against him when he'd left, and the way that anger had mellowed in the face of him again. He also remembered what it had felt like to have that young hope, so barely kindled, utterly guttered by the sight of Leo and Curtis holding hands in the grocery store barely a week after Leo had called it quits with him. It'd been a blessing when Leo had left with Curtis for Los Angeles.

Grant pinched the bridge of his nose. "There was a guy once. I thought I might be falling in love with him, but he didn't feel the same way."

"What happened?"

"He got back together with his ex-boyfriend and moved away. And that was that."

Leo swallowed and whispered, "*Grant.*"

Grant slapped his hands against his thighs and said, "So, now, it's my turn?"

Leo still stared at him, his eyes like stars, and Grant wanted so much to kiss him again.

"Grant—" Leo started again.

"Come on. Quid pro quo."

Leo acquiesced, but his eyes were still glowing, and Grant felt lighter just looking at them. "Okay, fine. Ask away," Leo said.

"All right then, I've been wondering this for a while now. Why the hell did you name that poor kid Lucky?" Grant said. "She's gonna get made fun of, you know."

"Hey, it's a cute name," Leo said, offended.

"For a dog. Or a rabbit. Or a cute little stuffed snake."

Leo rolled his eyes and laughed, sinking back into the sofa, licking his lips, and going distant, like he was remembering something fond and painful both. "Okay, so it's a long story."

Grant shrugged, took a swig from his cola. "I've got all night."

Leo pressed his hands nervously against his thighs and then sighed heavily. "Okay, then. Well, Hannah was a mess when she had Lucky. She'd moved out to Los Angeles, too. Not too long after I did. She wanted to be in films. You know, the usual. At first, we were helping her, and Curtis was introducing her to agents and directors. Then we started loaning her money, just a little here and there to get by, but in the end, we realized she was blowing it all on drugs."

Grant loosed a low grumbling noise.

Leo sighed. "I tried to get her help, you know? I mean, it's not like I didn't see how it happened. Drug use is rampant out there. But she didn't want to change. I don't know if it was the drugs or the boyfriend, but she wasn't interested in making her life better. I didn't even know she was pregnant. Honestly, I don't know how long *she knew* that she was pregnant before Lucky was actually born. It was a shock to everyone."

Grant had seen cases like that over the years: women too far gone into drugs or alcohol to notice their growing bellies until it was too late. He'd seen some messy and horrific attempts at illegal, late-term abortions from those situations, too. He was glad, for Leo's sake, that Hannah hadn't attempted something like that.

Leo went on, "Lucky was low birth weight, so small, and born strung out on drugs. We weren't even sure she was going to be okay."

Grant settled back against the sofa, tipping his head to rest it on the back, watching Leo carefully as he talked. He imagined little Lucky of the blabbing mouth and challenging eyes as a tiny infant detoxing in her hospital crib. His stomach tightened nauseously. Some people should never be allowed to breed.

"And then Hannah took off again, leaving Lucky in the hospital. Lucky was offered to Mom and Dad first, of course. But they were having money problems. Like they're never not having money problems, you know?"

Grant lifted his brows a little but stayed silent. He figured if he said anything it would be wrong, and then Leo would stop talking, or he'd start talking about something else, and this strange melancholy moment would lift away. And if it did, Grant would have lost something precious. He knew that for certain.

"I mean, Mom and Dad would have taken her anyway. Don't get me wrong. Of course they would have, but I was in LA, and Curtis had finally gotten to where his career was really taking off, and he was feeling good about himself and his opportunities. I was optimistic that maybe things would get better between us since he was doing so well, that we could make a family of our own, and build something really good."

"Makes sense," Grant murmured, not wanting to break the flow, wanting to stay right in the moment for as long as possible. Leo was so beautiful right now, with his skin still healthy and pink from freshly dialyzed blood, and his eyes burning with warm heat in the low light. Grant could watch Leo's hands move when he talked forever. The way they lifted and illustrated with gentle movements, the length of his fingers, and the elegant shape. Grant cleared his throat, focusing on Leo's words again.

"So, I said we'd take her."

Leo went quiet, and Grant sensed a struggle in him, as though he were weighing whether or not to reveal the next part of the story.

Leo took a breath and said, "Curtis wasn't too happy about it at first. He said that he wasn't sure he was ready, that he'd rather have waited, made the choice at a different time in our lives." Leo cleared his throat. "I talked him into it. I mean, what was I supposed to do? There she was, this tiny little thing that my sister had abandoned, and I couldn't just leave her there, Grant! I couldn't just leave that little baby alone and hope they found a good foster home, or that my parents wouldn't struggle taking care of her—" Leo was getting upset now.

Grant reached out a hand and put it on his shoulder. He didn't say anything. He didn't know what to say. Grant made hard choices every day, but Leo was a different person, and Hannah was his sister, and Lucky was his niece. Family was important to Leo, and so, no, he couldn't imagine that Leo would walk away from that. Grant would have been horrified if Leo had chosen to do anything different than he had.

"We fought about it. She was very sick, and it was awhile before we could bring her home anyway." Leo sighed. "I'm sorry, you didn't want to hear all of this. You just asked about her name."

"No, I do. It's fine. Tell me," Grant said. He wanted to know all of this more than Leo could possibly understand. He wanted to know it so very much. He wanted to know everything about Leo.

Leo brought up one shaking hand to run through his hair. "Yeah, well, I'll cut to the chase. Curtis eventually came around. I mean, she was so tiny, and kind of ugly, like a drowned kitten." Leo laughed, remembering. "He's the one who named her. We were arguing over the name. We used to argue over everything. Anyway, he wanted to name her after his mother, Harriet Roma was his preference. And I thought Marie Leona was nice—after my grandmother and me, since we were her blood."

"That makes sense," Grant said, though he wasn't sure that it did. Leo was confounding in so many ways. Still, it didn't hurt to agree.

"She was so tiny. She could fit in both of my hands. And I said to Curtis, 'We're so lucky to have her. We're going to make her life perfect in every way.'" Leo laughed then, a little bitterly, but he kept talking. "And Curtis said, 'That's it! Her name is Lucky!' And he was right. I took one look at her and knew that he was right. So she's been my good luck charm ever since."

Grant let out a slow breath, allowed his hand to move from Leo's shoulder, up to Leo's hair, and then massaged the back of Leo's neck gently. He didn't mention that between contracting myocarditis, requiring a heart transplant, and now having two bum kidneys, Leo's life had been anything but lucky since Lucky had been born.

"It's a terrible name," he said instead.

Leo laughed. "Yeah, well, it's actually Lucille Marie, and she can choose to go by either of those when she's older if she wants. For now, she's Lucky."

"Or Robot Twinklestars," Grant said, quipping a pretend game Lucky had been playing when he saw her the day before.

"Robot Twinklestars eats her breakfast," Leo said in a robotic monotone. "Robot Twinklestars brushes her teeth. All systems functioning. All systems ready for the day."

Grant laughed, his hand moving back to Leo's shoulder, feeling the heat of his body through his thin shirt. Leo sighed, rested his head back on the couch, and then turned to face Grant, his eyes wide and dark, and his lips wet, open, and inviting.

"Leo," Grant said softly, leaning closer. "I want to kiss you again."

Leo whispered, "I've wanted you to kiss me again for a long time now. For like, the last fifteen minutes."

"That *is* a long time," Grant murmured.

"Felt like eternity."

Leo's mouth was hot, and Grant couldn't get enough of it. He expected Leo to push him away, to stop it before things got heated like before, but Leo just slid down on the sofa, bringing Grant on top of him, and things grew intense very fast.

"I thought we were waiting for this," Grant said, panting into Leo's mouth.

"Changed my mind. I'm entitled." Leo laughed, kissing

Grant hard.

"Get your shirt off. I want to touch you."

"Later," Leo said, grinding up against him like a high schooler. "This is good. All systems functioning," Leo muttered, pushing his hips against Grant. "All systems ready for the day."

Grant shut him up with another kiss, and Leo wasn't long in giving in completely to the moment. He wrapped his legs around Grant's back, humping up. The sound of their blue jeans scraping together was almost as loud as Leo's hot breath in his ear. It was going to end a lot faster than Grant wanted it to, but the ache in his cock and the desire to be closer to Leo drove him on. They clutched each other and moved desperately together.

As Leo's wet mouth moved down onto Grant's neck, Grant could hear him babbling, pleas of *yeah*, and *good*, and *harder*. It was hot, so fucking hot.

"Leo," Grant murmured, and Leo shook against him, releasing a high, needy sound that ricocheted through Grant like a bullet of want. Grant clutched Leo's shoulders, buried his face in Leo's neck, and jerked in Leo's arms as he came, muffling his cry by biting down on Leo's straining throat.

Leo made a startled noise and then shook hard, trembling as he cried out and came, too. He arched against Grant, clutching Grant's head to his neck, and encouraging the pain.

After they both calmed, panting and kissing each other down from the height of orgasm, Grant kissed the mark he'd made on Leo's neck, and pulled away to examine it. The teeth marks were deeper than he'd thought, but when he looked into Leo's eyes, he saw nothing but hot, liquid warmth, affection, and gratitude.

"Did I hurt you?" Grant asked, his finger tracing the red mark.

Leo's legs relaxed down so that Grant was resting between them, and, chest to chest, Grant felt Leo's heart pounding. Leo blushed a deep red, averting his eyes and looking a little ashamed. In that moment, Grant knew that he *had* hurt him, and, more importantly, he knew that Leo had liked it.

"Well, that's good to know," Grant murmured.

"Yeah?" Leo asked.

"Very good to know."

Leo's already flushed face grew a bit darker, but he admitted, "I liked it. I liked that you didn't treat me like I'm fragile."

"You? Fragile? You're a strapping farm-bred piece of man meat," Grant said.

Leo laughed. "That makes me sound like bacon. Though, I remember you told me at Red's Breakfast Café last week that bacon is your one true love, so I should be flattered by any real or imagined comparison."

"Indeed. You should be. Bacon is sacred, after all. Like Jesus, or Mahatma, or the Dalai Lama, only so much better than all of them combined, because it actually does what it claims to do. It tastes like *bacon*."

"This is the most bizarre post-sex conversation I've ever had," Leo murmured.

"Oh, sorry, was superstar Mr. Curtis Banks more gracious? Should I tell you that you have beautiful eyes and that I want to be with you forever now?"

"If you wanted to say that, I wouldn't be offended." Leo laughed again, moving to the side, wedged between the sofa back and Grant's body. "But, really, right now I just want to clean up. It's getting a bit uncomfortable in here." He motioned toward his pants as he untangled himself from Grant.

Watching Leo wash off, staring at him in the bathroom mirror, Grant had to admit that at least part of what he'd joked about was definitely true. He stepped forward and wrapped his arms around Leo's waist. Leo caught his expression in the glass and smiled.

"It's true," Grant said.

"What is?"

"That you have beautiful eyes."

Leo lowered his lashes, and laughed a little, and then glanced up to Grant in the mirror. "Is that a compliment? A sincere compliment? I don't know what to say."

"Say thank you."

"Thank you."

Leo stared into Grant's eyes, and then turned around, looking at him directly. His voice was soft and so damn earnest as he asked, "So, do you think you could ever fall for somebody again?"

Grant narrowed his eyes. "I think that depends."

"On what?"

"On whether the guy is going to stick around this time."

Leo breathed, "Oh," and leaned in, pressing a soft, wet kiss to Grant's mouth.

Chapter Ten

*L*EO HADN'T SPENT the night, even though Grant had asked him to; instead, he'd headed home after cleaning up in the bathroom, saying something about needing to do some chores at the so-called 'farm' in the morning.

But the next morning, not long after ten, Leo arrived at Grant's apartment again just as Grant was dressing after his shower. He stood on Grant's doorstep with grocery bags full of the stuff to make pancakes from scratch and he smiled like the light of midday, brighter than the morning sun.

Grant couldn't look away from his happy face, and it lifted his spirits, which had been oddly dark since Leo had left the night before. He'd felt scratchy inside, like his brain was wearing an itchy wool sweater, and he couldn't sleep for wishing that Leo had stayed.

"Good morning," Leo said, dumping the bags of stuff onto the kitchen counter. "Sleep well?"

Grant scratched at his head, remembering the hours of frustration, and sighed. "Not really, no."

Leo looked worried, and then came around the counter and put his arms around Grant's waist, his face all sweet concern. "Did you miss me so much you couldn't sleep?"

"Something like that." Grant kissed Leo's mouth and found the minty taste of toothpaste still on his lips.

"Still want pancakes?" Leo asked, eyebrows lifting with the question.

"Absolutely," Grant said. "Where's Lucky?"

"Still with my parents. They're taking her to see a movie this afternoon, so I have all day. What's your schedule like?"

"I'm free." Grant's blood rushed harder, and he wondered whether making pancakes might turn into making love if he played his cards right.

Leo started opening and closing cabinets in Grant's kitchen, looking for something. "Uh, do you have a griddle or a frying pan?"

"This do?" Grant asked, handing over a barely used frying pan that he'd had since his internship in Seattle. He made grilled cheese with it occasionally, but he didn't really have the time or skills for much else.

Leo's phone rang and he glanced at the caller ID, dusting off his hands. "Sorry, I need to take this."

Leo moved to the window looking out over the parking lot and the cemetery next to the apartment building. "Mrs. Franklin, thank you for calling me back."

He paused and listened, and as he did his shoulders straightened and his chin went up. "I understand your concern, Mrs. Franklin, but perhaps you didn't understand my position. As you're aware, I've got some contacts on the school board who might be *interested* in your methods of discipline, and I have little doubt that they'd see my side of things quite clearly."

Leo's voice was low but serious, authoritative and firm. Grant had never heard this voice before. It was a 'Dad' voice for sure.

"Yes, Mrs. Franklin, the new library at the school *is* being funded via a substantial donation from Curtis Banks, Lucky's other father. And I agree that it is *very interesting* how that happened so recently, right around the time Lucky got into trouble in your class the first time. Funny how things can be coincidental that way, wouldn't you say?"

Grant pursed his lips and sat down at the table, relaxing there as Leo continued to essentially threaten one of Lucky's teachers.

"Now, Mrs. Franklin, do I need to review this with you again? Lucky is going through a very tough time in her life right now. She's moved across the country, leaving her friends and her other parent behind. She's coping with my illness, and she's not exactly fitting in with the other kids. And God knows the way you've been treating her hasn't helped with *that*."

Leo paced a little in front of the window, a small, kind of scary smile on his lips. Grant was impressed.

"So, this is how it's going to be: you'll sit down with the private instructor that Curtis is flying in on Monday afternoon to develop a plan of action for Lucky's education. This way, you'll have a game plan on hand, preapproved by both me and the instructor, for when Lucky inevitably finishes her work before the other kindergarteners. I suggest a letter writing exercise to start with—those skills will always come in handy, such as the letter I have drafted and stamped in my desk drawer. The one addressed to the principal and the school board."

Leo hummed in response to something Mrs. Franklin said and then went on, "You could start with local celebrities, such as letters to the weather man, the mayor, and the principal. Have Lucky send her regards and any thoughts she might want to share with them. Proofread it for acceptable content, and then mail it. At that point, move on to the state government, bigger celebrities, the King of Denmark, I don't care, but keep her thinking. Have her read about the people and places she'll be addressing. *Educate my daughter*, Mrs. Franklin, because that is your *job*, and if I hear that you've been putting her in a corner for acting out when she's bored, or that you've been pointing out to the other children that she's *odd* and has a *strange family*, which is, frankly, offensive and unprofessional on multiple levels, then I will be compelled, Mrs.

Franklin, to go to the school board, and I am *sure* that they will see my side of things. Am I clear?"

Leo paused to listen a moment, turning to catch Grant watching him. He lifted his chin defensively and ended the call. "Good. I thought we could come to an agreement. Have a wonderful weekend, Mrs. Franklin."

Leo tucked the cell phone into his pocket and cleared his throat. "So, pancakes," he said, going back to the batter and stirring it. He seemed tense, as though he were expecting Grant to say something about the call, though Grant had no idea what. Leo looked up and offered challengingly, "Well?"

Grant said, "I'd have her fired. She sounds like an imbecile who has no business near children."

Leo's lips twitched. "Really? So you don't think I over-stepped?"

Grant was confused. "The library may have been overkill, but if Curtis Banks has the money to burn, I say go for it. Leverage is good. And standing up for your daughter? How is that overstep-ping? I'd be angry if you didn't take that woman to task. Hell, if all you said is true, I think you were too easy on her."

Leo smiled, looking bashful and pleased. Grant felt pulled in by the expression, wanting to be closer, wanting to touch and kiss it, make Leo whimper the way he had the night before.

Leo was so confoundedly sexy in all of his iterations.

Leo began the process of making perfectly round pancakes in the frying pan, dividing his attention. He said, "She was my teacher once. A long time ago. I heard her husband passed away last year and that she doesn't really have the money to retire. I'm sure she's in pain. I don't really want to get her fired. I just want her to treat Lucky with respect."

"Maybe Curtis should take that library money, give it to the old lady, and spare a lot of kids future emotional scarring in the process."

Leo met his eye, a smile playing around his lips, and he said, "That's not exactly how Curtis works. This way he gets to flaunt it in the press, make something of it all." He flipped the pancakes and put them on the waiting plate, handing them to Grant. "Go ahead and eat them while they're hot. I shouldn't have any anyway. I have to watch my phosphorus intake."

Grant poured syrup on the pancakes, watching Leo make more. He took a bite and said, "Not bad."

Leo laughed again. "They're amazing. I can tell by the look on your face."

Grant dug into the pancakes feeling mixed up. He was confused by some of Leo's expressions, the way he'd seemed after Mrs. Franklin's phone call and the fact that he wasn't meeting Grant's eye.

"What?" Leo asked, glancing up from his work. "Why are you looking at me like that?"

"Just wondering why you doubt yourself. Seems pretty stupid for someone so smart."

Leo smiled and said, "Sorry, I'm having trouble parsing the compliment from the insult. Give me a minute."

Grant finished the pancakes and started on the one that Leo had just finished up. Leo began a new batch, keeping his eyes averted as he said, "Curtis really hated it when I did that kind of thing. He hated when I used his money or influence, whatever you want to call it, to get what I wanted. He said I was using him. And maybe I am. But when it comes to Lucky…"

"When it comes to Lucky, what does it matter?"

"Exactly. It's not like I used his name or money for myself. Now or in the past." The defensiveness in his tone made it clear that this had been a bone of contention many times. Leo waved his hand. "You know, forget it. I just wasn't expecting you to applaud me."

"When it comes to your kid, I'd expect you to do whatever it takes. It's something I admire. Require even."

"Require?"

"I already told you that I like 'em pretty." Grant said, standing up, approaching Leo, and taking hold of his chin. "But I also like 'em strong. It was one of the first things I noticed about you. No one can dispute how strong you are."

Leo kissed him fast and hard. Leo's mouth was greedy, and Grant groaned as Leo pulled his hair. Pushing Leo back against the counter, Grant nipped and licked, only the smell of burning pancakes made him pull away. Grant grabbed the potholder, jerked the frying pan from the stove, and dropped it with a clatter into the sink. Leo turned the burner off and met Grant's mouth again. The short distance to his bedroom was traversed with many stops against the wall, and bumps into corners and doorframes, and by the time they fell onto the unmade bed, still rumpled from Grant's sleepless night, they had their shirts off and pants undone.

Leo panted, clawing at Grant's back, seeming to want him closer than physically possible. Grant bit down on Leo's shoulder, making a mark, and Leo jerked underneath him, gasping and moaning, and then he started pulling at Grant's pants, trying to get them off.

"Oh, God," Leo muttered. "It's been…it's been a really long time," he said his breath coming fast and rough. "I'm not sure how long—God, Grant," and he was back, kissing Grant, moaning, and grasping him so hard that Grant had a hard time catching his breath.

Grant's hips ground down against Leo's, and he finally broke free enough to push his own pants down, and to get Leo's jeans over his hips. By then Leo had grabbed him back again, pulling him down, mouthing hot, wet lines up his neck and making soft noises of want and need.

When Grant ducked his head down and kissed behind Leo's ear, he was treated to a whimper, and when he bit down again on Leo's neck, making sure it was hard enough to leave another mark, Leo grunted, deep and resonant. He grasped Grant's hair and held him to his neck as Grant bit down again.

Leo whimpered when Grant pulled back to kick his pants off, and to jerk Leo's down all the way, too, throwing both pairs over the side of the bed. Leo's cock was big, thick, and incredibly hard. His body was beautiful—marred only by the transplant scar on his chest and the AV fistula in his forearm. Grant swallowed hard, surprised he hadn't noticed it before, remembering how Leo had declined to remove his shirt the night before. He wondered if this was part of the reason why.

"It doesn't hurt," Leo said, lifting his arm up, looking at the place where they put the needle in three times a week. "It's not pretty, though."

"Functional is good, too." He saw the flicker of worry in Leo's eyes, the sudden lessening arousal, and he quickly ran a hand down Leo's side and then grasped his thick, hard cock firmly. "I am so hot for you," Grant said, the truest thing he could think of to say at the moment. Leo's eyes sparked again, and he reached for Grant with his AV fistula arm and pulled him down to kiss.

It was less frantic this time, a little shy, and incredibly needy, so Grant slowed it down, running his fingers through Leo's hair, petting him, and drawing sweet little noises from his throat. Reveling in the length of Leo's body pressed against his, he moaned. Leo's thighs fell open and Grant rocked his hips, pressing their hard cocks together, rubbing off slowly as Grant drew the moments out long and hot.

"You need to tell me how far we're gonna go with this today," Grant whispered, his fingers teasing at Leo's jawline and wondering what on earth he was doing. He'd never asked that kind of thing before; he usually just let things play out as they would, ending up with an orgasm for the most part, no matter how the details went. In bed, Grant prided himself on reading a lover's messages.

But with Leo he had to be sure. He didn't know why, but he didn't trust himself. Not that he wouldn't stop the moment Leo said no, but rather he didn't trust himself to know the difference between Leo liking it rough and Leo not staying no when he should. He already knew Leo would take a lot, and Grant wanted it to be on the right terms. It wasn't a good time to wing it.

"I don't know," Leo gasped. "I, uh –" He blushed and swallowed hard. "I've never liked…you know. Anal. It hurts a lot. And not in the good way."

Grant nodded slowly, schooling his face carefully. "So, you and," Grant was loathe to mention Curtis's name, so he didn't. "You two didn't do that?" he asked. He hoped he didn't sound disappointed, because, God…he was disappointed. Confused, even. He'd never been with anyone who'd complained, especially not anyone who enjoyed sex a little rough.

"Twice," Leo said, and Grant could feel his heart pounding, thrumming so hard that Grant could feel it against his own chest. "I never liked it. So, we did other things, mainly. When we did things at all."

Grant could feel Leo's hard-on shrinking against his own, and he moved his hips a little, trying to tease it back to life.

"If you want to, though…" Leo said, his voice anxious and worried. "I mean, if you wanted to try?"

"What I want is to make you feel good. I want to see what you look like when you come. That's what I want. Anything else isn't important." He slapped Leo's hip kind of hard and said, "So show me what I want to see."

Leo eyes went dark and his cock fattened up again immediately.

Grant kissed Leo's mouth, and then ducked down, bypassing Leo's nipples, saving them for later, eager to get what he most wanted in his mouth. He grasped Leo's hips in both hands, holding him down against the bed as he sucked Leo's cock into his mouth, hard and fast. He wrapped his hand around the base, jerking in rhythm. Leo squirmed and groaned, until Grant pulled off with a pop.

Still moving his hand on Leo's cock, all sloppy and wet with spit, he bit down on the tendon where Leo's leg joined his groin. Leo jerked, laughing and yelping at once. Grant bit his way over Leo's inner thighs and then nipped softly at Leo's ballsack. Leo shuddered and twisted away from Grant, flopping over onto his stomach, but Grant kept hold of Leo's cock, squeezing and jerking it as Leo writhed. Leo gripped the pillow and arched his back, lifting his ass perfectly as Grant bit at the back of his thighs.

Taking the position as an invitation, Grant pulled Leo's ass cheeks apart and dove in, his tongue pressing against Leo's asshole.

Leo yelped in shock, and then scrambled a little, but Grant held him fast. Grant's tongue flicked at Leo's hole, feeling it grip and spasm against his mouth. Leo whimpered, whined, and twisted against Grant's grip desperately, but Grant held on. Leo shook hard and chill bumps rose up on his ass, as he released all sorts of wild sounds.

Grant pulled his tongue back and lifted up a little, using Leo's flailing movements to position his body the way he wanted. He pushed Leo's thighs up and apart, holding him open and vulnerable. He bit his ass cheeks and slapped them gently before diving in again to suck, lick, and gnaw at Leo's asshole. Every squirm and surprised yelp left his own cock convulsing and leaking pre-come. Soon, a relentless tremor took over Leo's whole body.

Grant knew the moment had come. Leo went very still instead of moving and twisting, and he ducked his head into the pillow, muffling his own breath as he tensed all over. Part of Grant wanted to make Leo come like this, to reach between his legs and jerk him while eating his ass until he spilled everywhere, but more than that, he wanted to see Leo come.

Grant pulled away, holding back his laughter at Leo's frustrated whine, and urged Leo to flip over. Leo's face was astounding. His cheeks were flushed and his gray eyes open. His expression was wrecked, vulnerable, and hot. The definition of defenseless.

"I want to see you come now," Grant said, and his voice sounded thick to his own ears.

"Yeah, okay," Leo said. "I need to. So much."

"I know. If it's okay, I'm going to put these inside," Grant said, holding up two fingers and then slicking them with spit. "And I'm going to make you come."

Leo nodded wordlessly, his eyes glassy and huge, and when Grant tapped against Leo's slick, worked-over asshole, his fingers sank in easily, just as he'd known they would. He smiled at Leo's surprised gasp.

Leo's steel-hard cock jerked, so on edge and ready to come for him.

"Please," Leo murmured, moving on Grant's fingers experimentally, and then groaning, obviously loving it. "Oh, God, it's been so long. Please."

"It's okay. I've got you," Grant murmured. "Just a little longer."

He wanted to make it last, wanted to see Leo squirming on his fingers for at least the next three days of his life, but it wasn't meant to be. Leo grabbed Grant's free hand, forced it to grip Leo's cock, and showed him the pace he liked. Then, as soon as Grant was jerking him at the rate he needed, Leo gave himself over to the pleasure. He clawed at the sheets as his face crumpled, and his body drew up on itself.

"Please, bite me," Leo whimpered.

Grant took some of Leo's inner thigh flesh into his mouth and bit down hard. Leo froze under him, seemed to struggle for a moment, and then Grant felt the tell-tale rhythmic clench around his fingers. Leo shouted as he came, shooting up onto his chest, hitting his own chin and even the wooden headboard, with seemingly endless, thick spurts.

Leo shuddered for a long time, whimpering and gasping. Grant left his fingers lodged in Leo's ass until he'd calmed down. He ran his other hand over Leo's stomach, down his side, and then up to wipe the come from Leo's chin. As Leo watched with wide eyes, Grant raised his jizz-covered hand to lick his fingers. His own cock ached. He was so hard he felt like he was going to lose his mind. But this was Leo's moment, his time, and Grant wanted him to feel as good as possible right now.

He slowly withdrew his fingers from Leo's ass and turned to get something to clean up when Leo surprised him. He sat up quickly, pushed Grant down, and enthusiastically held him against the mattress with the weight of his body. Leo's eyes were still hot, but less shocked, more challenging as he murmured, "That was great, but I think you forgot something."

"I—uh, yeah?" Grant swallowed hard.

"Oh, yeah," Leo said. "Definitely forgot the most important part."

"Oh," Grant said, his cock flexing against his stomach, and

his balls drawing up tight.

"You forgot how much I want to have you inside me," Leo said, and Grant thought he'd lost his mind for a second, until Leo's mouth suddenly descended onto his cock, and, holy fuck, he was *good at this*, really damn good.

Grant's head fell to the pillow and he gripped Leo's hair in his fist. He didn't pull Leo down on his cock or hold him in place. Instead he let Leo do his work and simply felt him there, under his command.

Quickly, Grant's legs drew up, his knees spreading, his stomach tensing, and his heart thudding so hard that the only thing he could hear over it were his own groans. And then, God, Leo made a deep sucking noise, and Grant's cock lodged deep in Leo's throat.

Grant pulled Leo's hair and came like the world was collapsing in on the bed. The orgasm was almost as harsh as it was sweet, and he jerked and trembled for long, powerful seconds after. His whole body twitched wildly, until Leo's voice brought him down.

"That was amazing."

Grant groaned and shivered again.

Leo grinned; his mouth still looked wet and bruised from their kisses and the blow job. "I left you speechless? Not gonna say anything about your own greatness in bed?" Leo teased.

"What's to say? I just showed you."

Leo collapsed against Grant's chest, his body sweaty and heaving, out of breath from his efforts. Grant held him there, thinking about how long it'd been since he'd felt this content, and coming to the conclusion that it was never. Never. Not even once.

"I liked it," Leo said, softly, as though a little embarrassed.

"I know," Grant said.

Leo batted at him and said, "I mean…your fingers. I liked that. I've never enjoyed it before."

"Well, there's an art to it," Grant said.

"Yeah?"

"It's called getting someone really turned on and then really wet and slippery down there. It's pretty simple, really."

Leo twisted and sighed as though both wanting to talk about it and not.

"Didn't you do it to yourself, ever?" Grant asked.

"I did. I do. I just…I don't know. I'd get tense, I guess, when I was with Curtis," Leo said, sounding guilty.

Grant said nothing as he stroked Leo's hair and willed him to drop the subject. He didn't want to talk about Curtis Banks every time they fucked. Or didn't fuck. As the case may be.

"I, uh, also like it when you, um," Leo laughed. "When you bite me. Or slap my ass. I don't know. Is that…don't you think that's a little—"

"Hot. It's hot. I like it. You like it. That's all there is to it."

"Okay," Leo said, and his relief was so obvious that Grant kissed the top of his head. Leo nuzzled Grant's neck. "I'm thirsty," he said. "I need to get some water."

Grant watched him get up, admiring his body as he walked, the fuzzy hair on his ass, the length of his legs, the way his shoulders tapered up to his neck. Leo paused in the doorway to the living room.

"Hey," Leo said.

"Mmm?"

Leo smiled fondly. "I, uh, well…how can I put this so that you'll understand?"

Grant waited.

"Grant, I like you better than bacon."

Grant laughed and Leo grinned, his eyes lighting up as he

turned to go into the living room.

Grant called out, "Leo, wait."

"Yeah?"

Grant sat up, narrowed his eyes, and said seriously, "The feeling is mutual. But, don't tell bacon."

"Never," Leo said, beaming. "Do you want some water, too?"

"Sure," Grant answered, suddenly exhausted. He slumped down onto the bed. "Absolutely."

But he was asleep before the water came, and when he woke up Leo was gone.

There was just a note that read: *Seriously. Better than bacon. <3 Leo.*

Chapter Eleven

Seven Months Ago

A MONTH AFTER the first time they'd played orgasm-friends together, Grant was coasting along, finding the ebb and flow of their relationship much more sanguine than he'd ever imagined.

Grant texted with Leo off and on every day, spoke to him at night if he hadn't seen him, and had sex with him as often as he could justify. The cog in that particular work was not the kid, which would have been Grant's original assumption. No, Lucky was asleep like clockwork by eight-thirty pm, and she slept more soundly than a patient under anesthesia.

Nor was the problem lack of desire. Grant couldn't ever remember being anywhere near as hot for another guy as he was for Leo. Grant wanted Leo all the time. He wanted to see him with his head back, his mouth open, and come splashing over his chest more then he wanted anything else in life, and that was saying something so huge that if Grant really thought about it a massive hole of terror opened up under his feet.

And it was obvious that Leo was on fire for Grant, too. It'd surprised and delighted Grant to discover that Leo was far kinkier than he would have ever expected from someone who usually projected such a wholesome image. He secretly gloated over the fact that it'd surprised Leo, too, and he reveled in the knowledge that a certain ex had never discovered that Leo had a thing for pain.

As much as Leo liked sappy stuff like candlelit dinners and walks out by the farm's pond holding hands, those things didn't turn Leo on even a fraction as much as when Grant forcefully demanded, "Get on your knees and suck me." Grant was half convinced that if Leo was asked what turned him on more, having Grant's mouth wrapped around his own cock or being ordered to suck Grant's cock, Leo would pick the latter.

No, the issue with sex was that Leo was still a sick man, and he had days of extreme fatigue and physical discomfort. On those days Grant usually brought take-out to the farm and helped get Lucky into bed. Sometimes he'd fall asleep sitting up on the farm's old, comfy living room sofa, holding Leo's feet on his lap, and wake up the next morning tucked up in a blanket with a soft pillow under his head.

Alec, of course, had to have his say, and he gloated so much about Grant and Leo's whatever-they-had-going that Grant had threatened to stop taking his phone calls.

"Admit it," Alec said. "You like it."

"I'm not denying it."

And, yeah, Grant liked it all. He never imagined that he could ever be the kind of man who would walk into the Wal-Mart for a few frozen dinners and leave with an Encyclopedia of the Human Body for Kids tucked under his arm because he'd walked past it on a display shelf and remembered Lucky asking him how kidneys worked.

He liked Leo's laugh, the way he smelled, the way he tasted, and the way he talked. Leo was, in so many ways, an endless mystery to Grant.

For one thing, Leo was a bundle of emotion that Grant didn't understand. He was warm and affectionate but also unpredictable. He was at turns playful, strong and determined, manipulative when he needed to be, and incredibly purposeful, and then he'd turn around and be timid, uncertain, and oversensitive. Their tender moments together, when Leo was so earnestly open and warm, Grant sometimes had a hard time believing that it was all for real. But it was; it was always real with Leo.

Grant also learned to like Leo's extended family, especially when they left him alone at the corner of the crowded table, stuffing his face with good food. In the sprawling clan of Garner cousins, there was always someone who was in love, or broken-hearted, or angry, or doing drugs, or having illegitimate babies, or getting caught in affairs or other unsavory activities. Or, as in Leo's case, someone who was sick.

One night, after an accidental family dinner at the farm—Grant had come over expecting Leo and Lucky to be alone, only to find Blaine, Felice, Meryl, Chuck, and four other people that Grant couldn't remember the names of despite seeing them around town for years—Leo asked, "So, did you learn anything interesting?"

"Yeah, I learned that chances are good you're going to look exactly like your mother in twenty years."

"Twenty years?" Leo asked. "Are you planning to be around in twenty years to see it?"

"Well, why play small?"

That night Grant had the honor of receiving Leo Garner's tongue in his ass, and while it seemed like it was probably the first time Leo had ever attempted such a thing, it was an incredibly *rewarding* experience, and Grant desperately wanted it to happen again. Soon.

Sitting alone in the cafeteria, pretending to read a newspaper, and shoveling green beans and mashed potatoes into his mouth, Grant made mental plans on how, exactly, to get Leo's tongue down there again. He alternated between going with a command—"Lick my hole"—and going with a reward approach—

"I'll lick your ass if you lick my ass." He was sure either one would work. It was just that the commanding approach would probably make Leo so hot that he'd be extra enthusiastic in carrying out the order, but the reward approach would reap Leo's bashful, sexy smile that made Grant's cock jerk just thinking about it.

His mind was lingering on such thoughts when, from the other side of the newspaper, he heard Leo's voice say, "Yeah, Grant's pretty amazing once you get to know him."

He opened his mouth to agree, but it was full. In the time it took for him to swallow, though, he changed his mind about announcing himself.

It wasn't as though Grant *planned* to listen to the conversation between Leo and his friends. It was just so…easy. After all, he was the one who was eating in the hospital cafeteria first. Was it his fault that they hadn't seen him behind the newspaper, or that he'd only just realized they were even there? He peeked around the corner of his paper to see whom Leo was talking to.

"Do *not* even begin to tell any sex stories about him," said Riley McCall, a friend of Leo's from high school who was currently working in radiology. At least he thought that's what Leo had said when he'd introduced Grant to his friends last week. Grant was just impressed with himself for remembering the guy's name. "I don't even want to know."

Ellen, a peds nurse and Riley's girlfriend from what Grant recalled, said, "Look at that smug smile, Riley. He's the cat who ate the cream."

"*Got* the cream!" Riley said, horrified. "That innuendo is gross enough without you making it worse. I'm telling you now, man, if you spill about the sex stuff, I'm so outta here, and I won't babysit for Lucky anymore, no matter how bad you beg."

"Oh, *beg*," Ellen said. "You asked for it, Riley. Look at him blush. Dr. Anderson totally makes him beg."

"That's it! I'm done!" Riley declared, and there was the sound of a chair scraping on the floor, and Leo's exclamation of innocence—"Ellen said it, not me!"—and then, once the laughter settled down, it was clear Riley hadn't actually left, because they were back to chatting again.

"So, I guess this is awkward and all," Riley said strangely. "Um, 'cause I know you're with Dr. Anderson now and all. But Curtis was our friend back in the day, too, so I guess we'd just like to know. You know?"

"Know what?" Leo asked.

Ellen answered for Riley, "What's going on with Curtis? Are you guys really over?"

Leo dragged some air though his teeth and let out a long sigh. "Looks like it. The forms have been signed, pretty reluctantly on his part to be fair, but I have them. Well, my attorney has them now."

"But *why*?" Riley asked.

"Yeah, Leo," Ellen said. "You guys were together a long time. How do you just turn your back on that?"

Leo sighed. "Ask Curtis. He turned his back on me and Lucky every chance he got."

"He came here and got you, man. Just like he promised. So don't tell me he turned his back on you," Riley said defensively."

"Hey," Ellen said. "Let him talk. Curtis is our friend, but Leo's not a dick."

"I know, it's just…"

"It's okay," Leo said, and Grant had a hard time remembering why he didn't want to stand up and clock Leo's pals. The last thing Leo needed was to get upset. But Leo went on, "I don't want to get into it too, much, but… At first, it was the little things. Like refusing to include me in his decision-making or his filming schedules. Be he always expected me to still be standing right where he'd left me when he wanted to come home. Never mind how it affected me or what I wanted in life. So I dealt with that for a long time."

"You couldn't travel with him?"

"No. He didn't want me around. He said I pulled focus from his work."

"What's that supposed to mean?" Riley asked.

"That I wanted too much attention and asked too much of him. Or at least that's what he said."

Grant ground his teeth together. He wanted to find Curtis Banks and kick him in the balls.

"But honestly, that was bullshit," Leo said sharply. "Truthfully? I don't think I asked enough of him. When I was deathly sick with myocarditis, and Lucky needed him? Do you think he was there for her? No. He sent a nanny to take care of her instead. He didn't even leave his filming location when I had the transplant."

Grant upped his fantasy from ball-kicking to throat-slitting.

"Yeah. I know, right? He said there was nothing he could do for me, really, so he just stayed on location and kept working."

"Oh," Ellen gasped. "My God, Leo. We had no idea."

Leo huffed a bitter laugh. "Yeah, it would be one thing if I'd chosen to put up with that kind of half-love for myself, but it's an entirely different thing to stay there and let it happen to your kid," Leo said, and his voice sounded tight.

Grant fought the urge to stand up and put a stop to it. Leo shouldn't have to explain himself. He didn't owe that to anybody.

Leo sighed. "I shouldn't have ever left Blountville with him. After his first big break in Los Angeles? When he came back here, sought me out, and promised me the world? I got swept up in the romance of it all. He'd just landed that big movie deal. I thought our lives would be a fairy tale. Ridiculous, right?"

"We all thought that," Ellen murmured.

Riley huffed.

"But the truth is, that was all for show, too. He wanted to be out, and his agent said that having a steady, non-celebrity boyfriend would make him look wholesome. Can you believe that? It was all for appearance's sake. And I thought it was love."

"Leo, man." Riley sounded pissed.

Grant couldn't blame him. He was pissed, too.

"Yeah, so, that's the truth. Curtis loved his work more than he loved me and Lucky. Not that he doesn't love Lucky, mind you. Because he does. In his way. But being famous, or trying to be, consumed him. For a long time I blamed myself. I thought it was my fault for being so…I don't know, so *me* that he couldn't put me first. But, in the end, when I got sick again, when my kidneys failed, and he couldn't be bothered to stay home to help me? That should have been the final straw, but, if you can believe it, it wasn't until he started shoving Lucky's needs aside and then trying to use his money to buy her love that I knew I had to go."

"So you came back to Blountville. I get that. It's home," Ellen said.

"No, not at first. I didn't really spread the word about all this, because I was ashamed. I felt like a failure. But, for the last year before I came home, I didn't live with Curtis. I moved out of our house and took Lucky with me."

"Oh, Leo, you could have told us."

"Yeah, man, you know we've got your back," Riley said, leading Grant to wonder if the man had already forgotten the jerky comments he'd made to Leo earlier. Because he hadn't.

Leo kept talking, like now that he was spilling his guts, he had to get it all out. "I got a house not too far from Curtis, and I tried to make it work. Or I told myself I was trying to make it work, but the truth is, I knew I wanted to leave LA, and I'd known that for a long time."

"You met someone," Ellen said knowingly.

"Not out in California, no. But before I left Blountville…yeah. I made a choice back then. I ended things with a guy I'd just started seeing in order to run back to Curtis. And I spent a lot of years thinking about that decision, and wondering if maybe I'd made the wrong one."

"It was Dr. Anderson?" Ellen asked.

"Yeah."

"So you regret going with Curtis?"

"Regret is such a weird word. If I'd done it differently, chosen him over Curtis, maybe Hannah wouldn't have gone to LA, and if she hadn't gone to LA, maybe there wouldn't be a Lucky. So, it's hard to say that I regret it, but…yeah, in a way, I guess I do. Things were miserable between me and Curtis for a very long time, and as much as I'd like to say that it was entirely on him, I've got to admit that sometimes I wondered if…if maybe it was my fault, too. You know, for ever choosing him to begin with, for indulging in that ridiculous fantasy." He grew quiet and Grant had to strain to hear him. "I've even wondered if maybe the myocarditis, the heart transplant, all these medications I have to take, everything I've gone though, and now my kidneys failing is some sort of cosmic punishment for going with Curtis to begin with."

"No!" Ellen cried.

"I know," Leo murmured. "Forget I said that."

"Dude, we had no idea," Riley said, sadly. "I feel like I just walked in on my parents having sex or something. All my illusions are blown."

"Sorry, Ri. I don't mean to bring you down."

"No worries, man. I'll get over it. At least there's no nudity to block out, or sagging skin and bouncing——"

"Oh, God, Riley, shut up!" Ellen said before turning back to Leo. "So, is Dr. Anderson the real reason you came back here?"

"No. I mean, it sure didn't hurt that I knew he was still around, but why would I think he'd be interested in sick ol' me after all these years? Especially after I chose Curtis instead of him?" He laughed again, this time in a weird, wondering way. "No, I came back here because when I got really sick, I didn't have any support from Curtis. He was traveling all the time, and when he was in town, there was just so much back and forth between us. It was complicated trying to raise Lucky that way. We fought so much. It started wearing me down. My health…everything. So I came back here to get help from my family."

"And we're glad you did," Ellen said.

"I have to admit, though, if it weren't for you guys, and for Grant, and Alec and Dennis, I might not stay."

Grant's stomach clenched and he put down the fork he'd been using to shovel in the mashed potatoes from his tray. It had only been a few months, but sometimes Grant felt certain that all of this *wonderful* in his life, all of the things he was growing revoltingly attached to, would simply disappear.

Leo went on, "My dad's great with Lucky, don't get me wrong, and Mom loves her, obviously. But Lucky's having a hard time coping with me and Curtis breaking up, and struggling with the culture here, too. If I don't make it—"

"Stop that!"

"It's a realistic thing to plan for, Ellen. If I don't make it, she might have been better off staying near Curtis. I don't know. But, for now, I'm planning to stay in Blountville. Mom and Dad are so helpful, and I have you all, and my cousins, and it's comfortable here for me. I'm hopeful Lucky will come to love it, too."

"Yeah, man, don't count on it," Riley said. "I mean, I don't know anything that you don't know, but this is Blountville and that child is a genius."

"I'm thinking of asking Curtis for money to send her to the private school in Nebo next year. It's just a thirty-minute drive north. But I hate to ask him for anything. He always thinks I'm using him."

"Asshole," Ellen sniffed, her opinion of her friend utterly changed. Rightfully so, in Grant's opinion. "So, this thing with Grant, though? It's different?"

Grant could hear Leo's smile. "Grant? Yeah. It's…well, it's surprising. I don't think either of us expected it, but it's become pretty serious, yeah. For me, anyway, and I think for him. I hope."

"Does he, you know, treat you okay? He seems like such a hard ass here in the hospital," Riley said. "And please don't turn that into a gay joke."

Leo chuckled. "He's surprisingly kind and amazingly human. Usually when you least expect it."

"Well…that's…good? I mean, what can I say, man? I'm happy if you're happy," Riley said.

"Thanks, Ri. The best thing is that I know you mean that."

"I do."

Grant heard the thud of a soft punch to the arm.

"But, yeah, it's been hard being back here," Leo said. "Even with my folks trying to be available when I need them, I have to admit that I'm having a hard time getting the help I need for Lucky sometimes. I mean, Ri, you know that better than anyone. How many times have I had to leave her with you or Carrie here at the hospital?"

"A lot," Riley agreed.

"Yeah," Leo's voice changed from frustrated to sweet and soft. "Grant, though, he's great with her. And she really likes him."

"Dr. Anderson and the kid? Really? Based on his reputation, I wouldn't have seen that coming," Riley said.

"Yeah, me either," Leo said.

"Alec says he's always been kind of great with Mina," Ellen offered. Grant had forgotten that she was friends with Alec. But then Alec was friends with everyone. Even him.

"It's really adorable actually," Leo said enthusiastically. "He's always so gruff and matter of fact with her, and Lucky just loves it. Though, she's not all sunshine and smiles when he's around or anything. Don't get me wrong."

It was true. Lucky was a pretty serious little kid.

Leo went on, "I don't know how to explain this, but it's like when she sees him walking toward her, she just relaxes. You can see her entire body just…let go. She's comfortable with him. Secure."

"That's wonderful," Ellen said.

"Yeah, she knows what to expect from him. And that's really important to Lucky right now. Everything's so unpredictable. She definitely trusts him. I think she likes knowing that if Grant says it, then it's true. Or true enough. Or true to Grant." Leo laughed. "When it comes to Lucky, there doesn't seem to be much difference. She's always telling me, 'Dr. Grant says,' and I have to laugh because, believe me, hearing Grant's words come out of my five-year-old's mouth?"

"Nothing funnier?" Riley supplied.

"Exactly."

"So, you really like him, then?" Ellen asked.

"Who? Grant?"

Riley said, "No, man, the guy at the cash register who was, for the record, so totally checking you out—not that I notice these things—*yeah*, Grant."

Grant sat his fork down, remembered the night before, Leo

naked on the bed at the farm, curled up around Grant, and breathing slowly as he drifted off to sleep. He remembered the way Leo had been so warm tucked against his side, and how right his own body had felt, sated, at peace. It scared him that all of that and a lot more was riding on Leo's response now.

"So much," Leo said, and the embarrassment in his voice was only topped by his earnest joy.

"Aw, Leo," Ellen said. "That makes me so happy. I'm so glad. And Curtis? You're totally over him? It's really done?"

"It's done," Leo said. "I just wish it'd been done a long time ago."

"Well, after this conversation, I'm so taking that guy off my Christmas card list," Riley said. "I had no idea he was such a douche."

"Oh, come on, Riley," Leo said. "Don't be that way. Curtis's still a good guy; he's still your friend. He's just not good for *me*. And, clearly, I'm not good for him either, so it's even this way. Don't deny him the pleasure of your rambling Christmas letter! He won't know if you and Ellen are ever gonna get married or not!"

"Hey, jerk!" Ellen said, and there was the sound of someone's arm being swatted pretty hard. Grant assumed it was Ellen hitting Leo.

"You've got to admit, you've been dragging this dating thing out for a long time now," Leo said, and his voice was so full of laughter that Grant felt it in his own throat.

"And if you keep that up, we won't watch Lucky for you this Friday night," Ellen said.

Grant frowned. A babysitter for Lucky? On Friday night? Had he forgotten some plans that they had together? He hoped he wasn't scheduled for rounds. He needed to check. Just his luck to forget something important right when things were really taking off between them.

"Why do you need us to watch her?" Riley asked. "Not that I mind! I mean, my goddaughter can stay over any time. I like it when she lectures me about Shakespeare and Zeus, man. It's bizarre. And she knows more than me!"

"Well, since you barely read anything in school that wasn't required, you can't be too surprised by that," Leo said.

"But, dude, she's *five*."

"She's precocious," Leo said. "In most ways she's like any other kid. She likes to play, get dirty, and laugh."

"Yeah, that's true! She totally beat me in that spitting contest last time, remember Ellen?"

"Don't remind me." Ellen said, dryly. "They didn't even do it off the back porch like I told them to. There was spit all over the kitchen floor. I don't even want to talk about it. No, Riley. Shut. Up."

"Hey, I cleaned it up!"

"If that's what you call cleaning it up—"

"Yeah, well, so, on Friday I have that test with the new nephrologist," Leo said, getting the conversation back on track. "It could last a while. I might be in overnight. I just don't want her to be worried, and Mom's flying to New York for some job-related reason or another, and Dad's going with her because it's their anniversary soon. So, guys, thank you. So much. I really appreciate it. You can't even begin to know."

"Did they find a donor?" Ellen asked.

"Maybe. It looks possible."

There was a lot of joy at the table then, slapping sounds and hugs. Leo put a stop to it, though, saying, "It's not a sure thing. It all depends on if this woman's kidneys are okay. She's on life support, and they're letting her go. The tests match up, but she's done a lot of drugs, apparently, and her kidneys might be affected."

Grant folded the newspaper carefully and turned to the table next to him, studying Leo's pale skin, the coloring not as healthy as right after a dialysis treatment. Leo's eyes looked tired, and his hands were a little shaky. Leo was very sick, and Grant couldn't forget it, not when they were alone, not when Leo was naked, and not now when he was sitting with his friends oblivious to Grant taking inventory. A donor. Leo needed one. The sooner the better.

Grant asked, "And was there some point in the near future when *I* was going to be privy to this information?"

"Grant! How long have you been there?" Leo said.

"Long enough," Grant said.

"Well, why didn't you say something?" Leo asked. "You could have joined us!"

Ellen raised a brow. "And miss the opportunity to eavesdrop?"

"Well, it was a very lucrative session," Grant admitted. "Especially hearing about Riley's spitting contest with the carrot."

"Carrot?" Ellen said.

"That's Lucky," Leo explained.

Grant focused on Leo. "How long have you known about this donor? What are the levels of the match?"

Leo didn't have a lot of information, but he said he'd probably have more after his meeting with Dr. Muresan in the afternoon. "I have to meet him in, oh…about ten minutes."

Riley and Ellen ended up leaving then. They both had to get back to work. Before they left, they re-established that they were taking care of Lucky on Friday night while Leo would be in the hospital, and Leo thanked them again.

After dumping their trays, Leo walked out of the cafeteria with Grant and took hold of his hand, saying, "I was going to tell you. Tonight, actually. When you came over to watch TV with me and Lucky. I was going to tell you when she went to bed."

Grant blinked at him, and he had a strange flash of Leo from the night before. On his big bed at the farm, his legs spread, knees up, and his eyes wide as Grant had fucked him with three fingers. Grant flushed hot with the memory, and then suddenly cold at the thought of Leo under the knife, followed by a surge of hope that Leo might be getting the kidney that he needed.

"Are you upset with me?" Leo asked.

"No," Grant answered. "Just surprised. I didn't expect to find out so many important things on my lunch break."

"Yeah? Like what?"

"Like that Radiology Riley is so squeamish about the concept of gay sex, or that his girlfriend is so perceptive about what you like in bed. Or that you like me *so much*."

Leo actually looked a little bashful, but he said, "Oh, you knew that. So much more than bacon, even."

"Given that you've never declared your abiding affection for said breakfast meat, I was never entirely certain just how much 'liking' that analogy entailed."

Leo bumped him with his shoulder as they walked. "You know how much I care about you, Grant. Stop kidding around."

Grant smiled and then said, "And then there were quite a few bombshells about your breakup with superstar Mr. Curtis Banks. Things I hadn't known before."

"I didn't want you to know," Leo said, the tips of his ears going red. "It's humiliating. I don't want you to think of me like that."

Grant paused in the middle of the hallway, put his hand on Leo's cheek, and spoke seriously. "You left."

Leo looked unsure but he turned his head and kissed Grant's palm. "And, besides, some of that information, like about how

I'd had doubts for a long time? That was something I feel like you really should have heard from me, Grant," Leo chided softly.

"I did hear it from you."

"You know what I mean. Face to face."

"This incredibly attractive visage before you is my face," Grant said.

Leo smiled and blinked slowly, flirtatiously for a moment, still looking timid. "Don't make me say it now. Not here."

Grant dropped his forehead to Leo's and Leo let out a soft sound. Grant kissed the end of his nose, palmed Leo's cheek, and changed the subject as he walked toward the stairs leading up to the second floor. "Then there was that little thing about a potential donor. All in all, a very interesting eavesdropping session."

"So, when do I get to eavesdrop on you?" Leo asked.

"Alas, I have no friends. So, never."

"You have Alec," Leo pointed out.

"True. I do like him. Though slightly less than I like bacon."

Leo grinned and looked down at his own feet and, much to Grant's amusement, actually shuffled them in embarrassment.

Grant's in-hospital beeper went off. One glance told him their conversation had to be over. "Sorry. Have to go."

"Okay," Leo said, taking Grant's hand again and squeezing it briefly. "See you tonight? I'll tell you what I find out from Dr. Muresan today."

Grant waved the beeper at him and said, "It depends on how long this takes. I'll call you."

• • •

Present

"WHAT IN THE hell is taking so long?" Grant asked.

"I don't know," Dennis said. "They might be having problems with Hannah. But, look, his heartbeat's steady, his blood pressure is sound. Have some patience."

"The kidney should be here by now," Grant said, cold sweat forming at the small of his back and panic sweeping through his body. "Maybe they got in there and Hannah's kidney isn't as healthy as they thought?"

"Maybe, but why borrow trouble?" Dennis said.

Grant had a strong urge to call Chuck, to insist that he bring Lucky to the hospital, because Grant needed her. He didn't know quite what he needed her for, but he wanted to see her face, maybe hold her, which he didn't do a lot because she had knobby knees that always dug into him, but he really wanted to hold her right now.

The observation room felt too small. How had he never noticed before how tiny the room was, how little air there was to breathe? He couldn't even pace properly because it was only nine steps that way and nine steps back, and suddenly he need an acre, a wide, open acre, or an endless ocean to fall into, because he was losing it. He was completely losing it.

"Grant," Dennis said. "You need to calm down. Things are just fine down there. Leo is going to be just fine."

Grant was past the point when he could tell Dennis to shut the hell up, he was past knowing anything other than the blip, blip, blip on the screens below, the numbers on the blood pressure monitor, and his own heart banging in his chest, making it hard to breath.

Lucky would ground him. She'd give him something to focus on that was real. But she couldn't be here. Not here in this room.

And Grant had to be here, too. He had to know every moment of what was happening with Leo.

"Grant, I don't know how to help you, buddy. What would Leo do? What would he say?" Dennis asked.

What would Leo do? He'd tell Grant to think of something that made him feel safe. He thought of being in bed with Leo, both of them sweaty and smiling, and then he thought of riding in the car with Leo driving Lucky to school, and he remembered kissing him in the middle of the hospital corridor just to make the nurses talk and to see Leo smile. His safe place? It *was* Leo, and, God, that made Grant feel as though he was going to turn inside out with fear.

"I can't," Grant said. He felt like he might pass out, black swirling dots speckled his vision. "Get Alec."

Dennis pulled out his phone and Grant heard him tell Alec to come to the hospital, Grant was flipping out, and Grant needed him.

He thought about Alec's soft hair, his warm cheek, and maybe if he were here, and he held Grant's hand, maybe this would be something he could tolerate. This staring down at Leo's unconscious body, cut open and waiting, still waiting, so *long* they'd been waiting, and it was really getting to be ridiculous. Maybe if he could breathe, he wouldn't be panicking so much.

"Grant, don't give yourself a heart attack, okay?"

Grant said nothing, watching the blood pressure monitor, keeping his eye on Leo's pulse.

Dennis kept talking, "This is a very common procedure. So get a grip."

At that moment the attendants from Hannah's OR came into the room with a cooler, and frantic activity began. The faster they got the kidney into Leo, the better the chances of it functioning properly, and the better the chance for a good outcome.

Grant pressed himself against the glass, trying to see if the kidney pinked up, if it started to produce urine immediately, but then there was a change in the room.

Something surprising, something unexpected.

Grant's heart stopped, he felt it go still and silent in his chest, and then thump with a mighty heave of adrenaline and fear. He didn't know how or when he broke down, or when he started pounding on the glass, but it was sometime after the numbers on the blood pressure monitor took a dive.

Grant watched them drop and drop as he yelled, and Dennis held him back, stronger than Grant had thought possible.

Chapter Twelve

Six Months Ago

"I WANT YOU to fuck me," Leo said, conversationally, while he poured boiling water over the teabag resting with the tag hanging outside of the mug. He passed it to Grant over the massive, wooden kitchen table. The house was quiet—just Grant and Leo. Lucky had already gone to bed before Grant had even made it over after his shift at the hospital.

Grant choked on his cookie. "Who, what, now?"

"I said that I want you to fuck me. I think maybe Curtis and I were doing it wrong. Maybe I just didn't want to open up to him, I don't know." Leo looked thoughtful. "Or maybe I wanted it too much, because I thought I'd never have what I *really* wanted with him, you know—acceptance, devotion, that sort of thing. But, yeah, I'm done with being that person. I want to try it. With you. I think I'll like it. I love when you do it with your fingers, and I'm ready."

Leo seemed to belatedly realize that he wasn't the only one who needed to agree to this for it to work out, and he added, "And, I really hope you are, too."

"I was more ready before you mentioned your ex," Grant said.

Leo rolled his eyes, amusement crinkling the corners. "Oh, come on, Grant, you have to know that if you trump him anywhere it's the bedroom, and, well, honestly, it's everywhere, so I don't know what you're even worried about."

"Who said I was worried? My superiority is indisputable in every way. It's just the idea of superstar Curtis Banks's dick anywhere near your ass makes my cock shrivel. I know you relate all too well."

Leo again rolled his eyes and started sipping at his small glass of water. "Whatever, Grant. I just want to try it with you, and if you don't like it, then we'll never have to—"

"Oh, *please*," Grant said. "I'm gonna like it, and if I have anything to do with it, so will you."

Leo smiled, his eyes liquid warmth. "I'm counting on it."

Grant said, "So, when are you thinking we should proceed with the initiation of your ass? Tonight? Tomorrow? This kitchen table seems plenty sturdy—"

"I need to talk to you first." Leo's voice had changed from the confident, eager tenor of before and suddenly sounded shy and maybe a little ashamed. Grant had a feeling he knew what was coming. And whose name would play a liberal role in whatever Leo was feeling tormented about.

"Okay," Grant said. "I'm listening."

Leo sighed. "There are things I haven't told you. About me. About my life. And I think you have a right to know. And they're important, too, if we're going to...you know."

"Fuck."

"Yeah." Leo fiddled with his water glass and then wiped his hands on his jeans. "I'm nervous. Some of this stuff I haven't told anyone. Curtis knew, but then he was there. So he knew. And now I have to tell you, and I don't want you to think less of me, or to want to leave, but I guess that's the risk I have to take. So I'm telling you, Grant."

Grant said nothing. He couldn't imagine that there was anything Leo could tell him to make him leave, but he wasn't one for false promises, and if anyone could surprise Grant, it would be

Leo, so he kept his mouth shut and just nodded.

"Okay, so…I might have some hang-ups," Leo began. "Or, I *do* have some hang-ups. Kind of big ones. But, God, it sounds so *insane* that I'm not even sure that you'd believe me. I mean, it's—"

"I'll believe you," Grant said.

Leo avoided looking at him, alternating between staring over Grant's shoulder and looking down at his mug of tea. "So, I don't know if I should start at the beginning or in the middle."

"Start where you need me to understand," Grant said.

Leo nodded, sucked his lips into his mouth like he was gearing up, and said, "Curtis and I…to say sex was difficult is kind of an understatement. He never seemed into it. We waited three years to have sex. We were in high school, so other kids were waiting too, so I believed him when he said it wasn't me."

"It wasn't you," Grant growled.

"Right. I know. But he said he wanted it to be right, and that seemed fair. In the end he just wasn't into it much, you know?"

"You don't have to—"

"I need you to understand," Leo said. "It was painful and embarrassing, and Curtis was perfunctory and sometimes strange. He'd put me off for so long, and then when we *did* do something, it was just such an effort, so much work, like it wasn't even fun."

Grant's stomach twisted up.

Leo met Grant's eyes, his lips trembling. "Until you, I didn't realize it could be fun."

"Leo…"

Leo held up a hand to stop Grant from going on. "He'd hold me after, but I could tell he wanted to get away as soon as possible. He'd get up and go shower, and we'd go back to the sexless life he seemed to prefer. Kissing? Sure. Holding hands? Sure. Cuddling? He liked a lot when he was around anyway. But getting down and dirty with me, being sweaty or adventurous?

He just wasn't up for that."

Grant couldn't imagine such a scenario. Not wanting Leo in a primal, deep way was something Grant couldn't begin to fathom.

Leo said, "I can't blame him for how that all made me feel. It's not my fault that he didn't like sex. Though, of course, I thought it was. But time and distance tells me that it's not *his* fault that he doesn't like it either. I don't know. He's never been willing to talk about his feelings on sex except to shame me and tell me that I was bad for enjoying it. Maybe he's asexual?"

"Possibly."

"I can't blame him if he didn't know that about himself. If that's even the situation? So I don't know. You can understand why I thought it was me."

"I can. It wasn't you. And he never should have shamed you, no matter what he likes or doesn't like."

"I know, I know. There were so many reasons it was bad between us. God, like, I thought the reason why sex wasn't good to begin with was because neither of us knew what the hell we were doing. High school sweethearts and all that. Virgins in every way." He blushed. "But after our first breakup, when he first went to LA to start his career? He never slept with anyone else. He said it was because he loved me too much. I suspect he just didn't want to. I think sex repulses him."

"Maybe. Who knows?"

"Yeah. And meanwhile, I started dating you, and we had insane chemistry."

"To put it lightly."

Leo swallowed hard and squeezed his eyes shut. "And it was scary to me."

"It was?" Grant frowned in concern. "I thought you—"

Leo's gray eyes popped open earnestly. "Yes! I wanted you so much. I'd never felt anyone want me back before. It was a lot."

"I…all right."

"So when Curtis showed up saying all the things I wanted to hear, I ran."

"I was there."

"I know. I have to tell you everything so that you're sure you want to be with me."

"Baby, I'm sure right now. I've been sure."

Leo blinked at him gently, but then he insisted on continuing. "I need to tell you everything."

"All right. I'm listening."

"Once we got back together—me and Curtis, I mean—it wasn't long after that when I *knew* I'd made a mistake. And yet I *stayed*, because he was breaking out in Hollywood, suddenly getting famous and rich, and I liked that. And I was humiliated by the idea that it might not work out between us after all I'd walked away from, and all I'd let myself believe. Worse, I didn't want to give up all the fairytales that might be waiting for us if I walked out. And my transplants, all the health problems, they're expensive. Curtis could afford to…" He shivered. "He could shoulder the financial burden of me. And so, in that way, what happened with Curtis *is* all my fault."

Grant understood that Leo had a driving need to take responsibility for things, and while he wished that he could tell Leo that, in this case, he was wrong, that it wasn't his fault at all, he couldn't say that. Leo had made a valid point, and so Grant held his peace.

"And, it's all left its mark, Grant. I'm afraid of disappointing you. I'm afraid of the day when you turn me down because you're too disgusted by my sickness to want to touch me. It's ridiculous, but I'm afraid of myself, afraid of what I might agree to, just to make sure you get what you want in bed, so that you'll want me again later. And I have to be careful of that. Draw lines sometimes. Because I never want sex between us to be bad. I never want to feel like it's work or a grudging gift to get me off your back. I want it to be good with us. The way it is now. The way it has been the last two months together."

"Leo—"

"No, I have to tell you this. It's important." Leo's face and neck grew more and more flushed, and his hands trembled as he held them out to stop Grant from talking. "I like when you bite me, or spank me, and I think it's really hot. But that's not what I'm talking about. I'm talking about being afraid that I'll give up a lot more than that."

"I know, Leo."

"And, wait, one last thing. I think I'm…well, just thinking about you makes me feel like I'm flying. I want so badly to believe in this, to believe in you and me, and I want you. I want *you*. And I am scared to death that I'm not going to get a new kidney. That I'm going to die. Or that I'll be so sick that you stop—"

"Shh, Leo. Stop."

"Wanting me," Leo finished, his chin trembling and tears in his eyes.

"I'll always want you," Grant said. No matter what. He would make it his mission in life if he had to, but never in his presence would Leo feel un*wanted*.

"You can't know that."

"I do know," Grant said.

"I could get really sick."

"You might. Or we might find a kidney for you. And a lot of people live for a very long time on dialysis."

"I don't want to live like that forever. I will if I have to—for Lucky, but—"

"For Lucky and for me," Grant said. "Because if I'm going to fall in love with you, I'm not going to lose you. You have to fight and stay as healthy as you possibly can. For me."

Leo's face dissolved into a soft, warm joy and he wiped the tears away with the back of his hand. "Do you plan to fall in love with me?"

"I don't think I have a choice," Grant said. "Planned or not, it's happened."

"Happened? Past tense? You already…."

"Yes."

Leo's head tilted to the side, his mouth open in surprise, and his eyes so warm and sweet. "I—"

"Don't say it," Grant said.

"But I want to," Leo said.

"Leo, there's no guilt here. You can feel it or not feel it, and it won't change a damn thing about what I feel for you. That's what's important right now."

Leo kissed him then, twining his fingers in Grant's hair, his tension draining away into heat and lust. Grant pushed aside the mugs of cold tea, the plate of cookies, and pressed Leo against the table, the wood digging into Grant's elbows and knees as they scooted back onto it. Their mouths never came apart, as their hands gripped and pulled at each other's clothes until smooth skin ran under fingertips.

Grant tugged at the button and zipper of Leo's jeans, getting his hand around Leo's fat cock. He pumped it hard as they kissed, going immediately to the rhythm that he now knew Leo liked best. He murmured against Leo's mouth, "That's good, Leo, come on, I've got you, come on now."

Just as Leo tensed, and Grant knew he was about to come, Grant ducked down and covered Leo's cockhead with his mouth, sucking and swallowing as Leo pumped out thick spurts. Leo's fingers curled and pulled at Grant's hair, and his stomach clenched under Grant's hand.

"Oh, God," Leo panted, flopping back against the table.

Grant crawled up, kissed his mouth, sharing his taste, and then straddled Leo's chest.

"Suck me," he murmured, unzipping his pants, and shoving them down on his hips. His cock bounced against his stomach, but Grant gripped it in his right hand, twined his left in Leo's hair, and lifted Leo's head up from the table a little.

"Open," he said, and Leo's wide eyes went hot again. He opened his lips and let Grant nudge his cock inside his hot, wet mouth.

Leo sucked cock so well that Grant wasn't sure he'd ever had it as good. And Grant had plenty of men's mouths to compare Leo's to, but no one had ever sucked cock like Leo. H moaned and groaned like he was on the verge of coming himself, just from the taste of Grant's dick on his tongue.

As Grant leaned up and forward, pushing back and down. Leo's throat opened around him and squeezed against the head of his dick as Leo swallowed. Leo's hard-won breath sucked past the tip of his cock, and Leo's eyes rolled up as he held Grant so deep.

"Yes, baby. That's it."

Leo pressed his tongue out until the tip of it brushed Grant's balls, tantalizing and slow. Grant bit down on his lip, trying to rein in the need to slam into Leo's mouth hard and fast. He held Leo's hair as he fucked his throat, backing off when Leo gagged, and then slowly easing in again, dragging it out, making it last because it was so fucking good when Leo took him this way, when Leo opened up and let him in.

The table beneath them creaked with their movements. Leo's hands grabbed Grant's ass, pulling him in deeper. His fingers dipped into Grant's crack to run over his hole in tantalizing brushes that only made it better.

Grant pulled back, let Leo suck on the head of his cock, and then slid all the way in, throwing his head back and giving himself up to the feeling.

"I'm gonna come," Grant said, grabbing a napkin from where it was about to fall off the edge of the table. He thrust into Leo's mouth hard and then pulled back to fuck the tip of his cock through Leo's tightened lips quickly. The suction was amazing and Leo's tongue flicked over the head at each thrust in.

Grant panted and fought hard to last just a little longer, but Leo's eager groans were just too fucking hot.

"I love you," Grant said, surprised that he wanted to say it with Leo's mouth working him over.

Leo's eyes were so hot, dark, and wide that Grant felt like he was falling into them. He pumped again and again, the head of his cock slamming through Leo's lips. He pulled Leo's hair as the orgasm built, using his grip to jerk Leo's face away from his cock. Grant covered himself with the rough napkin as he came and came, shaking and grunting, his eyes rolled back and his hand still buried in Leo's hair.

"Holy hell," Grant muttered, rocking down from the high to collapse against Leo's chest, rubbing his cheek against Leo's soft T-shirt. "That was so good."

Leo kissed the top of Grant's head softly.

Grant sighed, pulled away, got his pants back up and Leo's, too, before collapsing back down on the table, rattling the mugs and plate that were barely hanging on to the edge. It was a good thing the table was so big and strong, or they might have broken it in their enthusiasm.

"I wanted to swallow it." Leo pouted, his lips red and bruised looking. "You never let me swallow it anymore."

"You already know why. It's high in phosphorus," Grant said, slipping a hand under Leo's T-shirt to finger his chest hair and draw rings around his nipples. "And thus not on your special diet."

Leo groaned and closed his eyes, muttering, "Some day."

Grant kissed Leo's eyelids. "Yeah, some day."

"When are we going to get up?" Leo asked.

"When I can breathe again?" Grant said. "Why? Are you uncomfortable?"

"My doctor's going to wonder where I got all these bruises," Leo said, holding Grant as they panted together. "My spine must be covered with them."

"Just tell him that you like it rough."

Leo chuckled. "Yeah, I can just imagine that conversation now."

Leo's cell phone rang, a ring tone that Grant recognized as Meryl calling. "Don't get it," Grant said. "Let it go to voicemail."

"It's my mother. It might be important. I have to take it."

"Oh, hell," Grant muttered, moving out of Leo's way so that he could get up. His hips and elbows ached from the quickie on the table, and he stood up creakily.

Leo got his pants zipped up and got to his cell phone just in time. He grabbed Grant's hand, though, and kissed Grant's fingers, before turning his attention away. "Mom? Hey, what's up?"

During the long pause, Leo's expression lifted from blissed-out mellow to something like shining joy. "Really? Where was she? I can't believe it. When was this?"

Leo turned to Grant and said, "This is important. I'm going to take this out on the porch, okay?"

Grant nodded, cracking his back, and waving him off with his hand. He'd just had a mind-blowing orgasm, plus he had cookies and cold tea that he could heat up. He knew where Leo kept the milk and the pie if he wanted some. He was good to go.

Grant wiped down the table with an antibacterial wipe as he warmed up his mug. He got five more cookies from the jar, leaving three for Lucky. She was small. She didn't need as many cookies as he did.

He bit into one and moaned softly. They were so soft and delicious. He wished he knew how Leo had the power to make them taste this way. These were Leo's Memaw's recipe, as was the pie. It was something that Grant admired, how the Garners seemed to really value food and family.

"Hey," Lucky's voice came from the stairway separating the kitchen from the living room.

Grant turned toward her. "Shouldn't you be in bed, carrot?" He hoped she hadn't been there long, because if she had, then Leo was going to be facing some awkward questions. Assuming she saved them for Leo.

Grant cleared his throat, feeling a little anxious and sweaty at the thought of having to explain why he'd been shoving his penis into her daddy's mouth. Now that he thought about it, that had been pretty reckless. They should have kept it behind closed doors—with a lock.

Lucky asked, "Dr. Grant, will I ever see my Papa again?"

"Your—oh, well, I don't—it's, I..." Grant ran a hand through his hair and cleared his throat. "How long has it—I mean, I think you should ask Leo that, don't you?"

Lucky fiddled with the edge of her nightgown. "It makes him sad. I don't like to make Daddy sad. He used to always look sad." She sat down on the steps, not coming to join him at the table. "Did you know that when he was in LA, he cried sometimes? He'd hold me and cry."

Grant felt a low simmer of rage begin again; the idea of Leo in LA crying alone, while poor Lucky was in the middle of it? It was more than he could stand.

"I didn't know," Grant said.

"Papa was gone a lot. It scared me."

"It sounds...scary."

"Daddy hasn't cried since he met you," Lucky said. "And I like how you make him laugh by being mean. When Papa was mean, it never made him laugh."

"You know too much for a five-year-old," Grant said.

"I know. Mrs. Franklin says that all the time."

"No," Grant said, standing up and going to sit next to her on the stair, squeezing in beside her so that she was half on his lap. "Mrs. Franklin is an idiot. And that's not what I meant. I just mean that you're a little girl, and you should think about little girl things."

"Okay. Like wanna pretend I'm Medusa and you're Perseus, and you've come to cut off my head, but this time I freeze you and turn you into stone?"

Grant sighed, put his hand on Lucky's head, and said, "But then who will save Andromeda?"

Lucky puckered her lips, thinking. "Sometimes good people die. That's just the way it is."

• • •

Present

LEO WAS SEIZING on the table, and he was still open, they hadn't even had time to get him closed. They pushed meds faster than Grant could begin to understand what was going on.

"Let me go," Grant said, and he didn't recognize his own voice.

"No, Grant, you've got to calm down first. They'll get it under control. He's going to be—"

"Shut up!" Grant said. "He's not having a reaction to the anesthesia; it's a CNS infection, the immunosuppressant, it's—do they not understand what's going on?"

"Grant, calm down, or I'll have *you* put down with a sedative."

Grant shoved Dennis hard, nearly toppling him over. "Just you try."

"Grant!" Alec's voice cut through, high pitched and sharp. "What is going on in here?"

And then Alec made a strange noise, and he was in Grant's arms, holding him, squeezing him so tight Grant hoped he could keep him from turning inside out. He clenched Alec hard enough to hear him gasp, but he didn't let go.

"It's going to be okay," Alec murmured breathlessly.

"Don't lie to me," Grant said, starting to push him away. He didn't want that. He needed better than a lie to keep himself from going into that OR and taking over himself.

Alec clung to him. "Okay, okay. Just, shh. You can't help him this way. Calm down. Grant, he's gonna need you to stay sane, all right? Breathe for me. Breathe."

Grant looked into Alec's glitter-dusted eyes and took a long breath in, and then let it out; it sounded embarrassingly like a sob.

"That's it, that's good," Alec said, running his hands up and down Grant's arms. "Just look at you. Such a wreck. Welcome to the human race, Grant. It's tough stuff."

If this was the human race, if this was love and weakness, Grant really didn't think he was built for it. All of these emotions, all of this fear, it was too much for him. He hated it. He wanted it gone. But he wanted Leo more.

"What if he—"

Alec shook his head firmly and clenched Grant's forearms.

"Don't. Stop right there, mister. You can't think those kinds of things."

But he couldn't stop his mind from finishing the thought. His chest grew so tight with fear that he started hyperventilating again. He recognized the symptom, knew he needed to get it under control, but he couldn't regulate his breathing.

"Oh, baby," Alec said, putting his arms around him again. "Shhhh. Breathe. Breathe. He's in excellent hands."

Muresan was a hack. Grant knew that now; he should never have trusted him. He should have insisted that they bring in someone else. Someone better. He tried to turn toward the glass again, to look down at Leo, but Alec jerked his arms, making him face him. "Don't," he said. "Just stay focused on me right now."

"Is it still bad?" Grant asked.

"He's stopped seizing," Dennis said, glancing over his shoulder. "They're getting him closed up now. Once they get him out of the OR, we'll see what's what. He's going to be—"

"Say it again, and I'll kill you myself."

Chapter Thirteen

Six Months Ago

"HANNAH'S A MATCH?" Leo said. He sounded uncertain, like he couldn't even believe it. "And you're sure?"

"Yes, sugar-butt. Of course I'm sure. Your mother and father have her at the hospital now, detoxing and getting well enough for the surgery," Marie said, patting her gun like a habit. "And after all of that mess with that woman in Connecticut and her damaged kidneys, it's good to not get our hopes up in vain this time."

Little Apron was bustling with patrons and Grant glanced around to see who all was listening. He knew Blountville, and everything they talked about tonight would be fodder for gossip tomorrow. He could hear it now: *Leo Garner's little sister was giving him a kidney in exchange for him raising her kid.* Grant didn't want that version of the story getting back to Lucky.

"Can you believe she was living in that hovel in New York? It was disgusting, let me tell you. I wouldn't have even believed it, if I hadn't seen it for my own self," Marie said, resting her hand on her sidearm.

"It's a good thing Dad and Mom got there," Leo said. "It sounds like it was just in time."

"There was a *pig* living in the apartment, sugar-butt. An actual pig. It was one of her roommate's pets. I use both the words 'roommate' and 'pet' loosely, if you get what I'm saying."

"Gives Hell's Kitchen a whole new meaning," Grant said,

unable to keep the sarcasm out of his voice.

"Grant," Leo said softly.

"But the real question is, are her kidneys of any use?" Grant asked. "Drugs and healthy organs don't always go hand in hand."

Leo sounded sick when he interjected, "Grant, please. I don't want to even talk about that. I don't care about me right now. I'm just scared for Hannah. Is she okay? Is this completely voluntary, Memaw? Because I won't take her kidney if she doesn't want to give it to me."

Grant interrupted, "You might not care about yourself right now, but that's all I care about. I don't give a rat's ass about your sister's state of mind, or even about the validity of her consent. You will take this kidney and you will not think twice about that, do you understand?"

Leo's eyes took on a rare, angry glow.

Grant leaned forward, ready to press the point more if need be. It was essential that Leo accept the kidney.

"Well said," Marie said. "I agree wholeheartedly, Doc."

"How can you say that?" Leo asked, looking around, probably gauging how many people were eavesdropping, too. It had to be the entire restaurant at this point. "You're a doctor, Grant. You know what's at stake here if there's been coercion—"

"There's been no coercion," Marie said. "Hannah is very willing—eager even—to give her brother the help he needs. She wants to see you to tell you so herself."

Leo shook his head, breathing in through his nose. His mouth was set in a sad line. "Why do I doubt that? It's all my fault," he said. "I should have looked out for her better in LA; I should have known what was going on, made her get help, made her get clean."

Grant scoffed. "No one gets clean unless they're both determined and damned lucky."

Leo's jaw set tightly, and he glared at Grant. "You don't even know her. She's my baby sister, and I *love* her."

Grant cleared his throat and glanced at Marie, who was obviously very curious about just how Grant planned to handle Leo's anger.

"Yes, yes, of course. I understand. She's your sister. And you *should* love her. I get that. I just don't get why that means I have to think she's not exactly what she is: a drug addict who left her kid with you, went missing for a few years, worried her family sick, *including* you, and now suddenly wants to buy back everyone's affection and trust with a kidney for her big brother. Love her all you want, Leo. It doesn't change who she is."

"Grant. You know nothing about her. You have no idea what she's been through, or—"

"Oh, I think I do, pretty much the same as what you've been through, sans being, oh, gay and undergoing a heart transplant, and losing function of both kidneys, too, so I don't see what excuse—"

"You! You are such a jerk!" Leo tossed his napkin on the table and stormed out of the restaurant, leaving everyone gaping in his wake, and walking out into the rain without his umbrella.

Grant got up to go after him, but Marie grabbed his hand. "Well, you made a mess of that one, Doc. But give him a minute or twenty to cool off. You'll just make it worse right now. He needs to deal with this. On his own."

Grant was skeptical. Leo might interpret Grant not coming after him to mean that Grant didn't care, but he sank down into the chair, feeling the stares in the room boring into him.

"Well, I guess there is more than one way to announce that Leo Garner and I are a serious item. Personally, I'd just planned on holding his hand through thick and thin, for all the world to see, going to all the local weddings together, and maybe marrying him one day, but I guess having him throw a fit on me in public is just as good."

"That's right, Doc. There is more than one way to skin that cat," Marie whispered conspiratorially. "If you wanted to make for even more rumors, you could begin to sob into your wine glass while I console you. It would be the talk of the hospital tomorrow. Just imagine how much money will exchange hands if they see you cry."

Grant couldn't help but chuckle. "Oh, I already know there's a pool for how long it will be before Leo dumps me."

"Oh, well, don't worry. Tonight doesn't count. I'm sure you'll have it made up by morning." Marie patted Grant's shoulder with a firm hand.

"And if we don't?" Grant said.

Marie smiled and patted her gun again. Her accent was a bit thicker as she laid it out. "Tonight you'll go to him and you tell him that you're sorry, that of course his sister is an amazing, generous, loving girl, and that you're ever so thankful for her gift to him. And you'll try not to sound as sarcastic as I just did when you say it."

Grant harrumphed and took a sip of his wine. He hoped when he got back to his apartment Leo would be there waiting for him ready to make up. If he wasn't, then he supposed he'd have to drive over to the farm in the rainstorm and pound on the door until Leo let him in. Very dramatic, but, hell, he'd pull a *Say Anything* if he had to. He'd yell his love from the so-called pasture, while blasting that Peter Gabriel song from his car stereo. Leo could never say he lacked in the romance department again.

Grant smirked at the thought. At least those ridiculous romantic movies that his roommate in medical school used to watch might be good for something.

• • •

As it turned out he did have to drive to the farm. The rain was coming down in buckets, and he could barely see through his windshield, but Leo wasn't answering his phone, and Grant was starting to get worried.

Pulling up to the side of the house, Grant saw Leo sitting by the kitchen door in a wooden lawn chair, an umbrella in one hand, and a dark bottle in the other. As Grant got out, the rain washed over him in a sheet, instantly soaking him through. His shoes sank into mud and splashed through puddles as he crossed the driveway and stared down into Leo's dull eyes glaring up at him.

"What the hell are you doing?" Grant said, grabbing the bottle from Leo's hand.

"Having a drink. Getting fresh air," Leo said, belligerent annoyance in every word. "Oh, calm down, Grant. It's just ginger brew, non-alcoholic, get a grip."

Grant grabbed Leo by the arm and hauled him up. "No, you get a grip. It's barely forty degrees out here, your immune system is compromised, your body is weak, and you're drinking something that, while it isn't alcohol, still isn't any good for you. Leo, this pity party needs to be over right now."

Leo jerked his arm out of Grant's grasp. "Oh? And you get to tell me what to do?"

Grant shook his head. "No. I get to tell you that you're being an ass and that it's not a very attractive trait."

Leo sniffled and stared up at him with red-rimmed eyes. "Oh, well, of *course*, because what *really* matters right now is how *attractive* I am to you. I should've known—"

Grant sighed, grabbed Leo by the arm again, and guided him

more or less toward the door into the house. They were both freezing and wet, and Leo had dropped his umbrella, so now they were both soaked to the skin. Leo scuffled with him, though, refusing to enter.

"If you want to have a fight with me, let's at least do it inside where it's dry," Grant barked.

"No," Leo shook his head. "Lucky's in there. Don't want to scare her."

Grant scoffed. "Oh, of course not. Like it won't scare her when you're hospitalized with an infection your body would have otherwise been able to fight off if you hadn't submitted yourself to this ridiculous behavior tonight."

Leo stared at him and then turned to open the kitchen door, stalking inside, leaving wet, dark muddy prints everywhere. Grant had empathy for the floor.

"Lucky!" Leo called out. "Dad!"

They both entered from the living room, Lucky already in her nightgown, and Chuck looking pretty tired and ready for bed himself, with a thick five o'clock shadow and sleepy eyes.

"Leo, Grant," Chuck greeted, and then he did a double-take. "You two look like drowned rats. Did you forget your umbrellas? I'll get you some towels. Just a minute."

"You know, don't bother, Dad," Leo said, and Grant could see Chuck's face register that there was something wrong. "Come on, Lucky," Leo said. "It's time for bed."

Lucky's face scrunched with confusion and she started to complain. "But Dr. Grant just got here, and I wanted to—"

"It's bedtime," Leo snapped, rounding to the stairs. "Come on."

Lucky looked at Leo, then at Grant, and she bit her lower lip. She glanced to Chuck who nodded his head at her, as though telling her to go on, and she ran past her dad and up the stairs fast without looking back. Leo followed her, stomping as he went.

"Rough night?" Chuck asked, resting his arm against the back of a kitchen chair.

"You could say that," Grant replied, still staring at where Leo and Lucky had disappeared, wondering where to go from here. Wondering if this called for that *Say Anything* move he'd been considering. But he was too angry and frustrated to even fully imagine it now. He pinched the bridge of his nose and shook his head. "Ah, well, I guess I should be going. Tell Leo…hell, just tell him I left."

"Oh, come on, you're going to leave him just like that? I expected more from you." Chuck's gravelly voice was somehow tender in its scolding.

Grant took in Chuck's rough hands and kind smile, his old blue jeans, and plaid shirt. He was a good old country man, and he'd done his best by Leo when he came out and continued to do so even now. That much Grant knew. So, Chuck deserved a reply, even if he was coming across a little interfering now. "I'm not leaving *him*; I'm leaving his *house*. There's a difference."

Chuck sighed. "Look, I'm not going to try to tell you what to do. But I know my son. I've watched him grow from a baby to a man, and I know him very well."

Grant bit back the urge to demand that Chuck spare him the trip down memory lane to Leo's diaper days. Chuck wasn't to blame for the way the evening had gone down in flames, so taking his bad temper out on him would be fruitless and unkind. Besides, he wanted Chuck to like him, if only to make Leo happy.

"This is about Hannah," Chuck said.

Grant stuffed his hands into his wet pockets and nodded.

Chuck turned to a pantry on the left, opened it up, and pulled out a beach towel. "We keep these down here to use down at the pond in the summer," Chuck said. "Here's hoping it's not mildewed." He tossed it to Grant. "Dry off. Sit down and we'll talk."

"I don't know. This is between me and Leo."

"Not if it's about Hannah it's not. It's between Leo and his demons. I'm just offering you some insight. Take it or leave it."

Grant glanced toward the stairs. He wasn't sure how Leo would feel about him talking with Chuck about this, but he sat down at the table anyway. Chuck pulled out the chair across from Grant and sat down, too.

"So, Grant, I've had my eye on you."

"Great, is this when you threaten me and show me your shotgun?"

Chuck smiled, but not necessarily with reassurance. "Not quite. This is when I tell you that in all the years I've been Leo's father I've never seen him as happy as he's been lately. His illness, the stress he's still facing with the separation from Curtis, none of that is coming close to breaking his stride. And I believe that's because of you. I can't say that I understand why—frankly, I find you a bit off-putting—but *Leo* is happy with you, and that's all I give a damn about."

"Then we have the same goal."

"I believe we do."

"So, Hannah," Grant prompted.

That was, after all, why he'd stayed. He needed a little more information about Leo and his relationship with Hannah to fully understand what would bring Leo to this kind of breakdown. The temper fit in the restaurant was one thing but sitting outside in the rain drinking an indulgent brew that would leave him sicker than he needed to be before his next dialysis was something else entirely.

Chuck took in a deep breath and sighed. He started to fiddle with a napkin ring that had been left lonely on the table, and he said, "Hannah and Leo always had a special bond. I remember when Hannah first came home as a baby, Leo stayed the whole first night in the nursery, lying on the floor by her crib, because even then he insisted that she needed him to take care of her. Meryl had to step over him to get to Hannah in the middle of the night to nurse her."

That sounded like a little boy Leo. Grant could imagine it clearly.

"Meryl and I—we've had our money troubles in the past, and Hannah, especially, always took it really hard. Leo—well, Leo did too at times, but he would buck up and try to be a man for his sister. We never had a problem with Leo." Chuck chuckled in a kind of still-shocked disbelief. "But then Hannah hit her teenage years and, boy, did she more than make up for Leo being an easy child."

"Boy trouble?" Grant asked.

Chuck shook his head and raised his brow. "I can see how you might think so, but not exactly. That's when the drinking started. I assume you know about that."

Grant nodded curtly. He knew Leo's sister had a substance abuse problem. Those usually began with drinking.

"Drinking and lying, and then there were the events that led up to her going out to California. The drama after that…well, there was a lot of it. Drugs and drama. Then she got pregnant. Meryl and I …we didn't take it so well, to be honest." Chuck shook his head. "Leo is the one who held her together, or tried to, but he felt so ashamed that he hadn't protected her better from her own self."

Chuck stood up got a glass of water for himself and poured one for Grant, too.

"Thanks," Grant said, taking a sip, washing the remnants of

wine and anxiety out of his mouth. Grant rubbed the beach towel over his head as Chuck continued to talk.

"Always, though, in the background was Leo propping Hannah up, helping her through everything. I remember when they were just little things finding Hannah curled up at the foot of Leo's bed sometimes, even after he was much too old to have his sister in his room. Leo would tell me just to leave her, that she was scared from the storm or a bad dream. And I would. Leo was her rock. And he wanted to be that for her always. When things changed, when she changed, and Hannah went her own way, Leo didn't understand."

Grant cleared his throat. He took a sip of the water. He had little to contribute to this conversation, so he focused on just listening.

Chuck went on, "When Lucky was born, I wasn't surprised that Leo offered to take her. I suppose we should have stepped up, insisted that we raise her, but Leo and Curtis said they wanted a family of their own, and it seemed perfect for them." Chuck rubbed a finger over one tired eye and said, "Leo's a good father."

"He is," Grant agreed.

"Better than I am," Chuck said.

Grant said nothing, not sure if he had enough information to offer any real reassurance that Chuck wasn't to blame in any of this.

Chuck went on, "So, this thing with Hannah—running off to California and then New York, complicated by the drugs, and the abusive boyfriend. Leo's not handling it well. I think he sees it as the ultimate proof of his failure to protect her. Even taking Lucky as his own, even that was partially about protecting Hannah. He was still taking care of that baby whose crib he slept by. Do you understand what I'm saying, Grant? He loves Hannah fiercely, and this has broken his heart. Again."

"Does he always push people away when his heart is broken?" Grant asked.

Chuck nodded and gave a half-hearted chuckle. "Don't we all? Go on upstairs. Lucky should be asleep by now. He's probably waiting for you."

Grant shook Chuck's hand. "Thanks for the talking to."

"Go on. He won't send you home." Chuck shooed Grant on. "I'm gonna head on back to town."

The floorboards of the stairs creaked under Grant's feet as they always did. He went to Lucky's door first, opened it and looked inside. She was sprawled asleep on the bed, her long hair wrapped like a blindfold over her eyes, and her left leg kicked out from under the blankets.

Grant went to Leo's door next and knocked. He waited a moment and when there was no answer, he opened it slowly.

Leo lay on the bed staring at the ceiling. He'd changed from his wet clothes to a pair of sweats and a T-shirt that was so old it was nearly see-through. He looked comfortable and warm, and Grant's damp clothes felt clammy and cold against his skin.

"I thought you were going home," Leo said quietly.

"I thought I'd stay."

Leo sighed and rubbed his hands over his eyes. "I'm not always a nice person."

"No? Well, neither am I."

Leo breathed out a small laugh and scooted over on the bed, patting the place beside him. The storm outside grew louder, the wind and rain beating against Leo's window, and a sudden downpour rushed against the roof.

Grant sat down on the edge of the bed, running the backs of his fingers down Leo's arm, feeling the smooth skin and soft hair. He toed off his shoes and then he lay down next to Leo, his hand wrapped loosely around Leo's forearm.

"I'm sorry," Leo said.

"For what? Loving your sister? I can't blame you for that."

"For acting like an ass at the restaurant."

"You were very dramatic. I'll give you that much. A+ for making the whole town talk about us."

Leo chuckled. He rolled onto his side and Grant could feel him studying his profile. Grant kept his eyes on the ceiling, counting the faded-out green stars that someone, maybe Leo, maybe not, had put on the ceiling once upon a time.

"And I'm sorry for sitting out in the rain," Leo said.

"Well, that *was* stupid," Grant agreed.

"And for treating you like crap just because I was upset about Hannah."

Grant rolled onto his side, too, touching Leo's face, running his fingers along Leo's cheekbone. "Don't make a habit of it."

Leo's eyes were dark and yet clear, too, and Grant leaned forward to press a kiss to each lid. Leo wrapped his arms around Grant and held him close, burying his nose in Grant's neck and breathing in slowly.

"You're soaked," Leo murmured, as though he'd just realized how wet Grant still was. "Get these clothes off. You must be freezing."

Grant couldn't deny that he was. He was very cold, and damp, and really ready to feel warm again. Leo pushed at Grant's jacket, peeling it off his arms. He'd started on Grant's shirt buttons when Grant stilled his fingers. "Leo, I'm sorry, too."

"Why? I was the one who overreacted."

Grant said, "It's hard for me to understand what it means—being Hannah's older brother, having her as your sister. I'm an only child with a pretty weird family history, and I didn't get it."

Leo shrugged. "You got it eventually. That's all that matters, right?"

"I haven't entirely changed my mind about her," Grant warned. He still thought that every word he'd uttered about her was true. Now, though, he just had more information about why it was true and how that hurt Leo.

"That's okay. You're probably right." Leo went back to Grant's buttons. "Let's not talk about Hannah anymore. I want to get you dry and warm. Before *you* get sick."

It became obvious very quickly that Leo's idea of dry and warm was as naked as he could get Grant, and as much skin as he could manage to put under his hands and in his mouth. Grant was not complaining about that definition at all.

As Leo bit down gently on one nipple, Grant gasped, "Door. Locked."

Leo hopped up, pulled Grant's pants off, and threw them to the floor, not taking his eyes from Grant sprawled naked on the bed as he locked the door and moved a chair in front of it, too, for good measure.

Leo came back to straddle Grant, mouthing his neck, and sucking gently on an earlobe. Grant squirmed and laughed at the hot breath in his ear.

Leo blinked slowly, looking hesitant as he spoke. "So, the other night I told you I wanted to try something, and then my never-ending life drama got in the way and we never did. But we're finally alone again, so we could do it now. I mean, if you still want to, that is. I mean, I still want to, but if you've changed your mind or—"

"Oh, I still want to." Grant rolled Leo onto his back, brushed the hair off his face, and looked down at him for a long time. "Are you sure? Tonight? You've had an emotional evening. We can wait."

"No, please, Grant. I've waited so long. You have no idea

how much I want this," Leo said, his eyes earnest. So damn earnest.

"Tell me what you want."

Grant wanted to hear him say it. Leo almost never said 'fuck.' Grant didn't think he'd ever heard Leo say it at all before the previous night, and just imagining the word come out of Leo's mouth made Grant's gut curl with lust.

"I want you," Leo said, reaching down to grab Grant's cock.

Grant smirked and put his hand over Leo's, making Leo grip him even harder. "Say it. Just like you did last night."

"I want you to fuck me," Leo whispered, and Grant flared with want.

He climbed on top of Leo, holding his hands down against the bed, and said, "Say it again."

"Fuck me," Leo said.

"Again." He wanted Leo to beg for it, for him to tremble and shake, and *beg* to have Grant's cock in him.

Leo squirmed desperately under Grant, pushing his hips up against Grant's, begging with his body. Close, so close to what Grant wanted. "Tell me again, Leo. I want to hear how much you want it."

Leo grabbed handfuls of Grant's hair and gazed up at him. "Please, Grant. Fuck me. *Please.*"

It was perfect, just what Grant wanted, and he rewarded Leo by slapping his hip hard, and then soothing the mark by rubbing it.

"Grant, please. Please fuck me," Leo said again.

"Shhh," Grant said kissing him. Leo's lips were so soft, and Grant sucked the lower one into his mouth, and then deepened the kiss.

Leo arched under him, scrambling to jerk his sweat pants down as Grant continued to kiss him, until Grant pulled away to push Leo's shirt up and away as Leo kicked his sweats off the bed.

"Grant," Leo said, panting.

"Yeah?" Grant asked, pushing Leo back onto the bed and running his hands over the body he'd come to know well, feeling the outline of Leo's heart transplant scar and running his fingers down Leo's arm, avoiding touching the AV fistula.

"This isn't make-up sex," Leo said urgently. "Okay? Do you understand? That's not what I want this to be."

Grant huffed a small laugh and said, "Fine by me."

Leo relaxed back onto the bed, comforted by the clarification, and he whispered, "I want this because I love you."

Grant let out a low growl and whispered, "I love you, too."

"Was that special enough?" Leo laughed.

"No midnight picnic in a rose garden, but I'll take it," Grant said, and he knew he was smiling like a loon.

"Good," Leo said. "Because it's true, and I'm ready. So." He looked at Grant expectantly. "Get on with it."

Grant shook his head and couldn't stop from laughing. "It's gonna take a bit more than that. Where's the lube?" Though he knew exactly where it was. He opened the drawer beside the bed, bringing out the lubrication and the condoms Leo had shown him the other day after their talk. "Just in case," he'd said at the time.

"Do we need these?" Leo asked, picking up the box of condoms. "I know I'm okay."

Grant also knew that Leo was okay. He'd seen Leo's medical records, after all.

As for himself, even when Leo first arrived in town, it'd been a few months since he'd hooked up with anyone outside of a hand job. Easy tail was hard to come by in Blountville and required some special planning to avoid the uncomfortable scenario he'd faced when a young Grindr hookup decided they were boyfriends and followed him around town.

But Grant was STD-free. He tested. Regularly. And he'd always been careful. Except that first time, years ago, when he'd been too young, too horny, and too scared the guy would leave before the deed was done to insist on it. But, yes, he was fine.

"Yeah, I'm sure, too. We don't need them," Grant said.

Leo chucked the box to the floor and his eyes lit up. "Okay then."

Grant whispered, "Done it like this before? Without anything?"

Leo shook his head, a mix of bashfulness and pure lust on his face. Grant lay down on top of Leo, covering him with his body, rolling his hips so that their cocks pressed together.

He ran his hands over Leo's hair, as he gazed down into Leo's eyes. "You are so hot," Grant said. "Do you have any idea how hot you make me?"

Leo's smile was liquid and sweet, and he said, "Yeah. I make you pretty hot."

"Mmm," Grant turned Leo's head to the side and kissed his cheek, the side of his mouth, his ear, and breathed in the scent of his neck. Then he turned Leo's head to the other side and did the same. It was tender, and necessary, and he had to take care, make sure that Leo felt how much he wanted him, how much he *felt*.

Grant grabbed Leo's hands, careful of the forearm where the fistula went in, and pushed them down against the bed, forcing them back a little, and Leo's eyes went dark with want.

"We're going to do this my way, and I promise, Leo, I'll take care of you. You can tell me to stop at any point. I won't be upset. I want you to want this as much as I do."

"I do," Leo breathed. "Come on, Grant. Come on and do it already."

"Slowly, baby. Slowly."

. . .

LEO'S MOUTH WAS like the sea, wet and beautiful. Grant dove in for more before he moved down Leo's body, watching Leo squirm; he took his time, letting Leo's body and reactions move and direct the flow between them.

Leo's ass was gorgeous, and Grant loved to eat it, working his tongue in until Leo was a sobbing, aching, squirming mess on the bed. He loved to bite at Leo's hole and nip at his balls until Leo alternately stuck his ass out and scrambled to get away. He loved how Leo whimpered, "Grant, *Grant*, oh, God, Grant," either way.

It took a while to get Leo ready, to get his ass wet enough and loose enough that Grant would even consider putting more than lubed fingers inside. But eventually Leo was amply open, spread out on the bed like an offering, and Grant's fingers stroked in and out, fast and slow, keeping Leo on edge. He ran his hand up and down Leo's thigh, up to his chest and back down again, soothing him, talking him through the still-new sensation of anal orgasms. "I've got you, Leo. Shh, now. That's it. You're okay."

Leo's legs shook as another seized him, his cheeks stained pink beneath the damp hair on his forehead, as his hole convulsed on Grant's fingers. He crooned and moaned mindlessly, and his eyes burned with lust every time he opened them to stare at Grant. His cock was hard, flushed rosy against his stomach, and drooling there as Grant relentlessly worked his prostate. He was nearly incoherent with pleasure, begging with his body and his mouth. "Please, Grant. Please. I need you."

He was desperate enough now. He'd open up for Grant with just a little guidance.

Grant lubed up his cock and climbed between Leo's legs.

Bending down for a kiss, he caught Leo's sobs of frustrated need with his mouth. When he moved on to suck on the skin over Leo's collar bones, Leo begged him to get on with it, alternating pleas with urgent lifts of his hips, trying to get Grant's cock closer to his ass.

Finally, Grant pushed Leo's legs up, rubbing his cock in Leo's lubed crack, pushing slightly against the open pulse of Leo's hole. Hungrily, Leo arched up, pressing his hands against Grant's ass, trying to drag him inside.

Grant gazed down at Leo's face, wanting to see everything as he finally pressed in. And *fuck*, Leo was tight, so tight. But his sweet moan and expression of awe told Grant that it was good, and that if it hurt at all, it was a good hurt. Grant clenched his jaw, twined his fingers with Leo's, slick palms pressing together. "Just breathe for me now."

Leo stared up at him with wide eyes obeyed. On his exhale, Grant pushed. Both of them gasped, clutching each other as Leo opened up and took him in. He was velvet hot and so tight inside. Grant bit down on the inside of his cheek to keep from thrusting harder, wanting more, wanting it all now. He was shocked at how good it felt, how much better without a condom—wet, and raw, and somehow pure.

"Oh," Leo said, shocked. There was no pain or pleasure in his tone, just surprise. When Grant pushed a little more, sliding farther past the tight ring of Leo's asshole, Leo's eyes rolled up and his noise turned into a drawn out, "Ooooh." He grabbed Grant's arms and stilled him. "Oh, my God," he whimpered.

"It's a lot of sensation," Grant whispered. "You okay?"

Leo nodded, his eyes squeezed shut, and then he opened them, staring up at Grant in astonishment. "It's good. I'm okay, Grant. You feel so good."

Grant moved slowly, pumping in and out, going deeper with

each thrust. Leo's body seemed to melt under him, taking him more and more easily, until Leo was moving his hips along with him, taking him in, and squeezing Grant as he pulled out. He moaned, clutching at Grant's ass, pulling him in tighter, deeper, and struggling to keep him there longer. It became a heated push and pull of Grant trying to fuck Leo, and Leo trying to keep Grant as far inside him as he could manage.

"This is…oh, Grant," Leo murmured, his body arching greedily, his eyes rolling back, his toes curling and uncurling as Grant moved against him. His cock slid against Grant's stomach with each thrust, and pre-come slicked their skin.

Grant needed to take control, though. The grappling was hot, and it was good, but he wanted to show Leo what it could feel like, how it could be. He backed off, taking hold of Leo's hands when he tried to grab him back again. "Hold on, Leo. I've got you. Trust me."

Leo eased against the mattress, though his entire body seemed to jitter with want as Grant moved Leo's legs up to his shoulders. He grabbed Leo's hands and held them down on the pillow, watching closely as he started to move again. Thrusting hard, moving fast, Grant moaned with desire. Leo's face crumpled in pleasure, his mouth opened in a round O, and his body tensed and relaxed with each thrust. Grant licked his lips, looking down to see Leo's cock spill slick strings of pre-come between them.

"Oh, Grant," Leo said, and his voice was deep, thick with desire. He gasped and jerked as Grant plowed into him. "Oh, that—oh, *that*…I, oh…"

Leo shuddered and Grant stroked in and out at the same angle. Leo lit up and fall apart, his face shifting between pure ecstasy to a near fear of what he was feeling, and back again.

"It's okay, Leo. I'm right here," Grant said, moving faster, reaching between them to jerk Leo's cock. "I'm right here. Let go."

Leo trembled under him, nipples taut and eyes rolled up again. His body was tight and hot around Grant's cock. He quivered inside and out as he struggled beneath Grant, fighting the pleasure, unwilling to surrender to orgasm yet.

Grant's own pleasure was escalating out of control. He needed Leo to peak. "Come on, let me see you."

Leo's eyes squeezed shut and, as he shook his head, sweat flew from his hair. He jerked his arms free of where Grant had been holding them back, grabbed Grant's head and pulled him down for a kiss, whining into Grant's mouth and biting at his lips. "Please," he whispered. "Need you. Need you so much."

Grant understood what Leo couldn't seem to say. He slapped Leo's ass hard, driving in at the same time. Leo shouted and gripped handfuls of Grant's hair, guiding his mouth down. He bit Leo's neck hard enough to feel his ass clench on his dick, before pulling back to watch Leo tense, arch, and come around him.

Squeezing Grant's cock so tightly, Leo spurted between them with sweet, shocked whimpers. Grant touched Leo's cheek, wiping a stray bit of come that had made it that far, and he stared down into Leo's wrecked face as he fucked into Leo's still spasming ass.

"I love you," Leo whispered.

Grant was shocked, completely shocked that that declaration was what he needed. He bowed his head, resting his forehead on Leo's scarred chest as he came, aching to his soul with how damn good it was. Leo's hands rubbed up and down his back, and Grant trembled at Leo's breath against his hair.

This was love and he was deeply in it.

• • •

GRANT RESTED ON his side, his chin on Leo's shoulder and two fingers in Leo's sticky ass. He felt for his own come, smoothing it around Leo's hole, and then plunged his fingers in again. He kissed Leo's neck and whispered, "That was incredibly hot."

Leo was silent, and Grant propped up on his elbow and looked down at him, concerned. He pulled his fingers free, but Leo grabbed his hand and forced it back down.

"Don't stop," Leo said, his voice threaded with amazement.

Grant's eyes burned with surprise tears. He had to bury his face in Leo's neck for a moment as he pushed his fingers back in, feeling the slip of his own come. He cleared his throat. "You okay?"

"Yeah," Leo breathed. "Shell-shocked, but, yeah, I'm incredible. You're incredible. That was—"

"Incredible," Grant supplied.

Leo laughed, and Grant felt his body clench and release around his fingers.

"Grant," Leo said, his voice full of something Grant didn't understand.

"Mm-hmm?" Grant breathed, moving his fingers back and forth.

"I've never…I mean, I had no idea."

"I'm honored that I could show you."

"You were the best I could have ever dreamed of."

"You're sweet," Grant whispered.

"No, I'm not. I'm kind of stupid."

Grant laughed. "What? No. I don't date imbeciles."

"I just can't believe that I—"

"Shh," Grant hushed him. "I'm glad you liked it. Wait, you

did like it?"

Leo laughed so hard that Grant's fingers felt squeezed. "Yeah. I loved it." Leo grabbed Grant's chin and forced him to look into Leo's face. "Do it again."

"Now?" Grant asked.

Leo pushed the cover back and showed off his already hard cock.

Grant laughed. "I'll see what I can do, Leo. God knows I wouldn't want to disappoint you when you've missed out for so long."

Leo pulled Grant down for a kiss and whispered, "Missed out on you. Such a fool. Such a damned fool."

"Yeah, well, you said it," Grant said against Leo's lips, and Leo laughed before kissing him hard.

<h1 style="text-align:center">Chapter Fourteen</h1>

GRANT WALKED THROUGH the hospital corridors not noticing where he was going or even able to read the chart in his hands. He'd heard someone call his expression "dreamy," and he'd forced himself out of memories of Leo's body and the night they'd spent tangled up in each other long enough to look like he had it together. He'd glared at nurses as they'd scurried to their work, relieved that even if he was completely high on whatever these emotions for Leo were doing to him, he still had it in him to scare the pants off the underlings.

He rounded a corner, determined to focus on the task at hand before anyone else busted him on his love-sickness, when he noticed Leo and Lucky entering the half-open area set aside for visitation with the stable psych patients.

Grant tucked the chart up under his chin, and he skulked around a potted plant to get in a position to see into the room without much likelihood that he'd be seen in return.

It wasn't so much that he was spying as that he was *checking in* on Leo and Lucky. When he'd left the farm that morning, Leo still wasn't sure if he was going to come see Hannah today, and, if he did, he hadn't made up his mind about whether to bring Lucky. Grant just wanted to make sure that both Leo and the carrot were okay, and he didn't see any need for them to know he was there while he was doing that.

Apparently, things between Hannah and Lucky were more confusing than not. But given how careful Leo was to provide

Lucky with as much stability as he could muster, it surprised Grant to learn that things with Hannah were so messy.

That morning, before Lucky came downstairs, Leo had explained to Grant that Hannah had never officially given up her parental rights, but instead they had been deemed abdicated by California state law after Hannah had not contacted the state, the hospital, Leo, or any other family member with regards to Lucky in over a year. Lucky at that point was classified as abandoned and Curtis and Leo had become her adoptive parents.

"Lucky knows that Hannah is her biological mother," Leo explained. "But Hannah chose not to name a father on the birth certificate. I'm pretty sure the father was Hannah's boyfriend at the time, but someone at the hospital told her not to name paternity if she wanted to make it easier to give Lucky away."

Grant had listened to this while they ate breakfast as Leo shifted back and forth in his seat, sometimes flushing.

Grant had asked, "Sore?"

"A little," Leo had said. "It's nice."

"I'll get you something for it."

"No!" Leo exclaimed. "No, I'm okay. I like it."

Grant smirked. "Kinky. You love it."

Leo had rolled his eyes, and laughed, but then he'd come back to the subject at hand. Leo explained that, yes, Lucky was curious about Hannah, and when they'd first moved back to Blountville, Lucky had spent a lot of time looking at old photos of Hannah and asking about her mother's childhood, both with Leo and with Chuck and Meryl.

Leo had gone on, "I kept waiting for her to ask me why Hannah left. And when she finally did, I told her that her mom couldn't take care of her because she wasn't healthy. But then she pointed out that I'm sick, and she got scared that I'd leave her, too. I had to explain that her mom was sick in a different way, and that I wouldn't ever leave her, not until the day I die."

About that time they'd been interrupted by Lucky trotting down the stairs. She was excited about a field trip coming up at school, but Grant tuned it out, watching instead how Leo brightened when she talked.

Before Grant left to get back to his place for a change of clothes before heading to the hospital, Lucky had climbed up on his lap and said, with no segue at all, "Dr. Grant, do you have a mom?"

"Nope. I had an aunt once, but she died."

"Was she pretty?"

"No."

"Was she nice?"

Grant pursed his lips and looked at the ceiling. "Nope."

"Was she mean?"

"She was…frustrated."

"What else was she like?" Lucky wanted to know.

"Well." Grant let himself think about Aunt Jane and her red, fuzzy hair, her thick waist, and the way she'd tried to keep Uncle Kirk from drinking too much. "Well, she yelled at me a lot."

"About what?"

About letting them down and being a burden on them. "About taking baths and school," Grant fibbed. "She was a pain in my butt."

He remembered one night after Kirk nearly took his hide off with a belt for screwing up on a Chemistry test—it'd been a bad night—Jane had come in with a bowl of soup and a soft pillow for him to rest on. She'd clucked and touched his face gently and then ordered him to do better next time.

Grant sighed. "She could have been worse. She was kind of like a mom, I guess."

Lucky kicked her feet and wrapped a skinny arm around his

neck. "I have a mom that's kind of like an aunt," she said. "So, you and me, we're opposite."

Grant had rested his cheek against her warm, brown hair for a moment and then kissed the top of her head before dumping her on the ground. "I guess so. But on the bright side of this clusterfu…on the *bright side*, you got a pretty cool uncle for a dad."

Lucky had looked at Leo then with loving eyes. Then she tugged on Grant's hand. "Dr. Grant?"

Grant crouched down. "What's up, kiddo?"

Lucky kept her eyes on Leo as she whispered in Grant's ear, "Is my dad gonna be okay?"

Grant cupped his hand by her ear and said, "If I have anything to do with it, your dad is gonna get the best care possible so he has the best chance of getting better." Grant ran a hand over her hair, and added in his normal voice, "Now, eat your breakfast and practice your opening chess moves for tonight. I'm gonna cream you. Again."

Lucky narrowed her eyes at him and said seriously, "You just wait, Dr. Grant. One day, I'll kick your butt."

Leo had snorted laughter into his water glass, looking between them with happy eyes.

"You'd better," Grant had said, putting his hand on her head. He'd kissed Leo goodbye and waved at Lucky, who'd nodded him off with a smile.

Now Leo was at the hospital with Lucky, and they were clearly going to meet with Hannah today after all. Grant wasn't surprised that Leo hadn't informed him of his decision; it wasn't like Grant had a dog in the fight. It really was entirely up to Leo as Lucky's only present parent to make the choice. Grant just hoped it wasn't the wrong one.

He watched Leo and Lucky settle into the visiting area seats.

Lucky was obviously nervous, her small feet kicking back and forth, the fingers of her right hand knotted into the long sleeve of Leo's shirt.

Leo cuddled her close and whispered something in her ear. She nodded and faked a smile. Grant's stomach twisted up, and he licked his dry lips, thinking about how she'd looked the first few times he'd seen her—like she was inside of herself—and how she'd relaxed so much over the last few months. He hoped that Leo knew what he was doing and that this meeting with Hannah didn't set Lucky back or make her act out in school again.

Grant had seen photos of Hannah, but he wasn't prepared to see the woman the nurses escorted in. Though perhaps he should have been given what he knew of her recent life. She was so malnourished that the bones of her ankles and knees, visible beneath the short robe she wore over the hospital gown, stuck out with sharp edges. The smile on her face was tentative and faltering, and it fell off completely when she reached toward Lucky and the carrot pulled back under Leo's arm.

"She's feeling shy," Leo said, holding Lucky against his side as he stood up to embrace his sister.

Hannah seemed to recover from the surprise that whatever she'd imagined would play out between her and her estranged daughter wasn't, in fact, going to happen. It wasn't the Lifetime Movie of the week.

She smiled again and let her eyes wander over Lucky like she couldn't get enough of her. Then they all sat down without another word while Lucky hid against Leo and Hannah stared.

"She looks like you," Hannah said, and her voice sounded fragile and a little brittle, like broken glass, but she didn't look anything but contrite. "Like she's really yours."

"She is really mine," Leo said softly, and Hannah nodded, wiping the tears that welled in her eyes.

"Yeah, she is," Hannah said. "I know that. Of course I know that. I'm glad you adopted her. She's so beautiful, Leo."

"She's smart and funny, and she's the best thing that ever happened to me," Leo said. "So thank you for that."

Hannah sobbed a little and held the back of her hand to her mouth the way that Leo sometimes did when he cried. Grant clenched his jaw, holding back the urge to step into the midst of them and shake the girl.

"Ah, Hannah," Leo said. "I'm so glad you came home."

Leo rubbed Lucky's arm as she turned her head into his stomach and refused to look at her mother.

"I'm sorry," Hannah said through the tears. "For, you know, everything. For not being there for you, or for…Lucky. I like that name, you know. I was going to name her…well, something else. It doesn't matter now. I like Lucky better, anyway."

Leo said, "It's okay, Hannah. We're glad you're here, and we just want you to get better. That's all we want."

"I know," Hannah said. "And I want to get well, Leo. I really do. And I want to give you my kidney, because I want you to be around for a long time. She needs you. I need you, Leo."

"Don't, Hannah. Don't even worry about that right now. It's not important. All that matters is that you get healthy and well. Everything else can wait."

Grant rolled his eyes. Actually, it couldn't wait, he wanted to interject. Actually, it's *all that matters*. But he kept his mouth shut, though it was hard.

"I want to be better," Hannah said. "I don't want to be this person anymore. I want to come home."

"We want that, too," Leo said, reaching out to take Hannah's hand. "I've missed you so much, and Lucky—she should know her mom."

Hannah bowed her head and her shoulders started shaking.

Leo pulled her close and she wrapped her arms around his neck crying on his shoulder while Lucky still clung to Leo's middle.

They were an anxious, emotional clump of humanity, and Grant wanted to grab Lucky out of the middle of it and take her with him somewhere more peaceful, like the gossip-hell of the nurses' lounge. Because Lucky didn't need all of this. She didn't need these messy tears and declarations. She just needed Leo to be well, and if Hannah could give them that, then Grant didn't give a damn what else Hannah had to say.

Lucky slipped out of Leo's arms then, and Leo pulled away from Hannah to try to grab her. But she was fast, and she made a very obvious beeline toward the potted plant that Grant was not-so-well-hidden behind. Leo's eyes met his, and Grant gave a close-lipped smile as he bent down to pick Lucky up. She clung to his neck, and Grant stepped out with her, lifting his chin toward Leo and Hannah, saying, "Well, then…."

"This is my…this is Grant," Leo said, putting his hand on Hannah's shoulder. "He and I…well, we're…um, you've been gone a long time. Curtis and I…."

Grant shook Hannah's hand. "Dr. Grant Anderson. Leo and I are together. As for this one," he continued, patting Lucky's back, "I'm taking her to the nurses' lounge." He raised a brow firmly at Leo.

Leo nodded and put his own hand on Lucky's back, rubbing soothingly. "Lucky, I'll talk more with Hannah, and you go with Grant, okay?"

Lucky nodded against Grant's neck and refused to look at her father or mother. Grant nodded at Hannah and carried Lucky away toward the coffee and gossip of the nurses' lounge.

Lucky snuffled tearily against his shoulder and Grant's heart ached even as he made a mental note that he'd need to get a fresh lab coat and have this one laundered now that she'd snotted on it.

The lounge was full of too many nurses talking about a lot of nonsense, but most of them scattered when Grant came in with Lucky, and then the rest left, too, making noise about heading back to work.

Finally alone, Lucky lifted her tearstained face and looked at him solemnly. "I don't like her," she said finally. "I don't like Hannah."

"Yeah, well…" He plopped her down in one of the cushioned chairs the nurses had lobbied successfully for a few years ago. He scratched his fingers over his scalp and sighed. "Want some coffee?"

Lucky smiled and wiped at her tears and snotty nose with the back of her hands.

Grant rolled his eyes and pumped a handful of the liquid antibacterial soap from the dispenser on the wall. He rubbed it over her hands and passed a box of Kleenex her way.

"So, coffee?" he asked again.

"I'm too little," she said, giggling. "You know that."

Grant shrugged. "Suit yourself."

He poured himself a cup of coffee and grabbed someone's unopened cola from the fridge and handed it to Lucky. "Here," he said. "Wanna play chess?"

Lucky popped the cola and said, "I left my iPad in the car."

Grant nodded. He pulled out a sheet of white paper, drew the squares on the page, and passed a pen to Lucky. "Color in the black squares."

Lucky's eyes lit up and together they made a chess board out of a sheet of paper, and then they tore up small pieces marked to indicate the pieces. They had just started their first game when Leo came in, his eyes red-rimmed and worried.

Lucky ignored him, and Grant smiled up at him before making his next move when it was his turn. Leo stood nervously behind Lucky's chair and watched them until the game was over. Then Grant sipped his coffee and waited for Leo to make the right move for his daughter.

Leo knelt down next to Lucky and said, "Baby, I'm sorry. Come here."

Lucky chewed on her lip, glanced at Grant, and then launched herself into Leo's arms. "I don't want her to be my mom," she cried. "I just want you."

"You've got me, baby. Shhh, you've got me," Leo said rubbing her back and looking at Grant with sad, tired eyes.

Grant sighed, pinched his nose, and shook his head. Hannah better come through with that kidney if she was going to upset Lucky like this. The kid had already been through too much, and with Leo so sick, she might still have to go through more. Grant let out a short huff of fear and frustration thinking about it. The kidney—Grant had to focus on that. It was all that mattered.

Chapter Fifteen

Five Months Ago

"**S**HE'S DOING SO well," Leo enthused, threading his fingers through Grant's as they walked toward Meryl and Chuck's front door. They had to stop in to leave a check for the housekeeper because Meryl had forgotten to put it on the counter before going into work. But then it was back to the farm for Leo to rest and get ready for his stay at the hospital. It could be up to two weeks or more.

"She's really excited to help me, too. I can't believe it. I really can't believe that by this time tomorrow I'll have a functioning kidney, and Hannah will be starting her long-term drug counseling so that she can stay clean. Maybe, in the end, Lucky will be willing to give her a chance, too. I just…I feel like this all worked out this way for a reason."

Grant said nothing, preferring to let Leo ramble than to be the downer. The idea of Leo getting a new kidney made him so happy that he wanted to do something crazy like dance naked in the middle of the street. The idea of Leo going under the knife, though, made him sweat, toss around sleepless in the middle of the night, and generally feel like throwing up.

And *any* belief that Hannah would be able to complete her treatment was, essentially, nonexistent. He was just grateful that the girl was going to cough up a kidney for Leo, and he tried to keep the resentment that she was going to just turn around and break Leo's heart to himself.

Leo desperately needed the kidney, though. In the last month, the dialysis hadn't been working as well, and the AV fistula was becoming more and more unstable. There was some concern about the amount of fluid building up around Leo's lungs and transplanted heart, and there'd been some bandying around of the terms "iron overload" and the terrifying "heart failure." It'd become clear that whether or not Hannah was completely done with her rehab stint, time was of the essence. Leo was sick, and he needed help now.

"So, tomorrow, after the surgery, I know I'll be too out of it to remember to ask, but will you take Lucky out for celebratory ice cream? Because I know she's scared out of her mind right now, so—"

"Leo," a voice called from the side of the house.

Leo stopped in his tracks and his hand clenched hard in Grant's. Grant squinted into the afternoon sun, trying to make out the person by the house. Tall, dark hair, and he was walking their way.

"Of course," Grant said, gritting his teeth together. "Why am I not surprised?"

Though he was. He was quite surprised. As far as he knew, Curtis Banks hadn't even been in contact with Leo since things had gotten serious between the two of them, and now here he was, on the day before Leo's surgery to, what? Complicate things, of course.

"Curtis," Leo said, and his voice was tense, low. "What are you doing here? Is everything okay?"

Curtis smiled and scoffed. "Of course everything isn't okay. You're having surgery tomorrow. I couldn't let you go through that—" Curtis took in Grant and then his eyes fell down to where Leo held Grant's hand. "Alone."

Leo's fingers twitched, and Grant waited to see what he

would do. Let go? Or hold on?

"I can't believe you came all this way." Leo held on tighter. "I thought you were in Tuscany doing a film."

"I was," Curtis said, his voice loaded with implication and not all of it good. "And it looks like you were *busy*, too."

"How Alanis-ironic," Grant said.

Curtis crossed his arms over his chest. "I wasn't sure whether you were staying here at your folks' place or out on the farm still. I thought I'd check here first."

"If you ever called Lucky, you'd know," Leo said, coldly.

"The time difference is a lot to work around!" Curtis exclaimed. "And I did talk to her. That's how I even know about this surgery."

Leo sighed and rubbed a hand over his face.

"I'll wait inside your folks' place," Grant said to Leo. "If you need me, I'll be in the living room."

Leo attempted a reassuring smile. "It'll be fine."

Grant wasn't so sure of that, but he figured the best thing to do for now was to give them some time to talk it out, and he knew that Leo needed to do that on his own. He just wished that Curtis Banks wasn't so damn tall, dark, and handsome—because he looked like he might be gunning for a reunion, and Grant was cute enough, all right, but could he really compete with *that*?

"Where's Lucky?" Curtis asked as Grant went into the house.

"With Memaw," Leo replied, and Grant's stomach clenched at how tired, how gutted Leo already sounded, when only moments ago he'd been bright with anticipation and joy.

Shutting the door of Meryl and Chuck's house behind himself, Grant stuck his hands in his pockets, and rocked back on his heels. He stood in the middle of Meryl's cozily decorated living room as he tried to figure out what to do with himself. There was no good way to pass the time. The magazines on the table were all knitting, hunting, or fishing related, like he gave a damn about any of that.

He fought the urge to stand by the window and spy. Instead, he sat down on the sofa and opened his phone, stared at his emails blindly, then stood up again, pacing to the bookcase and back. There was the kitchen. He could make something to eat. But he wasn't hungry, not even close to hungry.

A few minutes into pacing, there was a crashing sound from the patio, and Grant raced to the door, jerking it open. His heart was in his throat and his hands in fists ready to attack. Rage and worry flooded him like a swollen river overflowing its banks.

Leo stood staring down at flowerpot shards next to his parents' patio table, his mouth twisted in a mask of sadness. "It's okay," Leo said, looking Grant's way. "I knocked it over."

"It was an accident," Curtis clarified, not taking his eyes from Leo. "Someone should fix that table. It shouldn't tip like that."

Leo sighed, stuffed his hands in his pockets, and swallowed hard. His skin was dull, and he was obviously having a hard time holding himself upright. That was happening more and more lately, but Grant blamed Curtis for Leo's current weakness. He'd been fine before.

"So, what do you say?" Curtis said. "I could stay here. Just— let me be clear before you answer—I *want* to stay."

"No, you should go," Leo said, his voice quiet and tired.

"Seriously, Leo? Are you sure about that? Because I've already looked into selling—"

"No, really, Curtis." Leo looked him in the eye and attempted a smile. "It's all right. I've got my mom and my dad to help me out—" He glanced toward the door. "And Grant."

Curtis crossed his arms over his chest again, glaring with startlingly handsome blue eyes. "So this is the famous Grant?" he gritted out.

"Yes," Leo agreed softly.

"Look, I don't know this guy from Adam. All I know is you were seeing him before, while we were broken up, and, well, I'm not sure I trust him around our kid."

"Oh, come on, Curtis," Leo said, his voice rising a little. "You've left Lucky with all kinds of paid strangers whenever you want. This is my boyfriend. And Grant loves Lucky."

"What's not to love?" Grant said, stepping out onto the porch before he realized that he was getting involved in something that he had no intention of being involved in. Leo did that to him. "Lucky is amazing." He put on a softer smile, trying not to sound as close to anger as he was. "Mr. Banks, I assure you, I'd rather have my fingernails pulled off one by one with dirty tweezers than see anything bad happen to her."

Leo sighed, his eyes cast down and his shoulders sagging. He was getting so tired. Grant could see that, why couldn't Curtis? Leo should be resting. The surgery was the next day. He needed to be in good condition for it.

"Curtis, you left *me*. Over and over you left me, remember?" Leo said.

"I'm not the one who moved across the country!"

"To get help with our daughter. Help that you weren't able to give."

"Would you just shut up and listen to me?" Curtis said to Leo, his face twisting with anger.

"I think you better go," Grant said, stepping forward.

"Grant, you're not helping," Leo whispered.

"You know what? I can't believe you," Curtis bellowed. "You haven't even been gone a year and you've already moved on. Did you plan this all along? Did you decide you'd made a mistake back then? Chose the wrong guy so you came back here to right your wrongs? Is that it, Leo?" His voice cracked, and he shook all over with rage or hurt, Grant wasn't sure. Either way, it was a good show. "Because I don't even know what to say about that!"

Curtis sounded so self-righteous, so accusatory that Grant had a hard time holding back from punching him in the mouth.

Leo's face crumpled, and there were tears in his eyes, but Grant saw clearly that underlying rage kept him still standing.

Leo jabbed his finger at Curtis. "You don't get to say that to me! You don't get to show up here one day—one *day*, Curtis— before my surgery and pass judgment on my life." Leo shook hard, and Grant reached out, putting a hand on his shoulder to steady him, to slow down the rage that could damage his already fragile body. But Leo jerked away, his focus still on Curtis.

"When we got Lucky, you promised you'd be there for her, for me, no matter what, but you never were. I don't even know if you really meant it—"

"Of course, I did. I just didn't know how hard it would be, Leo. You pushed her on me. I wasn't ready yet. You—"

"No!" Leo shouted, his body shaking so hard that Grant stepped even closer, afraid that Leo would fall. "Don't go there! Don't even start with that again! I've heard that enough in my lifetime, and I won't hear it again. You were there. You signed the papers. You walked away. None of it was my fault, Curtis. You did it all yourself. You're the one who screwed it up. Not me. It was never me."

"Leo, come on. That's not fair. You played your part. I never wanted it to be like this. I just needed a little breathing room to do my work, to get my focus—"

Leo pushed at Curtis's chest, yelling, "So, go! Go! That's what you do best! Why would today be any different?" Leo got in Curtis's face, spitting his words out slowly. "And after *everything*, why would I want it to be?"

"Leo—"

Leo shoved against Curtis again, and said, "*You* left *us*. You weren't there. So just…go." He moved back, shaking his head, his mouth trembling. "Go. I don't want you here."

Grant stood with his arms crossed over his chest and his chin down. He watched in blind rage as Leo clutched the doorframe to steady himself before retreating into his parents' house.

Curtis called after him, "Leo!"

Grant blocked Curtis's path to the door and narrowed his eyes. "Do you actually *want* to kill him? Because pushing him like that when his body is already breaking down is one good way to induce a heart attack."

Curtis had the decency to look scared. But then Curtis was all about decency and the appearance of devotion. It undoubtedly played well in the celebrity rags. And yet when the going got tough, Curtis sold out.

"He doesn't understand," Curtis said, pitifully. "It's not that I don't want him. Or them. It's that I needed time. Some space. That's all."

"And I care so little about what *you* need that I could not *begin* to express it. And as for Leo, it seems like he's heard it all before. Is it any wonder, Mr. Banks, if he doesn't believe you anymore?"

"Look, who are you to—"

"You know who I am to Leo. He told you to go."

"And if I don't?"

"Papa!" Lucky's voice called out from the driveway, and Grant turned to see her running toward them, her dark hair streaming out behind her. "Papa! You're here! I've missed you!"

Chuck walked down the driveway, a smile of greeting fading into an expression of concern when Leo stepped out from the doorway looking gray and tired. His skin was sweaty, and Grant wanted to check his pulse, but he didn't want to scare Lucky.

Chuck said, "Hey, son, over lunch with me and Memaw Lucky remembered she left her Sammy Spider here, but when Memaw couldn't get you on your cell, I offered to bring her over to grab it."

"Yeah, I had my phone on silent," Leo said, his eyes down and his shoulders hunched. "Sorry."

"Don't worry about it. We're here now." He looked between Grant and Curtis, and then glanced at Leo again, his jaw setting in obvious annoyance. "I'll just go in the house and grab it then?"

"Don't bother," Leo said. "I'll get it. Thanks, Dad, for taking care of Lucky. I really appreciate it. But I think Curtis would like to spend some time with her now."

Chuck nodded and patted Leo on the shoulder, jerked his chin Curtis's way, and gave Grant what was probably supposed to be a reassuring expression.

"Thanks for bringing that check by for the housekeeper, son. I guess I'll head on back into town and see if your mother can use any help in her office. Good to see you, Curtis. Grant. Love you, Lucky." He looked back twice as he walked away, and it seemed to Grant like he had something more he wanted to say, but he held it back for now, whatever it was.

Lucky clutched Curtis's neck in a massive hug. She grabbed his cheeks in excitement and said, "Papa, this is Dr. Grant! He's so cool! He takes care of me sometimes when Daddy's getting his treatment. He showed me this one room where we can see the operations and there was this man and his chest was open and I could see his beating *heart*! It was amazing, Papa! It was like, ba-boom, ba-boom, and so pretty!"

"Is that even legal?" Curtis asked, incredulous.

Leo ignored him and said, "Lucky, Papa is just here for a little visit while I'm in the hospital. He's staying at a hotel. Do you want to go have ice cream with him? See a movie with him?"

Curtis glared at Leo before turning a sweeter expression on Lucky. "What do you say, Luckster? Ice cream with your old man?"

Lucky, to Grant's surprise, seemed uncertain. She glanced between Leo, Grant, and Curtis, like she was trying to read their minds, and finally said, "Daddy's sick. He needs me."

"It's okay, baby," Leo said. "Go with Papa, all right? You'll have a good time with him. Maybe you could spend the night with him in the hotel, and you could be with him tomorrow while I'm in the hospital. Would that make you feel better?"

Lucky's eyes went straight to Grant, and she seemed torn. Her hands clenched in Curtis's shirt, and she finally said, "Okay, Daddy, I'll go with Papa."

"Give me a kiss," Leo said, reaching out for her. He clung to her for a long time, burying his face in her neck, and then handed her back to Curtis with his face down and his voice tight. "Have a good time. I'll see you tomorrow night, or the next morning. Be good for Papa."

Curtis looked like he wanted to say something else, but Lucky had scrambled down to the ground, taken hold of his hand and started dragging him away from the house. "Come on, Papa. I want ice cream. Chocolate chip! And maybe a cone, okay? A waffle cone!"

Only as she climbed into the rented BMW with Curtis did Grant realize she'd left Sammy Spider behind. He hoped she'd be okay without him.

• • •

LEO HELD SAMMY Spider close to his chest and stared at his parents' coffee table blankly. Grant sat next to him studying Leo's chin for signs of wobbling and saw only a slow burn of ongoing anger. Occasionally, Leo would shake his head, as if trying to make himself accept something that he didn't want to believe.

Finally, Leo spoke, "Can you believe him? Can you believe that he just *showed up* here? Like… like what? Like I'm supposed to be happy about that?"

"Yeah, well, from what you've said about him, that seems pretty typical," Grant commented.

Leo ignored that, saying, "I really did *not* need to see him today. And Lucky! She was just getting used to the idea that he wasn't around anymore. I mean, he calls her every few weeks; he's been pretty good about that. Better than he used to be, and I shouldn't have given him a hard time about it. But to show up like this? She's going to be so confused again!"

Leo looked fragile, physically and emotionally. Grant sat up to rub his back, but Leo tossed his hand away.

"Don't," Leo said. "Don't feel sorry for me."

"Why would I feel sorry for you?" Grant asked. "He's the idiot."

Leo shook his head again and covered his mouth with his hand. His eyes tumbled with emotions, like light on stained glass.

Grant wished he could go find Curtis and slug him. From what Grant knew about the situation Curtis had basically been designed as the perfect foil to Leo's self-esteem, effortlessly saying or doing just the thing that would take Leo down again and again.

Leo said, "It's always been on his terms. Right from the beginning. It was never about me, or what was good for me. He never supported me in *anything*, not unless it was reluctantly, begrudgingly given, and I just thought that *of course* that's what I deserved. That's what I was worth, obviously, because that's all I was worth to him, and I loved him."

Grant said, "He never valued you."

"Wow. Thanks for the ego boost." Leo sank back in the sofa, his skin sweaty and his pallor poor.

"You're welcome," Grant said. His hands itched for his stethoscope; he wanted to have a listen to Leo's heart.

Leo whispered, "Because it feels so good to know the man you devoted part of your life to, built a family with, never *really* thought you were worth a damn."

"His loss."

And it was a huge loss. Grant was acutely aware of that fact. The idea of Leo no longer being in his life cut Grant down the middle. So, yes, what Curtis had let slip through his hands was huge, vast even, but the thing was—if Curtis had never truly understood or appreciated what he had in Leo to begin with, not even in the losing of him, then Grant could only sneer. Despite being an almost-superstar who appeared to have the world at his feet, Curtis was the biggest fool he'd ever met. And Grant had met a lot of fools.

Leo shook his head. "Yeah, well…." He lifted and dropped his hands in defeat.

"It's his loss," Grant said again. "You're the best thing that ever happened to him."

"Yeah, well, tell *him* that." Leo laughed. "You know what? Don't. He's certainly not the best thing that ever happened to *me*. What do I care what he thinks?"

Grant risked putting his hand on Leo's shoulder again, and this time Leo let it remain. "Beats the hell outta me."

"And you really think so?" Leo asked.

"What?"

"You think I'm the best thing that ever happened to somebody?" Leo gazed at Grant with his clear, gray eyes, half teasing and half begging Grant to say the right thing.

"Oh, wait, I was wrong. You *are* an idiot."

Leo rolled his eyes.

"You're the best thing that ever happened to about a dozen somebodies, and while I might be the only one lucky enough to know it, it doesn't make it less true," Grant said, rubbing his fingers gently over the soft fabric of Leo's T-shirt. He would have liked to work out the tight muscles of Leo's shoulders, but he didn't want to release additional toxins. Leo's kidney was working hard enough.

"Thought you didn't believe in luck," Leo whispered.

"Maybe I need to change my stance on that."

Leo smiled, and he let himself fall over into Grant's lap, twisting until his feet were hanging over the edge of the sofa's arm and his head was cradled against Grant's legs.

"I'm so in love with you," Leo murmured, gazing up at Grant with a soft expression.

"I know," Grant said, and ran his fingers through Leo's hair.

Leo smiled sweetly and after a few minutes his breathing slowed down.

Grant pressed one palm to Leo's chest to feel his heartbeat and when Leo relaxed enough to fall asleep, he pressed a kiss to Leo's temple and rested his own head on the back of the sofa.

Chapter Sixteen

Present

GRANT THOUGHT HE was going to have to kill Leo's mother if she didn't shut up and listen.

"What are you saying, Doctor? Are you saying something went wrong?" Meryl asked.

Chuck held Meryl, his strong arms around her sturdy frame, and said, "Honey, shh, let's hear what the doctor has to say before we panic."

"Panic?" Meryl reacted to the word like it was a bomb. "Do we *need* to panic? Grant? Dr. McGraw? Dr. Muresan? Do we need to panic?"

Grant glanced to Muresan, and then back to Dennis, waiting for someone to tell them *something* about what the hell had happened in there, and what the prognosis was, and whether or not Grant needed to go find a loaded gun and put himself down, because he was not doing *this* without Leo. If there was no Leo at the end of this, he wanted none of it.

But then he looked down the hall and saw Lucky standing there holding the nurse Carrie's hand, looking terrified and abandoned in the shuffle as the doctors had exited the ORs. She stared right at him, and as his eyes met hers, they bore into him with a deep, old wisdom that made him feel sick to his stomach. He stared back at her, torn between going to her side immediately to offer some kind of reassurance that he could never honestly offer and staying to hear what Muresan had to say about it all.

"Mrs. Garner," Dr. Muresan started for the third time. "Please, your son will need you to be calm and—"

"Forget that," Grant interrupted. "Skip the niceties. Tell me what the *hell* went wrong in there, because from what I saw, it was—"

"Grant," Dennis cut him off. "Let's focus on the situation at hand."

Muresan took that opportunity to actually talk, thank God, and said, "Leo is stable. He had an unusual reaction on the table, and we suspect that he's contracted a CNS infection—"

"CNS? What's that? Is it serious?" Meryl asked, clasping James's hand that clutched her shoulder.

"Central Nervous System infection, and, yes, it is always serious. For someone on immunosuppressants it's even more so. He suffered a seizure on the table, and his blood pressure dropped a great deal. We believe, however, that we can control this infection—"

"How did he get it?" Meryl asked.

"There's always a risk with long-term immunosuppressant patients for the introduction of—"

"The anti-rejection drugs for his heart made him susceptible," Grant interrupted. "He could have been infected at any point recently—introduction of foreign bodies into the AV fistula—"

"But Leo is fastidious," Meryl said. "He always cleans that carefully."

"I know," Grant interrupted. "There's no telling how it happened. It's happened."

Dr. Muresan turned to Dennis. "We're getting Dr. Lynn Gregor in from Raleigh via helicopter. She's an expert at these situations. In the meantime, we have all hands on deck for Leo."

Dennis clapped Muresan on the arm. "Dr. Muresan, aside from the uncontrollable—good surgery."

Grant clenched his teeth, glared at Muresan, and said nothing.

Chuck said to Dr. Muresan, "This Dr. Gregor—she's the best?"

Grant noticed Carrie walking toward them with Lucky as Muresan said, "She is."

Grant interrupted. "Time for brave faces, Chuck and Meryl, here she comes."

Lucky clutched Sammy Spider in one arm and Carrie's hand in the other. She didn't take her eyes off Grant, not even when Chuck lifted her up, and Meryl told her that her daddy was out of the surgery and he was okay.

"Don't lie to her," Grant said. "She's not stupid. You're just scaring her more by lying to her."

Lucky swallowed hard, and her lips started to tremble. Chuck cleared his throat and looked at Meryl, but then nodded toward Grant, agreeing with him.

"Lucky," Grant said. "Leo had a problem, but we've got the best doctor in the entire world coming to help—"

"You're the best doctor in the entire world," Lucky whispered.

Grant's throat went tight, and he had to clear it to say, "This lady's better than me."

"Don't lie," Lucky said.

"She's better than me at dealing with CNS infections. She's better at what your daddy has, and I couldn't treat Leo anyway, even if I was the best."

"Which you're not," Lucky said.

Grant swallowed. "Right. Not at this. She's the best."

"Like how Daddy is better at ping-pong, but you're better at chess."

"Exactly."

"Will this doctor fix him?" Lucky sniffled against the top of Sammy Spider's head. "Will he die?"

"No!" Grant said, so vehemently that everyone jumped a little. "Leo won't die." He said it like a promise.

Lucky stared at him, measuring Grant's words, and she said, "Sometimes people tell lies by accident."

Grant remembered when she'd told him something like that before and he said, "No. Not this time."

He knew he couldn't guarantee anything. He'd never made a promise like this before, but he couldn't entertain the idea that what he said might not be true. He had to stay focused and make sure that Leo got the treatment that he needed, and that Lucky got her daddy back as soon as possible. There were no other options he was willing to consider.

Lucky nodded at him solemnly, as though they'd made a pact, and then she buried her head in Chuck's neck and started to sob. Meryl comforted her, and Chuck stroked her back. Grant swallowed hard, and then turned on his heel, leaving them there with Dennis calling after him.

He headed directly to Recovery, because even though he knew Leo wouldn't be waking up in an hour, wouldn't be smiling up at him and asking for that wonderful meal he'd planned, Grant still had to see him.

He had to look at him and *know*.

• • •

Two Months Ago

"SHE'S NOT IN New York," Leo said, drowsy from the sedative they'd given him for the more invasive tests. "At least not at the place where she used to be. Memaw said that no one in the…the hovel had any clue where Hannah might be. Hadn't heard from her since before. Before…you know, before."

It'd been a month since Hannah had bolted the night before the surgery. While Lucky had been eating ice cream with Curtis, and Leo had been sleeping on Grant's lap, Hannah had signed herself out of the hospital, gone to God knows where, and didn't seem to be hurrying back.

Conversations about Hannah always resulted in Leo losing his shit in some way or another, or trying to blame himself for Hannah's behavior. Grant braced himself for it and sighed when it began almost immediately.

"I put too much pressure on her. She never should have felt ob—obli—obligated to give me a kidney," Leo said. "If I hadn't, she'd be here getting straight. Wait. She is straight. Getting… narrow. Getting good? What's she getting, Grant?"

Grant didn't say "drugs" and instead sat down next to Leo's hospital bed and brushed Leo's hair off his face. "Shh, you should be resting."

"Sick of resting," Leo said. "Wanna go home."

"You and every other patient in this place," Grant said.

"Tests are over. They should let me leave."

"Not until the drugs wear off."

"Yeah, I'm a menace to society," Leo said loopily. "Menace? *Menace.* Why does that sound wrong?"

"Because you're high."

"Right!" Leo said. "You should use this opportunity to ask me inappropriate questions!"

Grant chuckled. "What do you suggest?"

Leo looked hilariously thoughtful as he considered. "How I keep my teeth so white? No, I know! Why I'm so darn attractive to you, even though I'm a mess?"

"Getting cocky, aren't we?"

"Admit it. You're kind of hot for me," Leo tried to lean over, but Grant pushed him back against the bed. Leo took the opportunity to run his hand over Grant's hair and breathe in Grant's ear.

Grant shivered and planted a kiss on Leo's forehead.

Leo said, "See? I told you."

"Yes, obviously, you turn me on like no other," Grant said, sarcastically.

"Charmer," Leo laughed.

"Leo," Grant began, but was interrupted by a nurse coming into the room, dragging a cart along with him.

"Sorry, Dr. Anderson," the nurse said. It was the same nurse who for whatever reason often flirted with Grant, and now he gave Grant the same look through his lashes that he always did. "I just need to get his vitals."

Grant moved away from Leo to give the guy some space to take Leo's temperature and blood pressure. But the nurse couldn't seem to stop looking Grant's way and smiling softly. Grant huffed in annoyance.

"Seriously?" Grant asked.

The guy was going to flirt with him in front of his sick, morphine-filled boyfriend? Grant was going to have to learn this kid's name and make his life hell. Clearly, he didn't understand how this worked at all, or that Grant was *not interested.*

Leo looked between the nurse and Grant, and then giggled. "Oh, he likes you," Leo said to Grant. "He thinks you're hot."

The nurse flushed a little, though he couldn't seem to stop himself from looking at Grant again.

Grant rolled his eyes, saying to the nurse, "You didn't think you were being subtle, did you? If a man high on painkillers can see what you're doing, I can assure you that I've figured it out by now, too."

"He's a doctor," Leo slurred. "He knows things." Then Leo laughed again. "You're pretty cute, though. Should I be jealous?" And Leo looked up at the nurse with such a coy, flirtatious expression that Grant's stomach curled with possessive irritation.

The nurse, whom Grant would *definitely* soon make sorry for all of this, smiled down at Leo and said, "No need to worry at all, Leo. He doesn't even look at me once, much less twice."

Leo laughed loopily. "Yeah, he's kinda in love with me."

The nurse grinned. "I know. *Everyone* knows."

Leo nodded and closed his eyes happily as the blood pressure cuff swelled on his arm. "Yeah," Leo sighed. "He's great."

The nurse bit his lip and looked like he was trying not to laugh. "Now, Leo, don't rub it in."

Leo snorted and chuckled again. "I can't help it! You should know! Everyone should know!"

Grant rolled his eyes. Leo was exuberant when high. To say the least. Grant wondered if Leo was also like this when drunk. He'd probably never get a chance to find out.

The nurse patted Leo's arm as he took the blood pressure cuff off. "126 over 89," he reported. "You'll be out of here in a few hours, Leo," he said. "My name's Aiden if you need anything, okay?"

Leo nodded and waved him off.

Aiden took the opportunity to smile at Grant again and mouthed, "He's cute."

Grant glared at him, and Aiden just laughed and left the room, pulling the cart behind him. Grant leaned over Leo's bed and whispered, "You're ruining my reputation."

"He's hot," Leo said. "Should I worry?"

"Yeah, you should worry," Grant said. "Worry that I'm going to make his life hell."

"Aw, Grant, he can't help it!" Leo said. "You're just so sexy!"

Grant couldn't help but laugh at that.

"It's bound to happen. Just don't encourage him," Leo said, and yawned. "I'm tired."

"Rest. I've got to go check on some patients. Is it safe to leave you here alone? Or will you be calling Aiden in for extracurricular fun?"

Leo waggled his eyebrows. "I'm high. I can't be responsible for my actions."

"Uh-*huh*." He kissed Leo's forehead again. "I'll be back."

"A'right," Leo murmured. "Be sleepin'."

Grant paused in the doorway, and Leo was already out. He glanced around, saw that no one was looking, and he blew a small kiss toward Leo's bed.

• • •

A FEW HOURS later, Grant groaned as he walked out of the elevators on Leo's hospital floor to find Curtis Banks standing at the nurses' desk outside of Leo's room, surrounded by ogling fangirl nurses. And one fanboy nurse—the very flirty Aiden.

"I thought you left," Grant said to him. "A month ago."

"I came back," Curtis said.

"Obviously," Grant muttered, crossing his arms over his chest. "You should star in more horror films."

"What's that supposed to mean?" Curtis asked, crossing his arms over his chest, too, and squinting at Grant angrily.

"You know, that clichéd ending where the monster just won't stay dead? You've got that part down pat, don't you? Coming back again for more?"

Curtis's lips twisted into a sneer. "You don't know anything about me. Or about me and Leo."

Grant pursed his lips. "I know enough. Enough to say I don't want you here. And enough to know he doesn't either."

The nurses' eyes flicked between Grant and Curtis with interest. Grant thought that at any minute a magical bowl of popcorn would appear in their hands to go along with the show.

Curtis shook his head. "You know, if I were a different person…. You know what? Never mind," Curtis said throwing up his hands and starting to turn away.

Good riddance, Grant thought.

He paused and turned back, "Look, I have Hannah. She showed up at my place in LA, and my assistants there contacted me. I left my film set to go back to California and talk with her. I've brought her to Blountville to do the right thing by Leo, okay? That's all I'm here for, so take your attitude and—"

"What's going on here?" Leo stood by the door of his room, his hospital gown flapping open in the back, lines hanging loose from his arms, and his face looking swollen with retained fluids. "Curtis?"

Grant and Aiden rushed to Leo to help hold him up. "You're supposed to be in bed," Grant said irritably.

The other nurses busied themselves with coming to aid Leo, too.

"I'm fine," Leo said, pushing Aiden, Grant, and the other nurses away, his focus back on Curtis. "What are you doing here? I thought I told you that I didn't want to see you anymore? If this is about Lucky, we had an agreement—"

Grant swallowed, taking hold of Leo's arm again. He raised an eyebrow at Curtis, waiting for him to pass on to Leo the bomb he'd just dropped.

"It's Hannah," Curtis said.

Leo glared at Curtis, his lips tight, and his head tilted with suspicion. "Hannah?"

"Yeah—it's a long story, Leo. Maybe you should get back in

bed. You don't look so good."

"Is she okay?" Leo asked, and Grant felt Leo tremble under his hand.

"Yeah, she's fine," Curtis said. "Well, kinda. I mean, she's here. In the hospital. I just checked her in. She needs a few weeks to get clean again, and then she's going to donate her kidney."

Leo shook his head. "No, that's…I can't take it." His eyes were wide and wild. "She needs to take care of herself, and she…she's a drug addict, and she might need that kidney—"

Grant steered Leo from the doorway back into his room and then into the bed with Aiden's help. Leo's skin was gray, and a film of sweat stood on his upper lip. Grant motioned at Aiden to get the crash cart ready just in case, and Curtis bent down in front of Leo, his blue eyes full of worry as Leo swallowed and seemed to fight for a good breath.

"Shh," Grant murmured pulling out his stethoscope to listen to Leo's heart. "Be calm, Leo."

"Be calm! How can you say that?" Leo exclaimed, but then he clutched his chest and moaned, before going gray and limp.

"What is it?" Curtis asked, looking desperately to Grant. "What's wrong?"

Aiden bustled around pressing buttons and calling the doctor on duty, as Grant said, "It might be his heart. You need to back away. Now."

Curtis lurched away from the bed, and Grant moved aside, too, as Dr. Matthews and Dr. Muresan both came into the room. Though it took everything in him, Grant managed to stay back while the other doctors examined Leo and meds were pushed. He released his long-held breath as Leo's skin pinked up again.

Dr. Matthews shook his head at Grant and motioned for him to step outside the room. "You've got to keep him calm. Everything in his system is taxed right now. You know this,

Grant."

Grant nodded, unable to speak over his racing heart.

"For now, for the immediate time frame, he's okay. We want him checked back in, though, after this incident," Dr. Matthews said with a deep frown. "I know he'll fight us on that, but he needs to consider this a warning. And, dammit, Grant, we need to find a kidney."

Dr. Muresan nodded at Dr. Matthew's final statement as he exited Leo's room. "The sooner the better," he added.

Grant let out a shaky breath and stood in the door, watching as Curtis took Leo's hand and said things that Grant couldn't hear. Leo gazed at Curtis with conflicted, tired eyes. They needed a kidney. The sooner, the better, like Muresan had said. And Curtis had brought Hannah back to them.

Grant pinched the bridge of his nose and sighed. Now, he had to convince Leo to take what his sister could give. They were running out of options, and Grant's shaking knees and trembling fingers told him that he'd never been more terrified.

Chapter Seventeen

"HEY, DOC," AIDEN said, passing Grant a patient chart. "I checked in on Leo earlier, and he had a visitor I thought you'd want to know about."

After the scare the other day, Leo had been checked into the hospital until they could figure out how to best handle the congestion around his heart. Lasix was usually a good option for draining the excess fluid, but Leo's kidneys couldn't handle the strain, and so they were monitoring him closely, trying to strike a balance.

"Curtis again?" Grant asked.

Curtis had been visiting daily, and Grant was trying to be patient about it, but it was starting to wear thin. At least Curtis wasn't making Leo angry anymore, instead claiming that he understood that they were over, and that he just wanted to see Leo get well. Grant wanted that, too, but he wanted Curtis to be on the other side of the country when it happened.

"No, Dr. Anderson," Aiden said. He caught his breath when Grant turned his full attention on him, and then he blushed. "Um, sorry. You just—um, anyway." Aiden laughed and said, "Right. It was his sister."

"Okay, then," Grant said, sighing. "Great. Is she still in there?"

"No, she went back to the psych and detox unit a little while ago. She was smiling when she left? So, maybe that's a good sign."

Grant nodded his thanks and stepped into Leo's room prepared for anything at all. Leo's emotions were unpredictable when it came to Hannah.

"Hey," Leo said as soon as Grant shut the door. "How were rounds?"

Grant rubbed his face and groaned, "Boring. Not a single patient with any exciting diagnoses today. Maybe tomorrow."

Leo smiled and waved Grant closer. "Aw, are you okay? Need a serious car accident with perforated lungs to make it all better?" he cooed.

"Yeah," Grant said. "That'd be good. Arrange that for me."

Leo snorted. "I'll work on it."

"No," Grant said. "You'll work on getting better. So, your sister's kidney…" Grant raised his brows.

Leo sighed and adjusted his blankets. "I guess Aiden told you she was in here. He's trying to get on your good side. Probably in case I kick it. You realize he's positioning himself to cheer you up after my death with blowjobs and casseroles."

"I wish that were funny."

"What? You can't joke about my death? Does it scare you too much?" Leo laughed.

"Uh, yeah," Grant said. "As a matter of fact."

Leo's face softened, and he waved Grant even closer.

When Grant was close enough, Leo jerked him down by the collar of his shirt. "I love you," he whispered.

"And I love you too," Grant said irritably, rubbing his eyes, not finding the jokes at all amusing. Casseroles and blowjobs from Nurse Aiden were no substitute for Leo. "So, your sister's kidney. You're going to take it."

"You sound like Memaw," Leo said. "She's already called to tell me the same thing."

"Then it's settled."

"Yeah," Leo agreed.

Grant stared at Leo in surprise. He'd expected another fight, and he'd been ready to deal with whatever upset Hannah's visit might have caused, but Leo seemed calm, relaxed even, as he stared at the opposite wall and nodded slowly.

"Yeah, it's settled," Leo said. "She's got to detox, and then we'll schedule the operation. She's…*different* this time." Leo shrugged. "I can't explain it. But she really wants this, and her doctor thinks that it might even help her stay clean, give her an added incentive to keep healthy. I don't know." Leo raked a hand through his hair and looked stressed again. "I just know I promised Lucky to be here for her, and I'm running out of options, Grant. I guess I have to do this."

Grant pulled up the chair and sat beside Leo's bed, taking his hand. "I'll bring that little girl in here every day and make her tell you how scared she is that you'll die if that's what it takes."

"No," Leo said. "I know how scared she is. And I have to do what I have to do. For her. Hannah doesn't come first anymore."

Grant nodded, raised Leo's hand and kissed Leo's knuckles. Leo squeezed Grant's hand and gave him a wan smile. He shifted in the bed and sat up slowly.

"Curtis's been here again," Leo said, sighing. "He wants to know if he can have Lucky for a few weeks this summer."

"Oh?"

"He wants to take her to Scotland with him. He's filming a movie with dragons."

"Huh, strange. I thought dragons were *make-believe*. Leave it to Mr. Banks to school me," Grant said, flipping through Leo's chart, darting his eyes over the information the nurses had been recording like clockwork every two hours.

Leo laughed, but his heart wasn't in it. "Yeah, well, that part's all going to be CGI'd in later. Curtis went into great detail about all of that. He's pretty excited to do so much work with a green screen. He likes to exercise his imagination, he says."

"You don't sound happy at the idea of her going." Grant snapped Leo's chart shut, satisfied with what he'd seen there. If things continued at this pace, Leo might be able to go home for a few weeks before the surgery. That would be good.

"I'm not," Leo said. "I mean, I guess I should be glad that he wants her around and in his life, that he's making the effort, but…I'm not." Leo looked at Grant, searching his face. "How do you feel about it?"

Grant shrugged. "I like the carrot home with us where she belongs, but it's your choice. He's still part of her life. And I'm not her father, so…" Grant pressed his lips together. "That's that."

Leo swallowed. "Yeah, but if you were, you know, her father. What would you think?"

Grant said, "I'm not. But Scotland's not a third world country. He loves her. And that's all I've got to say on the matter." Grant stood up and tucked Leo's blanket in around his feet, taking a moment to run his hand over Leo's warm skin.

Leo looked a little disappointed, but he nodded and lifted his head up to meet Grant's kiss goodbye. Leo's lips were soft, and Grant tried to deepen the contact, but Leo pulled back, smiling and blinking slowly, as if dazed.

"Later," Leo said softly.

"That better be a promise," Grant said, and Leo nodded, looking breathless and aroused.

At that moment, a nurse buzzed through. "This is Patricia. Is everything okay?"

"Yeah, fine," Leo said.

"All right. Your heart rate jumped, and we just needed to check."

"S'all good," Leo said.

Grant smirked and Leo smiled, ducking his head.

Grant was anxious for Leo to get home for a lot of reasons, one of which was purely selfish. Their sex life had been put on hold with Leo always hooked up to monitors. The nurses would know if they got up to anything just by Leo's heart rate.

Grant kissed Leo's cheek softly and turned to go. "By the way, I'm stopping by the farm tonight."

"You are?" Leo asked.

Grant said, "Yeah, even though your mom and dad are staying out there with Lucky, for some reason the carrot wants *me* to be the one to tuck her in. So…" Grant shrugged.

He didn't mind doing anything for Lucky. He just didn't know what he was *supposed* to do.

"Thank you," Leo said, his eyes soft. "Thank you for being there for her."

"Yeah, well. She's a good kid," Grant said, leaving out that he cared about Lucky, that he wanted her to be happy, and that he wanted the three of them to be happy together, whatever the hell that meant.

"She really likes you," Leo said.

"I like her, too." Grant waggled his fingers. "Adios."

Leo smiled and called out a quiet goodbye as Grant left the room.

As soon as Grant was around the corner from the curious and observant Aiden, Grant pulled out his cell phone and dialed Sheriff Memaw Marie's number.

"Mission accomplished," Grant said.

"He's taking the kidney?" Marie demanded.

"Indeed he is."

"Well, hallelujah!" she said emphatically. "I knew I could count on you to make him see reason."

Grant leaned against the wall in the corridor and said, "Well, surprisingly the credit isn't mine. The kidney donor herself made the plea, and Lucky was the glue that sealed the deal."

"Excellent news," Marie said. "Hannah—for all her problems—loves her brother. She won't screw it up this time. I'll see to that."

Grant made a noise of agreement.

"No matter what. Leo will get that kidney if I have to harvest it my own damn self."

"Same, Marie," Grant said softly. "Same."

• • •

Present

GRANT PULLED A chair up next to Leo's bed in the recovery room. He watched Leo's heart rate beep on the monitor, steady and regular, and then he let himself really look at Leo's sleeping face. They'd removed the oxygen mask; he was still puffy from the surgery, but the bag attached to the catheter showed that Hannah's harvested kidney was working, producing urine well, and in copious amounts, which was good.

"Hey," Grant said softly. He had become one of those people who stood by their unconscious loved one's bed and talked to them. But he had to make sure Leo knew how important he was to Grant, and to Lucky. So he'd know that he had to make it through this.

"Hey," Grant started again. "Leo, you better get your ass in gear and get better, because I..." His voice cracked a little, and he cleared his throat, looking over his shoulder to make sure he was still alone. "I need you. I love you. So, I'm counting on you. Don't leave me. Don't leave Lucky."

Grant wiped at his face quickly when he heard footsteps, and

Dennis stepped between the curtains to put his hand on Grant's shoulder. "Listen, the tests are looking really good, okay? Dr. Gregor's landing shortly, but, Grant, I think he's already fighting this thing. We might not even need her."

Grant nodded, wiped at his nose, and kept his eyes on Leo.

Dennis sighed, squeezed Grant's shoulder, and said, "Come on, you can't do anything for him right now, and you need to calm down. Let's get out of the hospital. Alec can take you—"

Grant shook Dennis' hand off. "No," he said. "I'll be here. At the hospital. Until Dr. Gregor gets here and I hear what she has to say."

Dennis loosed a sound of frustration and said, "Grant, what about Lucky? She really needs you now."

Grant closed his eyes. He put his hand in Leo's unresponsive fingers and swallowed. "She's with Chuck and Meryl. It's fine."

"Come with me, buddy. We both know that for whatever reason the person Lucky most trusts in this world is you. She needs you right now. Leo wanted that."

"*Wants* that," Grant said. No one would talk about Leo in the past tense. Not now, not with things still so touch and go.

"Exactly," Dennis said. "So, get your act together, and go be the person that kid needs."

Leo's eyes were swollen and ringed in blue, and his fingers warm and pliable in Grant's hand. His lips were dry and slightly open, but he was breathing, and his new kidney was working. The seizing had stopped, and if Dennis was right then it was possible that the meds they'd already pushed were making headway with the infection.

"Give me a minute," Grant said.

Dennis crossed his arms over his chest, but moved behind the curtain, leaving Grant as alone as he could be right now with Leo.

Grant leaned over and kissed the stubble along Leo's cheek,

and whispered, "You left me once. You can't do that to me again." Grant ran his hand through Leo's hair, kissed his cheek again, and said, "You're needed, Leo. Kick this infection's ass and come back to us."

He pushed away, rubbed his hands over his face, and left the room with a defiant glare at Dennis, avoiding the empathetic gaze every nurse and doctor seemed to be trying to send his way.

He was in love and scared. He didn't need their googly eyes gazing at him. What he needed was Leo, and unless they could provide him with that, he wasn't interested in what they had to offer.

Chapter Eighteen

G RANT AND LUCKY played endless games of chess, mostly in silence, with little instruction going on at all. When Lucky lost, Grant didn't explain to her why, or how she could've prolonged the inevitable, but just cleared the board and started over. Neither of them wanted to talk.

Meryl paced the room like a caged bear, fretting and worrying, and asking all kinds of questions that Grant wouldn't answer, until Chuck reminded her, "Honey, Grant's hurting too. Leave him be for a while, okay."

"But he's just playing chess."

Lucky had turned to her then and said, "No, he's waiting, and he's scared like me. He loves Daddy."

Grant put his hand on her head. She didn't need to defend him, even if her furious little face did warm his heart. "Meryl, I assure you, I've told you everything I know. I'm waiting, just like you're waiting."

Chuck put his arm around Meryl and led her toward the couch. An hour later, she finally came back over and put her hand on Grant's shoulder, saying, "I'm sorry. I know you care about him."

Care about him. Grant had almost laughed. It was the biggest understatement he'd ever heard. *Care* about Leo? Leo was his safe place, his everything. His love for Leo was a once in a lifetime thing. It wouldn't fluctuate and it wouldn't fade. So, no, he didn't *care* for Leo. What he felt was so much more.

At that point, Lucky had abandoned her seat beside him to wrap her arms around his waist and bury her face in his chest, breathing slowly, clinging and worried. Grant patted her arm and she relaxed a little against him.

Dr. Gregor appeared several hours later, harried and frowning. Grant hefted Lucky up, standing as Dr. Gregor entered.

"And?" he asked. "Did you see the test results? What's the—"

"Dr. Anderson," she cut him off. "Are these the patient's next of kin?"

Meryl and Chuck stood up. "We're his parents, yes."

She turned her focus onto them. "Well, it's not the best news. I've seen the latest tests and examined the patient. As I said, it's not good. I've confirmed that it's progressive multifocal leukoencephalopathy, a rare brain infection that occurs mostly in patients who have been on immunosuppressants for an extended period of time. It's often fatal. I should warn you in advance, this is a difficult diagnosis."

Grant was washed in cold, and he held Lucky tighter. He stared at Dr. Gregor, waiting for her to tell them more.

"The good news is that I've had success fighting this virus. There's a new protocol that I'm willing to try. I had a good outcome with my last PML patient. Methfloquine," she said.

"An anti-malarial drug," Grant said.

"Yes, this past June we reversed the virus in a case much worse than Leo's using methfloquine," she said.

Hearing Dr. Gregor use Leo's name for the first time, like he was a person, not a thing, made Grant's stomach relax a little, and he nodded and swallowed. "Do it then," Grant said.

Dr. Gregor looked to Chuck and Meryl. "It's not Dr. Anderson's call."

"Whatever you can do to save our son," Meryl said, gripping Chuck's hand on her shoulder.

Lucky clutched Grant's neck harder at Meryl's words, and Grant held her a little tighter. He took a breath and closed his eyes, terrified that he'd accidentally told Lucky a lie. And if he had…if he lost Leo now…what would that do to him, to her, to both of them? He opened his eyes and glared at Dr. Gregor, willing her to fix this.

"All right," Dr. Gregor said. "We'll know by the morning if the treatment is working. I'll start it right away."

Lucky whispered against Grant's ear, "Don't leave me. Promise. Don't leave."

Grant said nothing, rubbing her back, and sat down with her on his lap. It was going to be a long night.

• • •

AT ABOUT TWO in the morning, Grant put a sleeping Lucky down on the sofa in his office and turned to Chuck, who was standing by his open office door.

Chuck beckoned Grant closer and said, "Thank you for being with Lucky. She needs you right now. Listen, I, uh, was thinking. Someone should let Curtis know about this."

"Why?" Grant asked. "He's filming in Scotland. There's nothing he can do. By tomorrow morning we might have word that there's no reason for Curtis to catch a flight, or cancel production, or whatever it is he might do in a hurry so that he can feel like a hero."

Chuck looked at Grant and said, "Son, I understand that things between you and Curtis are tense at best. But he was part of Leo's life for a very long time. He deserves to know. I can call him, or Meryl can. Someone's going to let him know, though. It'll be morning there soon enough."

Grant grimaced and rubbed a hand through his hair. "Why

bother telling me? I can't stop you."

He turned back to Lucky and sat down at the foot of the couch; there was just enough room. He studied at her sleeping face, her limp body, and sighed. He looked back toward the door to find that Chuck had left, probably to go call Curtis, and Grant sighed again. Even if the experimental protocol managed to work, Curtis always added so much drama to Leo's life. It wasn't healthy, and it wasn't what Leo needed right now. But Grant would fight that battle later when Curtis was actually here. He'd have him banned from Leo's room if he needed to. He'd do whatever it took for Leo to get well.

It was quite early in the morning in Scotland. Grant supposed if Curtis caught a flight as soon as possible, he could be in Blountville by the following day. One thing was for sure, if they made it through this, he was going to talk to Leo about setting up some paperwork giving him power of attorney over Leo's health care and vice versa. Assuming Leo would want that. He knew he did.

He sighed again, glanced at Lucky, and thought about her trip to Scotland with Curtis earlier in the month. She'd been reluctant to go, and she hadn't even been gone a week when she'd called home one night and begged Leo to come get her.

It wasn't surprising to Grant that Lucky hadn't handled the separation well. Grant knew how attached Lucky was to Leo, and, over the last few months, she'd grown habituated to Grant, too. Lucky was like Leo in more than just her looks—she was loyal, and devoted to her home and family—but, she was different in the way she expressed those things. No, Grant hadn't been surprised at all that Scotland had been a bust.

In the end, Curtis had brought her home, and he'd even been unexpectedly relaxed about it, given that his time with her was thwarted. Leo said he'd grown up. Grant speculated that taking care of Lucky on his own while trying to star in a film in another country had been more of a pain in the ass than Curtis had thought it would be. In the end, Lucky's version of events made Grant think he was right.

Now, Grant watched Lucky sleep and stared at the clock. The hours went by slowly and he swallowed back fear over and over. He'd never felt this way before. After he'd left his aunt and uncle's home, he'd never put himself in a position again where he couldn't win.

Now, though, he was in love. And it wasn't just Leo who had a hold on him, but Lucky and her little earnest face and her deep need for someone to trust. Every moment, every second, it became clearer that he needed them in his life, and he didn't trust anyone else with their well-being.

He looked at the clock. Only six more hours and they should know something. Six more hours of hell. He felt suspended in time, as though each second were longer than he ever imagined possible. He'd never been so helpless.

When this was over, Grant decided, he was going to do something about all of this. He was going to get back some control. He was going to ask Leo to make this thing between them legal. In the common vernacular, he supposed, he was going to ask Leo to marry him.

Grant didn't sleep. He watched the clock and when it said eight in the morning, he waited, and he waited. Lucky dreamed on, and he didn't wake her. He waited some more.

When Chuck finally showed up at Grant's office door, grinning and giving him a thumbs up, the rush and whirl in Grant's ears was so loud that he couldn't hear over it. He stared into Chuck's eyes, trying to make sure he understood correctly.

"He's going to be all right. It's working. The treatment is working," Chuck said. He hugged him, and Grant hugged the man in return. Chuck thumped Grant's back hard over and over, saying, "He'll make it. He's gonna make it."

Grant nodded and let out a long breath. He swallowed, rubbed at his eyes, and then he looked down at Lucky. She would probably wake at any moment.

Heart in his throat, Grant said to Chuck, "Watch Lucky."

Then he rushed from his office. He passed Alec and Dennis hugging in the hallway, and when they called out to him happily, he ignored them, heading directly toward the ICU.

Because he wasn't going to tell Lucky another damn thing until he'd seen Leo and talked to Dr. Gregor herself. It'd been too close. *Too close*, and he had to know for sure before he renewed his promise to Lucky that Leo would be okay.

He'd been an imbecile, a cocky, terrified, son of a bitch to make a promise like that to begin with. They'd been lucky. Damned lucky.

Now they needed to stay lucky.

<h1 style="text-align:center">Chapter Nineteen</h1>

A Week Later

CHUCK AND MERYL were late picking up Lucky from Grant in the hospital cafeteria after they'd spent most of the day going back and forth between Leo's hospital room, and Hannah's new set-up in the rehab unit. The unit was not the best in the state, but Leo, Hannah, and their parents seemed to believe that Hannah would have better success getting off to a clean, new start if she remained in Blountville.

Lucky was still anxious about her mother, though, and she told Grant while they ate together that she didn't want to see Hannah. At least not yet.

"I don't have to like her now, do I?" Lucky asked him, sipping her chocolate milk and gazing at him with her clear eyes.

"Nah," Grant said. "Why should you like her? You don't even know her."

Lucky picked at her green beans and shrugged, not meeting his gaze.

"Who said you had to like her?" Grant asked.

Lucky bit the end off a green bean and chewed it for a long time before saying, "Denise at school says that everyone loves their mommy. That they *have* to love their mommy. She says it's just the way it is."

Grant snarled up his lip and said, "Is Denise a psychologist?"

Lucky laughed. "No, she's five. She's the line leader on every other Monday, though."

"So, who are you going to believe? Me or a line leader? She's not even line leader every Monday."

Lucky grinned and took another bite of her food. "Sometimes I'm line leader," she said. "On every other Wednesday."

"Cool," Grant said.

Lucky sighed. "So, it's okay then, if I don't love Hannah?"

"Seems okay to me," Grant said, stealing one of Lucky's fries because he'd already finished his own.

"Dad will be sad that I don't love her, though," Lucky said.

"Your dad will understand," Grant said. "Love isn't something that you feel because you're supposed to." Grant sat back in his seat. "It's not something you control. Sometimes you even feel it when you shouldn't. Or when you don't want to."

"Why wouldn't you want to?" Lucky asked.

Grant thought about Leo in the OR seizing on the table and the terror that had ripped through him, and he thought of Leo pale, gray, and puffy in the recovery room, and he thought of Leo's gray eyes crinkled in laughter, and his smile that made Grant's stomach flip, and the desperate way that Leo clung to him in bed, and the expression on Leo's face when he came.

"Beats the hell outta me," Grant said, though it scared the pants off him even still.

"I wish I loved my mom," Lucky said. "But I don't."

"Your dad would probably say to give her a chance," he said.

"Do you think I should give her a chance, Dr. Grant?" Lucky asked, all earnest eyes and worried face.

"I say wait it out. See if she sticks around."

Lucky nodded and looked thoughtful as she ate the last of her fries and started to unwrap the cookie. "Yeah, that's a good plan," she said. "And Denise is stupid. She doesn't even know her multiplication tables."

"Oh, well, in that case, never listen to a word she says," Grant muttered.

"But Granny Meryl says that she's only five and most five-year-olds don't know that yet."

"It's never too early to start with intellectual snobbery."

Lucky gave him a look that made Grant smile. It was a look he'd seen on Leo before. It said very clearly, "You're full of shit."

Grant liked that Lucky already knew when that look was appropriate and he said, "Give me part of your cookie."

"No!" she said. "It's not yours!"

"Give me," he said waggling fingers at her.

She laughed and took a huge bite and shook her head. Grant sighed mournfully and sat back to watch her eat it.

A few minutes later, after Lucky had devoured her cookie, Chuck and Meryl finally showed up looking anxious and tired.

"How's my girl?" Chuck asked, hefting Lucky up and hugging her close.

"I see Grant has fed you dinner already," Meryl said, wrapping her arm through Chuck's, and smiling warmly.

"Green beans, French fries, and a cookie," Lucky said.

"Healthy," Meryl said, raising an eyebrow at Grant, but her eyes were full of good humor.

Grant shrugged, picked up his tray, and said, "I've got rounds."

"So late?" Meryl asked.

"Yep, well, I had a little company this afternoon." He narrowed his eyes fondly at Lucky and winked at her.

"Dr. Grant's patients get mad when he brings me with him," Lucky said.

"You took her on some of your rounds?" Meryl sounded a lot like Leo.

Grant shrugged. "Only the boring ones. I could do those with my eyes shut."

"That's what he told them," Lucky said.

Grant winked at her again and headed out of the cafeteria, leaving Lucky with Chuck and Meryl. He wasn't sure where they would take her for the night, but either way she was sorted, and now he only had to see a few patients, and then he could go to Leo.

. . .

Leo was awake.

Aiden told him when they passed in the hall. And even if Aiden *was* trying to get on Grant's good side in the hopes of a payoff in some completely delusional future, Grant had to admit the guy was a good nurse. He'd taken very fine care of Leo.

When Grant knocked on Leo's door, Leo himself called out for him to enter. He thrilled to hear his voice again. Leo looked exhausted, but he was alive, breathing, and smiling at Grant like he was the best thing he'd seen all day. Possibly in his life.

Grant felt shot through with warmth at the sight of him.

"Hey," Grant said, and pulled up a chair to sit close to Leo's bed. "How do you feel?"

"Alive," Leo muttered through chapped lips. It was the first time in almost a week that Leo wasn't half-asleep on painkillers. Leo smiled lazily up at Grant and said, "Gotta reward me for that soon."

"Yeah, well." Grant gazed at Leo warmly. "I can't wait to reward you for that feat."

Leo's eyes widened in mock surprise. "Really?"

"I can't wait to give you everything you want for the rest of your life in reward for that." Grant pushed Leo's hair off his forehead. "I gotta say," Grant said, keeping his voice low. "This, uh, being in love with you thing? Made me pretty worthless."

Leo's eyebrows lifted and his eyes were soft. "How's that?"

Grant swallowed, brushed his hand over Leo's hair, and shrugged again. "I panicked. I'm a doctor. I keep my cool in moments of disaster. I do my job. But seeing you—" Grant shook his head and pressed his lips together. "I couldn't...I couldn't even think about anything. Or anyone."

"But you were good with Lucky," Leo said, taking Grant's hand and kissing it. "Dad said she only wanted you."

"Yeah." Grant nodded. "I could stay focused for her. I don't know what else I would have done." Grant gazed down at Leo intently, studying his face, the curve of his lips and cheeks. "Don't ever do this again. Do you hear me? I won't lose you."

Leo laughed softly and said, "I'm not making any promises, but I'll do my best."

"You better. I've never been so scared."

Leo blinked slowly, his eyes so tender and full of emotion. "I'm sorry."

"Don't be sorry. Just get well. And stay well. Forever."

Leo laughed. "Okay, I'll just find a sparkly vampire to bite me and become immortal then."

Grant nodded and said, "That's fine with me. Whatever it takes."

Leo snorted and motioned for some water. Grant handed it to him and watched as Leo sipped out of the straw. Grant took a deep, steadying breath, and put the cup back on the tray.

"Leo, I never thought I'd ever ask anyone this question. It's not part of the plan."

Leo tilted his head and said, "Plan?"

"I never wanted a family, but I never wanted a lot of things. And now there's you, and this situation—and the kid. She needs stability. She loves me. I love her. And—"

"Wait, you love Lucky?" Leo asked.

Grant blinked and his mouth opened and closed a few times.

"Yes. I mean, yes…is that a problem? Of course I love her. Why do you think I spend time with her? It's sure as hell not her chess game."

"No, of course not," Leo said, smiling. "You love her?"

"Yes."

"Grant, that makes me so happy."

"Well, good. And you love me. And we love each other. It's how it works? Right?" Grant didn't think he'd ever said the word 'love' so many times in his life. "That's what's supposed to make a family. And I know I'm babbling, and I might be freaking you out, but this—I'm serious and I've thought about it. It's legal to do it now, and it's…I…just…marry me."

Leo's smile was like summer and pie and cookies and casseroles and ice cream and everything that Grant loved best in the world.

"You're such a jerk," Leo said.

Grant swallowed. That was not the response he was expecting. "Well, yeah. But—but you knew that," he stuttered. "And what did I do now?"

"What did you do? I was going to ask *you*. I had a whole romantic thing planned, you jerk. You stole my thunder!"

"Oh," Grant said, his heart pounding and his stomach twisting. "So…what does this mean? Is that no? Or yes? Or…?"

"It's yes, jerk. It's a big, fat, hell yes," Leo said, lifting up enough to grab Grant's face in both hands and pull him down for a kiss. "Yes," he said again. "I love you."

"Love you," Grant murmured, kissing Leo back, wrapping his arms around Leo's body to pull him close. He practically crawled into the bed, hovering over Leo, careful not to put pressure on Leo's body or side. It was probably his knee that hit the call nurse button.

The buzzer by the bed announced, "This is Janet at the nurse's station. You called us?"

Leo started laughing, and Grant cursed.

"Oh, sorry, Dr. Anderson," Janet said. "I'll just cancel it out."

Grant kissed Leo again and then crawled out of the bed carefully, saying, "You need to get well and get home."

"Yeah," Leo agreed. "I've got to get my hands on you. I can't wait much longer. Or Aiden is gonna catch you in a weak moment."

Grant kissed Leo again and muttered, "I'd have to be unconscious or dead."

"Well, that's a weak moment," Leo said earnestly.

Grant's face went soft with affection, and he teased, "I'm starting to think he's wanting a threesome. You in?"

Leo snorted softly and shook his head no. Then he grinned. "So…you wanna marry me?"

Grant grunted his agreement and ran his hands over Leo's hair again, and said, "Yep, Leo. You did something to me. I drank the Kool-Aid."

"You like Kool-Aid," Leo said, his eyes glowing with happiness.

"Mind-altering red dyes," Grant said softly, leaning closer for a kiss. "Smashed bugs. Coal by-product."

"You love me," Leo said against Grant's lips, and there was a touch of wonder in his voice like he still didn't entirely believe it.

"Yeah," Grant admitted, kissing Leo again.

"I must be pretty delicious Kool-Aid," Leo said softly.

Grant smirked. "And now that you have a new kidney, you can finally taste mine."

Leo's eyes went wide with amusement and lust. "*Grant.*"

Grant nodded and cupped Leo's cheek. "Hurry up and get well. I'll let you drink all you could want."

Leo pulled Grant down by his collar and kissed him hard. Grant laughed against his lips, and they both groaned when Janet beeped in again to check on the sudden rise in Leo's heart rate.

Chapter Twenty

Four Weeks Later

THE FIRST NIGHT home from the hospital, Leo sat at the kitchen table at the farm supervising Lucky's homework and watching as Grant and Chuck carried the last of his luggage from the hospital out to the truck.

"Well," Chuck said, clapping Grant on the shoulder. "That's the last of it. Your mom will want you all to come to dinner tomorrow night. Hannah's arranged to have a family pass for the evening."

Grant noticed Lucky shrink a little in her chair and duck her head so that she wouldn't have to meet Chuck's eye.

"Your mom's looking forward to having everyone together," Chuck said. "What about you, Grant? Can you make it?"

"I've got rounds. And—I'm not sure Leo will be up to a night out yet," Grant said, widening his eyes at Leo and then inclining his head toward Lucky a little. "You've been overdoing it since you got home," he added. "You just had major surgery and recovered from a near fatal CNS infection. Stop being a hero and rest.

Leo glanced at Lucky, and then flashed his confusion to Grant before saying, "I'm sure we can be there, Dad. I can rest all day while Lucky's at school, and I'm sure I'll be able to—"

Lucky slammed her notebook shut and ran up the stairs. A few seconds later the sound of her door banging closed reached them all.

Leo and Chuck looked after her in confusion. Grant sighed, turned to the cookie jar, and said, "Okay then. Cookie time."

Grant pulled out two cookies and opened the refrigerator for the milk. He poured a glass and leaned against the counter, taking a bite, and waited. He wasn't happy that Lucky was upset, but it had been bound to all go down sooner or later, and cookies would make it more palatable. For him anyway.

"Grant?" Leo asked. "Do you know what's going on with Lucky?"

"Doctor-Patient confidentiality," Grant cited.

Leo narrowed his eyes and leaned forward on the kitchen table staring Grant down. "You're not her doctor."

"I put antibiotic ointment and a Band-Aid on her knee just yesterday," Grant said, waving his glass of milk in Leo's direction, and then taking a stalling swallow.

"Grant," Leo said. "What's going on with our kid?"

Grant almost choked on the cookie, and he stared at Leo, coughing into his elbow, until Chuck pounded him on the back, and his milk sloshed on the floor.

"What?" Leo asked.

Grant said, "I didn't realize she was mine."

Leo's eyes softened, and a small smile curved his lips. He leaned back in his chair and said, "Yeah. Of course she is."

"Well," Chuck said, shaking Grant's shoulder. "I'm concerned about Lucky, but this seems like it's verging on being personal and private, so I'll head on home. Leo, call me later. Let me know if there's anything I can do for Lucky." Chuck squeezed Grant's shoulder again and said, "Grant, son. See you later."

Grant stuffed more cookie into his mouth before he said something to Chuck that would make Leo frown and possibly derail this very interesting conversation about *their* kid.

The kitchen door shut, and Leo stood up, walking slowly

toward Grant.

He put the cookie and milk down on the counter and ran a hand through his hair. Slow blinks and a sweet smile made Grant's heart thump, and a quiver of lust shot through him. Leo was hot when he was in love. Grant swallowed, thanking all that was awesome that Leo was in love with *him*.

"We're getting married," Leo said, taking Grant's left hand, threading his fingers through, and then pressing his still too-thin body against Grant's. "You love me. You love Lucky. You wanted to be a family."

When Leo put it like that, it kind of made Grant feel like he should run as fast as possible to another state. Another country. Except for the fact that Leo was right there, and he was smiling, and Grant was physically incapable of denying anything about that smile. Leo could look at him that way and Grant would cheerfully break every rule or law just to make Leo look at him that way again.

"So, she's your kid, too, now, Grant." Leo said. "When we're married, we can make it legal. Curtis's already agreed to give up custody. And so—"

"Wait, what? Make it legal?"

"I told you," Leo said. "I was going to ask you. I had plans. Romantic, hot, sexy plans. And you ruined them. Remember?"

Grant stared at Leo.

"Part of those plans included making sure that if you said yes, if you wanted to make a family out of the three of us, then it could be official. Lucky deserves that. Don't you think?"

Of course Lucky deserved that. But Grant had never really considered being her father. Not like *that*. He'd thought he'd just stay Dr. Grant, a kind of uncle-ish figure. A friend who was married to her father.

Leo continued, "So, I had it out with Curtis before the surgery. It was part of what we agreed on. In exchange, I agreed that she could be with him for two weeks every year. Only if she wants to go. I told him that I wouldn't force her. And I think, after Scotland, he might not even be all that eager to try again. Though he'll always be part of her life. I know he'll send Christmas presents, and birthday cards, and probably drop in to see her when we'd really rather he didn't. You know, nothing new."

Grant wasn't sure what to make of the sensations racing through his body. He was hot, he was cold, and he was starting to sweat.

"Grant?" Leo asked, clearly concerned now. His eyes dimmed and his smile faltered considerably. "What are you thinking?"

Grant rubbed at his face and backed away, looking away from Leo, but not really seeing anything. "I never said I wanted to be her father."

Leo's quick indrawn breath made Grant look up. Leo looked like he'd been slapped. Grant rubbed his face again, shook his head, and tried to figure out a different take. "Leo—"

"Oh," Leo said, and he sounded hurt, too. "I thought…well, I guess you know what I thought. I feel like such an idiot right now."

"No," Grant started, but Leo pulled away, moving toward the doorway heading upstairs. "That didn't—"

"Fine," Leo said. "I can't believe I actually thought—I just… Wow. I didn't expect this." Leo shook his head, his mouth open in sadness. "I thought you loved her."

"I do!"

"I can't talk about this right now," Leo said, his eyes bright with tears. "I need to go see my daughter and find out what's wrong with her because I guess it's my responsibility, since she's mine."

"Can we cut the drama?" Grant said.

"No," Leo said. "We can't." And he stomped up the stairs.

Grant threw up his hands and groaned. He tossed the cookie in the garbage and he poured the milk down the drain.

Dammit, Leo didn't get it. He didn't understand, and he hadn't stuck around long enough for Grant to explain. Not that Grant knew how to explain. It was all wrapped up in expectations.

Leo expected that Grant would become Lucky's father legally, and Grant had expected to be…what? What had he expected? He hadn't expected anything, really.

He thought that he and Leo would get married to make it legal between them, and they'd move in together. It looked like that mutual living area was going to be the farm because Lucky wanted to stay, and Leo thought it was best not to uproot her again.

Grant had assumed they'd live here and things would be…the way they are now. He'd be Dr. Grant, and she'd be Lucky, and Leo would be his hot dish of Leo goodness, and Grant would be that strange thing known as *happy*.

So…this other thing? This thing that Leo had proposed? What did that really mean? If Grant became Lucky's father, what changed in that scenario? In so many ways, it would be better. He'd have legal rights to Lucky if she were sick or hurt, and if something happened to Leo…

Grant squeezed his eyes closed at the thought.

He'd be Lucky's parent. No one could take her from him. His stomach flipped, and his chest felt tight. He didn't know if what he felt was fear, excitement, happiness, or some mixture of them all, because he wasn't sure he could do it. He wasn't sure he could be Lucky's father. At the same time, he didn't trust anyone else to even try. As far as he was concerned, Lucky and Leo were his now, and he might fuck up, but there was no way he was going to walk away from them.

Grant headed to the stairs, walked up slowly, and stopped at Lucky's room. She was sitting on the bed with her knees drawn up and her face buried in them, as Leo rubbed her back and spoke to her softly.

"I know you're upset, honey, but you and I aren't going anywhere. And Grant's not going anywhere." Leo met Grant's eye. "Right, Grant?"

Lucky's head came up and Grant forced a smile. "Just to the hospital for work and back."

Lucky shrugged. "I don't care about that."

"Then what, baby?" Leo was confused. "Just tell me what you're upset about."

Lucky shook her head, and Grant stepped into the room. He sat down on the other side of the bed. "We'll play a game," Grant said. "It's called Quid Pro Quo."

Leo looked at him with a wary expression but said nothing.

"What?" Lucky asked.

"Just…listen. I told you I never had a mom," Grant said, and Lucky looked nervously at Leo and back at Grant again, obviously afraid Grant was going to tell Leo how she felt about Hannah. "Well, I never had a dad, either."

Leo shifted on the bed, turning toward Grant with a yielding, curious expression on his face. Grant knew that Leo wanted to know more about Grant's family, about his childhood, and that he was usually disappointed when Grant shot those conversations down or snarked his way out of them.

"You didn't?" Lucky asked.

"No, I had an uncle."

"You had an uncle for a dad, too?" Lucky asked brightly. "We have that in common."

Grant looked down at the patchwork quilt on Lucky's bed,

and picked at the loose edge of one of the patches. "Not exactly," Grant said. "My uncle was a jerk."

Leo's head came up and he focused on Grant, understanding starting to show in his eyes.

"Yeah, that kind of jerk," Grant said to Leo.

"What kind?" Lucky asked.

"He called me names, pushed me around. Once when I didn't pass a test with the kind of grade he expected from me, he belted me five times for each wrong answer." Grant cleared his throat. "He said, 'This is how you pay me back for keeping you alive all these years.'"

"Oh, my God, Grant," Leo whispered.

Lucky took his hand, kissed the palm, and said, "I hate him."

Grant put his arm around her and pulled her close. "Sometimes I hated him, too."

"Why was he so mean to you?" Lucky asked. "Were you mean back?"

Grant smiled at that and caught Leo's eye. He swallowed and didn't tell Lucky all of the things he'd done to the old man, all of the ways he'd tried to make him pay, the tricks he'd played on him, the pranks, and how he'd humiliated his uncle by walking out of his house after announcing his full ride to medical school and never returning again.

Instead he said, "This is a crappy bedtime story."

"Grant, please," Leo's voice was so sad, so warm, and full of how much he didn't want that to have been Grant's childhood.

Grant didn't look at Leo, though. He looked down at Lucky, took her chin in his hand and he searched her hazel eyes. He remembered the tantrum she'd thrown the day before when she hadn't wanted to help wash the dishes. He recalled the full-on screaming, the stomping, and the tears. Grant had been flabbergasted, and he'd stared at her then thinking she had been replaced in her sleep by an alien. But he'd have never hurt her, or called her names, or slapped her face.

Grant said, "I'm better than that."

Lucky looked confused but said, "You're the best in the whole world."

Grant smiled a little at her sweet confidence in him, and Leo said, "Grant—you could never."

Grant shrugged and said, "Okay, carrot, I told my secret. So, your turn. Spill it."

Lucky looked at Leo and squeezed Grant's hand harder like she was seeking his strength. "I don't want Hannah to be my mommy. I don't want her. Ever."

Leo's face dissolved with affection. "Baby, she's always going to be the woman that you grew inside of, but I'm your dad. Me and Grant are your parents."

"Dr. Grant?" Lucky asked, looking up at him.

"Yup," Grant said. "We can make it official. You can be my kid. But only if you want that."

"What about Papa?" Lucky asked.

"He'll always be your Papa," Leo said. "He loves you. But this way you'll have me and Grant, and if I can't be around—"

"Why wouldn't you be around?" Lucky asked, warily. She wasn't anywhere close to being over having almost lost Leo.

"Hopefully, I'm going to be around for a long time," Leo said. "But if I couldn't be around for some reason, you could be with Grant. Would you like that? Do you want Grant to be your other dad?"

Lucky thought about it for a long time, and Grant's gut started to churn. His palms began to sweat, and he felt sick. He didn't know if he could stomach how much it would hurt if she said no.

"And Papa will be Papa?"

Leo nodded.

"And if you…if you…then Dr. Grant will take care of me? Forever?"

"Yes," Grant said.

Lucky nodded her head. "Okay. That's good. I like that."

Leo said, "You could call him Pop, or—"

"Or Dr. Grant," Grant said.

Leo looked at him like he was being a jerk.

"Dr. Grant," Lucky said, clapping her hands together happily.

"It's a little formal, don't you think, *Grant*," Leo said, and he widened his eyes at Grant like he should change his mind.

"No one calls him that but me," Lucky said. "It's mine. I like it."

Grant nodded and gave her a high five.

Leo rolled his eyes and said, "Fine. Whatever. You guys are the least—"

"Sentimental romantic boobs," Grant supplied.

"I've ever met," Leo finished.

"I'm going to grow boobs one day," Lucky said sounding a little worried about that.

Grant flashed to a future of boys—or girls—knocking on the door to take her out on dates, and he imagined her coming down to greet them with her freshly grown breasts on display in some too-small dress, and he shuddered. What had he just agreed to in becoming her other dad?

Leo laughed and agreed that breasts would grace her chest when she was older, and Grant had to shake away the horrible feeling in the pit of his stomach.

"I love you, Daddy," Lucky said as Grant and Leo left the room together.

Grant noticed that Leo moved slowly, stiff from the transplant wound which was healing nicely, but still had a way to go.

"'Night, Lucky. I love you, too," Leo said.

Grant blew her a kiss and had the door almost closed when Lucky called out, "I love you, Dr. Grant."

He opened it a little and gazed in at her little face staring earnestly at in him the darkened room. "I love you too, carrot."

Chapter Twenty-One

"GRANT," LEO BREATHED as he shut the bedroom door behind them, and then leaned back against it. "You never told me."

Grant shrugged, starting on the buttons of his shirt and kicking his shoes off next to the closet door. "Yeah, well." He shrugged again.

He tossed his shirt in the hamper in the closet and unbuckled his belt. He could feel Leo's eyes on him, the sadness and worry pouring across the room in a steady, thick stream of affection. Grant sighed.

Leo pushed off from the door, and Grant let Leo wrap his arms around Grant's waist and closed his eyes as Leo pressed kisses to his shoulders and collar bone.

"It was a long time ago," Grant said, lifting Leo's chin. "It sucked. I lived through it. Chalk one up for the resilience of kids."

Leo didn't look convinced. "Did he hurt you a lot?"

Grant looked at the ceiling, and his lips pressed into a thin line, considering. "The physical abuse was minimal. My aunt took the brunt of that."

Leo's eyes went even wider, and tears shone in them. His lips pressed into a trembling frown, and Grant wanted to kiss the worry away, but he knew better. Leo was going to drag this out of him. He might as well just spill it, get it over with, and move on to the sex he was sure to get as compensation for sharing the horror of his childhood. It might make up for having to dredge it all up at least.

"Grant…" Leo murmured. "Did he hit her?"

Grant groaned and pulled away, moving toward the bed, but not sitting down. He stared at the blue quilt that Leo had pulled out of one of the hallway closets when he got home from the hospital, saying it was his favorite and that Memaw's mother had made it.

"It wasn't every day," Grant said. "He was brusque. Rude. Insulting. Demanding. A perfectionist."

"Oh," Leo said softly.

Grant said with a half-smile, "Yeah. Well, let's just say I fell short of his expertise in assholery. Hard to believe, I know." Grant looked down as Leo's arms wrapped around him from behind.

"How often did he hit you, too?"

Grant felt Leo kiss the back of his shoulders and up his neck, nothing passionate. Soothing kisses, like Leo wanted Grant to know that he was adored now, even if he wasn't then. Grant still thought that might be the craziest part about this thing with Leo.

"It happened," Grant said. "I won't deny that it did. But it was worse when he hit her."

"Did he drink?" Leo asked.

Grant nodded and turned around in Leo's arms, meeting his eyes. "Yeah, he drank."

"I'm sorry."

"It's not your fault."

Leo bit his lip and his face showed that he was feeling emotionally wobbly. Grant wanted to smooth it away, to get Leo to smile again, but he knew Leo well enough to know they weren't done.

Leo said, "I promise you, Grant. Our house won't ever be like that. I would never do that to you or to Lucky."

Grant laughed and said, "Is that what you think? That I'm worried you'll turn into my uncle?" Grant laughed again. "I cannot even begin to tell you how much I'm *not* worried about that."

"You won't turn into him either," Leo said earnestly.

"I know," Grant said. "I know that."

"Because you're not him," Leo said. "You're a good man."

Grant lifted Leo's chin and kissed his soft, warm lips that opened and grew desperate and eager so fast. Lust was always quick to ignite between them. Grant pulled at Leo's shirt, getting it up and over his head, breaking away as little as possible, just wanting skin under his hands.

Leo shivered and pressed against Grant, drawing his fingers down Grant's stomach, before grabbing Grant's hips and dragging him hard against his body. Grant wrapped his arms around Leo and the fresh scar on Leo's side rubbed against Grant's forearm. He pulled away from Leo's mouth, kissing down his neck and chest to Leo's heart transplant scar, pressing kisses the whole way. Then he moved down to the fresh, new purple scar on his side. He got his mouth on the sensitive tissue, kissing and sucking lightly, as Leo tossed his head back and forth and made soft gasping noises.

When Grant came back to Leo's mouth, he found Leo's face a mess of emotions. Grant picked through them—awe, surprise, worry, love, lust. It all made Grant feel hungry, possessive, furious in his desire to never let Leo go.

"Make love to me," Leo whispered.

A burst of affection crashed inside him. It was intense and it broke him, but he wanted it every day for the rest of their lives.

"How do you want me to do that?" Grant asked. "Like this?"

Grant kissed Leo's neck and then bit down until he felt Leo jerk and heard his gasp.

"Yeah," Leo whimpered.

"Like this?" Grant ran his fingers over Leo's scars, and then brought his hands up to pinch Leo's nipples so hard that Leo's knees buckled a little.

"Oh," Leo said, trembling and breathing hard. "Please."

Grant gazed at him, pinching harder until Leo whimpered and humped against Grant's hip. "I could fuck you," Grant said.

"Yeah," Leo said, desperation all over his face. "Fuck me."

"Maybe," Grant said, releasing his tits. "How much do you want it?"

Leo's trembling turned into outright shaking and Leo scrabbled at his own jeans, trying to get them off. "So much. Please, Grant. Please."

"Get on the bed. On your back," Grant said, stripping his own pants off.

Leo spread on himself out on the bed wantonly. His thick, hot cock arched up, flexing, with a pearl of pre-come dropping down to his stomach.

"I can't wait," Leo said. "It's been too long. Thought I might never..."

Grant pushed him down into the mattress, kneeling over Leo, dragging his own balls over the length of Leo's cock. They'd done a lot—even during the last week in the hospital—they'd used hands and mouths, but Grant hadn't fucked him since several weeks before the surgery. Leo had been too sick before, and after, until now, he'd been too fragile.

It wasn't how Grant had planned it. He'd wanted to give Leo some absurd and romantic fuck, something long and drawn out, something to show how much he loved everything about Leo and his body, and how much he'd missed it. He'd thought that's what Leo would want. But that wasn't what happened.

Grant shoved Leo's legs back, less rough than he would have

been before the surgery, but not gently because he knew Leo liked it when Grant was forceful with him. He knelt below Leo's exposed ass, and ran a finger down Leo's his crack, teasing is hole. Leo's legs started shaking hard. A coarse and needy lust gripped Grant, and he spread Leo's ass cheeks, and bent low, pressing his mouth to Leo's asshole. He licked and sucked, getting Leo as wet as possible, and then he sat up and reached into the bedside drawer for lube. Carefully, he opened Leo up, and then slicked himself.

"Ready, baby?"

"Yes, please, please."

With a groan, Grant worked his cock in. Leo was tight, not as prepared as Grant usually insisted on, but Grant couldn't wait, and Leo's eyes were so wide and pleading.

As he moved deeper, Leo made a noise that wasn't entirely good, but when Grant started to back out, Leo reached up and grabbed Grant's face, pulling him down for a kiss. As their tongues moved together, Leo lifted his hips, trying to take more inside.

"Hold on," Grant said, pulling away. "Wait a second."

"No waiting," Leo whimpered. "Now. Now, Grant. *Now.*"

Grant grabbed hold of Leo's hands and forced them down, pulled back enough to spill more lube on Leo's asshole, and then pressed in.

Leo's legs jerked and then his asshole seemed to tremble around Grant's cock and give way. Another good squirt of lube slicked the rest of the push inside, and Grant was satisfied that the fuck would be good for Leo now.

He came back to Leo's mouth, kissing him, as he screwed him with steady, surging thrusts. Leo squirmed beneath him, trying to get it faster and harder, jittering all over, and begging with everything he had. He kissed all the skin he could find—

Grant's mouth, chin, neck, ear—whatever he could get his lips against as he whined and moaned.

Grant trailed his hands down Leo's body, feeling the thick transplant scars, and thinking of how close it'd been, how fragile, how touch and go. He closed his eyes and drove into Leo's slick, convulsing heat, overwhelmed by how good it was to fuck him hard, to know that Leo was resilient and strong enough to take it.

Leo groaned under him, whimpered, and babbled. When the first trembling of Leo's haunches heralded an anal orgasm on the wat, Leo threw his head back, surrendering easily to the pleasure, and babbling incoherent gratitude. He thanked Grant for fucking him and for making him come like that. Taking aim, Grant fucked Leo harder, not being very careful, not taking his time, because Leo's body could take it, thank God, and Leo wanted it.

"Oh, God, Grant!" Leo's cock rubbed against Grant's stomach and, looking down at Leo's pleasure-torn face, he knew Leo was seconds away from losing his load. If Leo touched himself, he'd burst in just a few strokes, but Grant wanted to see if Leo could come just from this. Just from Grant fucking him hard.

When Leo started to reach for his own cock, Grant grabbed Leo's hands and held them both against the mattress. Fucking Leo faster, harder, making sure that his stomach rubbed over Leo's cock on each thrust, he stared down at Leo's wrecked face as Leo tossed his head on the pillow.

"*Grant*," Leo whimpered. "Please, oh…oh, ah!" Leo's eyes flew wide and he tensed, pressed his ass up to receive Grant's thrusts, and his mouth opened in a sweet O as he stared up into Grant's eyes and came hard with a small cry. Come burst from his straining cock, and slicked their stomachs.

Grant slowed down then, dragging his cock in and out more slowly as Leo jerked through aftershocks beneath him. Grant kissed Leo's eyes, his cheeks, and his lips. He stared down at him, studying every precious expression.

A few minutes later, Leo quivered, oversensitive, and Grant knew that it was hurting a little. So he slid in and out of him gently, still close to coming, but holding back, loving the way Leo shivered and bit his lip with each thrust.

It was strange, given how frantic the fuck had been, but, when his orgasm finally hit, it was sweet. A slow roll that started with Leo whispering Grant's name, and then pulsed through Grant's body with warm, intense heat. It left him sated, amazed, and somehow even more in love with Leo than before.

"I love you," Leo said.

Grant rubbed his nose against Leo's and then kissed his mouth. "I love you, too."

Leo smiled and laughed a little, his ass squeezing Grant's cock and setting off a series of sweet aftershocks that made Grant close his eyes and shiver.

"You make me happy," Leo said softly.

"Good." Grant ran his fingers lightly through Leo's hair. "That was my plan."

"You make good plans then."

Grant kissed him softly. His entire world held in the beating heart of the man in his arms.

• • •

Two Days Later

"HE'S GOING TO be my dad, so shut up," Lucky said with her hands on her hips.

Grant's eyes narrowed as he took in the small boy Lucky was talking to. The kid was wearing a pair of jeans and a T-shirt that proclaimed he was God's gift to football. Grant doubted that very much.

The small sea of children and their parents separating him from where Lucky was standing on the opposite side of the classroom didn't part for him. He tried to shoo some kids aside, but then it all went to hell.

"My dad said that doctor is a queer!" the boy said. "Your dads are fags!"

As Grant watched, Lucky's eyes went bright with rage. She balled her hand up into a fist and socked the hell out of the kid. He fell back about a foot. He blinked wildly and then he started to wail.

"You're mean!" Lucky yelled. "And I'll hit you again if you ever say mean things about my dads!"

The other parents and kids went silent. Everyone turned toward the drama, and Grant had an even harder time pushing through. He was only supposed to pick Lucky up from school because Leo had a follow-up appointment with Dr. Gregor in Raleigh. Grant hadn't expected picking her up to be an *event*.

The teacher, Mrs. Franklin, Grant believed her name was, got there before Grant. She hitched up her skirt and knelt by the boy, looking at his cheek where a bruise was swelling. Her wrinkled face twisted at what she found, and then she turned to Lucky. "There's never any call for violence, Miss Lucky Garner-Banks!"

At that, Grant shoved through the parents and said, "I beg to differ. She has my permission to slug anyone who calls her dad a fag."

Mrs. Franklin looked up from where she was tending the boy and said, "Mr. Anderson—"

"*Doctor* Anderson," Grant replied.

Mrs. Franklin looked pissed at that, but Grant was pretty sure he could take the bitch. The murmur from the parents behind him didn't surprise him either. He couldn't care less. Lucky could beat the shit out of anyone who tried to make her feel less for having two—or three—fathers.

"Dr. Anderson," Mrs. Franklin said nastily. She straightened her skirt as she rose. "There are rules at this school, and the number one rule has always been that violence of any kind will not be tolerated for any reason."

Grant put his hand on Lucky's head. "Well, Mrs. Franklin, I think I recall a big issue at the high school a few years ago? A Michael Dunfee? A bullying incident I believe it was, and it led to his suicide. I recall a huge march against hate speech. So let me say this now: it starts—and will stop—here."

Mrs. Franklin said, "Dr. Anderson, I'm not condoning what Robby said, but—"

Suddenly a small woman with dark hair and a nervous face was at Robby's side, saying, "Oh, baby, what happened? Are you okay?"

Grant rolled his eyes. The kid's mother. Great.

"He's fine," Grant said. "I'm a doctor. He'll live."

"He called my dad a fag," Lucky said, her arms crossed over her chest. "That's hate speech."

Grant bit the inside of his lip to keep the smirk from showing. Robby's mother looked up at Grant and Lucky and then down at the floor. She blushed and when she turned to her son she said, "Come on, Robby. Enough crying. If you can't take it, then don't dish it out."

"I just said—" the boy wailed.

His mother shook her head and said, "We'll talk about it at home." She looked at Grant as she got up from her crouching position and said, "Dr. Anderson, I apologize. My ex-husband and I have different views of life. I'll talk to my son."

Grant said, "See that you do. Or my daughter might break his nose next time." He took Lucky's arm, turned his back on

Mrs. Franklin, and said, "Come on. Let's go."

"Dr. Anderson, tell Mr. Garner that he'll be hearing from me," Mrs. Franklin called.

Grant clucked his tongue and said, "You do that. I'm sure that Leo will be thrilled talk to you again."

Mrs. Franklin blinked with gray, round eyes. Grant turned away from her, pushing his way through the waiting parents. He said with a chuckle, "Excuse us, please, or I'll sic my kid on you. She's got a great right hook."

"Really, Dr. Anderson," some other mother said, though she was smiling like she was amused. "Making a little girl fight for you?"

Grant held up his hand that wasn't holding onto Lucky's and said, "Surgeon. Gotta protect the hands."

The woman rolled her lips in like she was fighting off a laugh, though some of the other parents didn't look so amused. Grant pushed by the woman and ignored the other parents and their kids.

Lucky followed behind him and, once they were in the car, Lucky got strapped into her booster in the backseat. The booster seat had initially kind of given Grant pause when Leo installed it, but he'd quickly just rolled his eyes at himself and thought, "You have a kid. Get over it."

"Dr. Grant," Lucky said. "What's Mrs. Franklin gonna do? Is she gonna hate me now?"

Grant thought about the shiny new library Curtis was paying for, and Leo's face when he was determined. "Well, carrot, if she does, she'll regret it."

"Yeah?" Lucky asked.

"Yup." Grant pulled out of the school parking lot and said, "So ice cream?"

"What about dinner?" Lucky asked.

"Ice cream for dinner is a perfectly valid lifestyle choice," Grant said.

"What about Daddy?" Lucky said, and Grant looked at her in the rearview mirror. She was looking out the window with a peaceful expression on her face. She sat still and quiet in her seat. Along for the ride.

"We'll take a pint home for him."

Lucky laughed. "No, silly. He'll be mad that we ate ice cream instead of real food for dinner!"

"Oh," Grant said, shrugging. "Maybe. But he'll get over it."

Lucky sighed.

Grant looked at her in the mirror again. She smiled and rested her head against the back of the seat.

"It's okay to be mad sometimes, right?" she said.

Grant nodded. He reached back and patted her leg. "Yep. No matter what. You can get mad at me even. It won't make a difference. I'm not going anywhere."

"Yeah," Lucky said.

She sounded sure, as absolutely certain as Grant.

Chapter Twenty-Two

Four Weeks Later

GRANT HAD NEVER been fucked like this before. He'd been fucked into the mattress; he'd been screwed against a wall, and in a sling, and bent over holding onto the side of the bed for dear life. He'd been fucked slowly, and badly, and boringly, but he'd never been fucked like this.

He'd never been penetrated by a trembling, wild-eyed Leo Garner who stared at his face instead of his ass, and bit his own lip, and looked like he might cry. He'd never been made love to like this. In his life, he'd been fucked a lot, but what he was doing with Leo was an entirely new continent of sex, and it was kind of freaking him out.

When, earlier, Leo had looked at him through his lashes, flushing and bashful, Grant would have agreed to anything. But when Leo asked him if he could be the one to…and he'd gestured at Grant in a ridiculous way that somehow made it clear that Leo wanted to try topping, Grant had been more than happy to say hell yes. It'd been a long time. Sure, he preferred to top, but being fucked was pretty great, so he'd helped Leo through the preparation, and reconciled himself to the idea that since Leo had never done this before, it would probably be over before it had even begun.

But Leo was taking his time. He was slow, and thorough, and taking long breaks to just stare at Grant with shining eyes, to lean down to kiss his mouth, and be inside of him.

Leo didn't say much, didn't make much noise at all, which was so different from when he was underneath Grant taking dick that it was confusing at first. But Leo's intense gaze, the breathless wonder on his face as he stroked in and out in long, deep thrusts, made it clear that he loved it, and that he was overwhelmed in a completely different way.

When Leo had pushed in the first time, and Grant pressed down to open for him, Leo's eyes widened with a strange look of near-fear that'd passed into trembling tenderness. Then Grant had grunted, adjusting to the girth of Leo's cock, and Leo had almost come right then. Grant knew by the way Leo fought it back, biting his lip and closing his eyes, taking long breaths in and out. It'd taken Leo ages to get all the way inside Grant, and Leo had to stop and breathe through the urge to come several times.

Now Leo's lips were bitten red as he breathed, "Grant," and then bowed his head. His face broke into such sweet emotion that Grant's heart clenched. Tears stung his eyes.

It shocked him. It frightened him. He'd never felt this kind of thing before during sex. He'd felt love for Leo, and a need to bring *Leo* to a place like this, a place where Leo was open, and vulnerable to him, but this turnabout was something he'd never expected.

Grant took a shaky breath and gazed at the pulse throbbing in Leo's neck. Fear that Leo might see vulnerable Grant was twined through him. He was entirely out of control—not in a heated, crazed way, but in a fragile, slipping way that Grant could barely contain or understand. He was undone, like every bit of him was about to be exposed—his secrets, his weaknesses, his fears—and he couldn't meet Leo's gaze for fear that Leo would suddenly know them all.

Leo shifted on the next thrust.

"Ah!" Grant cried out, twisting under Leo as pleasure jolted like a livewire through his body.

"There," Leo whispered, pride in his tone.

Grant keened as his cock ached, jerked, and spilled pre-come.

Leo stroked against his prostate again. Grant clenched his hands in the sheets and went still under Leo's next thrust, groaning and breaking out into a sweat all over his body as the thrust hit the mark once more.

"Oh, God, Grant," Leo whispered. "I love watching you."

Grant ground his teeth together, twisting his hands in the sheets, trying to get a grip on his emotions. He shook as chills raced over him, and broken noises wrenched from his throat when Leo hit his prostate again and again. Grant's cock flexed, enervated beyond endurance, a good grip would bring him to a screaming climax. Leo reached between them running his fingers lightly over the wet head of Grant's cock, a zing of sensation that made Grant convulse. Licking the collected pre-come from his fingers, Leo said, "I love how you taste. I love it. I love you."

Leo focused on Grant's face again, like he couldn't get enough of Grant's pleasure, and the fuck grew even more intense. Leo was now faultless in his angle of penetration, raking his cock over Grant's prostate with every thrust. The jolting pleasure, the electric arcs of chills, and the buzz of too-much-but-so-good had set up camp in Grant's pelvis and brain. He was freaking out. It wasn't the sensations, it wasn't the fuck itself, it was Leo gazing down at him, Leo moving in him, Leo acting like Grant was so fucking precious and loved.

Grant whimpered. He tensed against how good it felt when Leo thrust again. He closed his eyes, taking a deep breath, trying to tell himself that he wouldn't fall apart from a fuck. But it wasn't a fuck; it was Leo, and Leo was making love to him. Grant felt stripped to his soul under so much adoration.

"Grant," Leo said. "Please look at me."

Grant opened his eyes, and Leo slammed his hips forward. The long slide of his cock into Grant was so fucking intense that Grant arched up and broke into jittery convulsions. He hooked his feet around Leo's waist, wanting to slow him down, to control the depth of each thrust because he couldn't take much more.

Leo didn't stop, though. He just cocked his head and studied Grant intently, his lips rolled inward with concentration, as he kept to the rhythm. Grant cried out, kicked at his back, scrabbled at the sheets with his fingers, and finally cracked open with pleasure. He sobbed, riding too much sensation, too much emotion, and Leo's eyes ate him up in his shuddering madness. Leo took him, and adored him, loved him so hard that Grant ached through and through. Grant wanted that love, he wanted it more than he could ever say, but he didn't know if... didn't know....

"You're scared," Leo said, seeming in awe of his own understanding. "You're scared for me to see you like this."

Oh, God. Leo knew. He knew what he was doing with his cock, what he was doing to Grant, how he was breaking him open emotionally. Leo kissed him again, and then redoubled his efforts, fucking him harder now, not faster, but forcefully, commanding Grant's body to respond. Grant's heart pounded, his dick throbbed, and he squirmed on Leo's cock. He pushed his hips up to take it easier, feeling like he was going to twist out of his skin it was so good. So scary.

God, he was terrified for Leo to see.

"Just look at me. Please, Grant, look at me," Leo whispered, thrusting in a rhythm that didn't give Grant time to get a better grip on his reactions, or to hold his face in some kind of expression that didn't reveal *everything*.

Leo was so tender, so in love, that Grant couldn't hold on

anymore, not when Leo murmured, "*I love you so much*," and gazed at him with open-mouthed adulation.

Grant slipped his hand between them, grabbed his own cock and squeezed it with Leo's thrusts. He wasn't going to last much longer, not with Leo staring at him like that, not with Leo pummeling his prostate, and not with Leo forcing Grant to look at him, to see how Leo loved him.

"It's okay," Leo said softly. "I've got you."

Grant would have laughed, but he was too far on the edge, too far out there, and wildly desperate for it to be true. He hoped that it was. He fell, dropped over into the terrifying fall of the fuck, of the love that Leo was making to him. He trusted Leo to have him, to be there when he hit bottom and smashed into hundreds of thousands of pieces, and then he did.

Grant came hard, sweaty, trembling, pulling at the sheets and struggling to keep his eyes open as Leo demanded, "Look at me. Don't take your eyes off me." And through the near-white-out of his own orgasm, he saw Leo's expression as Grant's ass tightened around Leo's cock, watched Leo's face collapse as he lost control, and they fell together, entangled, twitching, whimpering as they came and cried out as one.

Afterward, Leo didn't pull out, holding Grant close and staring down at him for a long time.

"I love you," Grant said. He hadn't intended to say it with so much need for reassurance in his voice. It just came out that way.

Leo stroked a hand over Grant's cheek. "I know. I love you, too. And whoever made you think that you weren't good enough for this was wrong. You're everything to me, Grant."

Grant swallowed and looked away. Leo took hold of his chin and made him look back.

"Did I do it okay?" Leo asked, eyes worried. "Was it all right?"

Grant blinked at him. Leo had just taken him apart, torn him down, and broken him completely with that *making love* thing he'd just done, and now Leo wanted to know if it was all right? Grant didn't *know*, actually. It'd been terrifying. He was a mess. He had no idea.

"Grant?" Leo asked.

"Yeah," Grant said, shifting a little. "You were amazing." The thickness of Leo's cock in his ass was still soul-shiveringly good, and he licked his lips. "You're still hard," he observed.

Leo nodded, looking worried, and Grant had to get that look off of his face. "I came, though," Leo said like he thought Grant didn't know.

"I remember," Grant said. "You've got me."

Leo's face softened in understanding and he said, "Yeah. I've got you, Grant. You don't have to worry. I've got you."

Grant nodded and said, "Well, then, maybe you should have me again."

Leo brushed his fingertips over Grant's eyebrows, down across his cheekbones, and leaned down to kiss his lips. Leo moved his hips, thrusting. Grant was still sensitive, and it was almost too much, but he relaxed and tried to open up for Leo, to let it happen. He gripped Leo's shoulders, holding him close, burying his face in Leo's neck as the pace picked up again. He could feel Leo's come squishing out of his ass with each thrust of Leo's cock easing the friction of the fuck. He wrapped his legs around Leo's waist, feeling the new transplant scar rub against his thigh as Leo moved.

Leo kissed Grant's neck and murmured romantic nonsense in his ear. Grant listened hard, taking in every word.

"I love you," Leo said. "I love you so much. You're amazing. Everything to me."

Grant's eyes rolled up as Leo fucked him harder, clinging to

Leo as he was taken apart again. This time, it wasn't as hard to let go, to fall, and to let Leo have him. It was better, even, because this time he knew he was going to be okay. Leo loved him.

And Leo wasn't letting go.

Chapter Twenty-Three

One Month Later

THE OUTDOOR RECEPTION at the farm was relatively low-key, and exactly the way that Leo had wanted it. Grant, for his part, hadn't cared so long as they got married and he didn't have to profess a belief in God in order to do it in a church. So, they'd chosen the open space by the Garner Pond, and Leo had decided that the reception could be held around the barn.

There was a dance floor set up inside the barn, and a DJ that Hannah had arranged. She was dating the guy. Apparently, he was in her Narcotics Anonymous group, though Grant wasn't supposed to know that, but he might have been privy to Sheriff Marie's plan to put a tail on the skinny-looking kid when Hannah first mentioned him. In fact, Grant might have been the one to call Marie to suggest the idea.

"Oh, my God, Grant! It was beautiful!" Alec said, dragging Grant into a hug and holding him tight.

When Alec released him, Grant grabbed a second piece of wedding cake and shoveled a bite into his mouth. He pointed his fork to where Leo was dancing with his mother.

"It wasn't *The English Patient.*"

"Nope," Alec agreed, nodding, and looking ridiculously pleased with himself. "It was, however, a triumph of the human heart."

"No," Grant said. "It was a terrible, over-the-top, tear-jerker. I'd be demanding my money back if Leo somehow convinced me to see it in the theater."

Alec rolled his eyes and huffed. "Oh, come on. It was epic."

Grant caught Leo's eye and his heart clenched at the smile aimed his way. He lifted his chin in acknowledgment of it, wanting to go over and kiss the grin off of his brand-spanking-new husband's face.

"Yeah, it was," Grant agreed.

Alec placed a hand over his chest, faking a heart attack from shock. "You agree with me?"

Grant handed him the now empty plate and his empty champagne glass, too. "Hold these."

As he moved through the crowded dance floor, he saw Lucky dancing with one of her cousins, and he laughed at how she kept stomping on the boy's toes. He noticed Nurse Aiden chatting up Mr. Superstar Banks in the corner by the punch bowl, and he rolled his eyes imagining the drama that might unfold from that potential connection.

Grant tapped Meryl's shoulder and asked, "May I cut in?"

She kissed his cheek and said, "Of course you can. He's your husband after all."

Leo grinned and wrapped his arm around Grant's waist, pulling him closer than their ridiculous dance lessons had allowed in the mirror-lined classroom.

"So," Leo said, happily. "What's the plan for tonight?"

"Well, you'd better be the blushing virgin you've made yourself out to be, or I'll have the wedding annulled before you can say cheese-whiz tomato."

Leo cracked up, and Grant pressed their foreheads together. Leo whispered, "Holy crap, we're married, Grant."

Grant brought his hand to Leo's cheek and kissed him hard. He heard the whistles and cheers, but he didn't let go. He kissed Leo until he needed to see his face to know that Leo felt the same.

Grant pulled back and gazed into Leo's eyes.

"I love you," Leo said.

Grant nodded, kissed him again, and was about to answer that he loved Leo, too, when the noise of a low-flying prop plane droned so close that it was impossible to ignore.

"C'mon," Leo said, tugging him out of the barn and toward the pasture. Once they were both out there, Leo pointed up at the sky.

MORE THAN BACON

The banner flying behind the plane proclaimed it for all the world to read. Grant snorted and started laughing. Leo laughed, too, as he asked, "Isn't it great?"

Grant rolled his eyes. It was horrible. And he couldn't stop smiling. He thought his face was going to break from it. "You're ridiculous."

Leo nodded, wrapped his arms around Grant's waist, and pointed up at the sky again. "And you love me more than bacon."

Grant shrugged helplessly. What could he say? It was true. More than true. "I love you more than anything."

Leo's grin was beautifully bright. If Grant could, he'd frame Leo's happiness and hang it on the wall. He'd look at it every day and it'd be the greatest accomplishment of his life.

As the plane circled around to leave, Grant noticed that on the reverse side of the banner, there was an odd imperative.

"Does that mean something?" Grant asked. The words didn't ring a bell to him.

Leo shrugged. "I don't know. Maybe it's a wedding wish from the pilot."

Grant's eyes narrowed against the bright light of the sky. Lucky ran up to them, shouting excitedly about the plane, demanding to know what the banner meant. Grant picked her up, and the three of them stood together watching the plane fly into the distance until the words became unreadable.

Then Leo kissed Grant's cheek, and Lucky struggled down from his arms. A new song filled the silence left by the plane, and Leo and Lucky whooped together as the dancing began again. Grant stared up at the blue, brilliant sky.

After several long moments, Grant turned back to the party, grinning at the sight of his kid and his husband dancing in the grass in front of the barn. Things weren't perfect. Leo's health was always going to be fragile. The average life expectancy post heart-transplant wasn't anything Grant wanted to dwell too long on, even with a new kidney helping out. Still, this farm, these people, and this life was everything to him. It was all his to have and love as long as he could hold on to it.

He threw self-consciousness aside to swoop Lucky into his arms and move to the music with Leo. Clinging to each other, a brand-new family, they laughed and kissed and danced. Through it all, the words on the back of the banner burned through Grant with a fiery hope.

STAY LUCKY

THE END

If you loved Leo and Grant and want to read SIX steamy bonus stories with them, sign up for my newsletter for immediate access!

Dear Reader,

Thank you so much for reading *Stay Lucky*! I hope you enjoyed reading it as much as I enjoyed writing it. Originally released under the same title via my former pen name, Halsey Harlow, this retouched version has been released now under my main nom de plume—your very own Leta Blake!

Be sure to follow me on BookBub or Goodreads to be notified of upcoming and new releases. And look for me on Facebook for snippets of the day-to-day writing life, or join my Facebook Group for announcements and special giveaways. To see some sources of my inspiration, you can follow my Pinterest boards or Instagram.

If you enjoyed the book, please take a moment to leave a review! Reviews not only help readers determine if a book is for them, but also help a book show up in site searches.

Also, for the audiobook connoisseurs out there, many of my other books are now available in audio, narrated by John Solo or Michael Ferraiuolo. I hope to eventually add my entire backlist to my audiobook offerings over the next few years.

Thank you for being a reader!
Leta

Standalone

VESPERTINE

by Leta Blake & Indra Vaughn

Can a priest and a rock star obey love's call?

Seventeen years ago, Jasper Hendricks and Nicholas Blumfeld's childhood friendship turned into a secret, blissful love affair. They spent several idyllic months together until Jasper's calling to the Catholic priesthood became impossible to ignore. Left floundering, Nicky followed his own trajectory into rock stardom, but he never stopped looking back.

Today, Jasper pushes boundaries as an out, gay priest, working hard to help vulnerable LGBTQ youth. He's determined to bring change to the church and the world. Respected, admired, and settled in his skin, Jasper has long ignored his loneliness.

As Nico Blue, guitarist and songwriter for the band Vespertine, Nicky owns the hearts of millions. He and his bandmates have toured the world, lighting their fans on fire with their music. Numbed by drugs and fueled by simmering anger, Nicky feels completely alone. When Vespertine is forced to get sober, Nicky returns home to where it all started.

Jasper and Nicky's careers have ruled their lives since they parted as teens. When they come face to face again, they must choose between the past's lingering ghosts or the promise of a new future.

ANY GIVEN LIFETIME

by Leta Blake

He'll love him in any lifetime.

Neil isn't a ghost, but he feels like one. Reincarnated with all his memories from his prior life, he spent twenty years trapped in a child's body, wanting nothing more than to grow up and reclaim the love of his life.

As an adult, Neil finds there's more than lost time separating them. Joshua has built a beautiful life since Neil's death, and how exactly is Neil supposed to introduce himself? As Joshua's long-dead lover in a new body? Heartbroken and hopeless, Neil takes refuge in his work, developing microscopic robots called nanites that can produce medical miracles.

When Joshua meets a young scientist working on a medical project, his soul senses something his rational mind can't believe. Has Neil truly come back to him after twenty years? And if the impossible is real, can they be together at long last?

Any Given Lifetime is a stand-alone, slow burn, second chance gay romance by Leta Blake featuring reincarnation and true love. This story includes some angst, some steam, an age gap, and, of course, a happy ending.

Book One in the Heat of Love series

SLOW HEAT

by Leta Blake

A lustful young alpha meets his match in an older omega with a past.

Professor Vale Aman has crafted a good life for himself. An unbonded omega in his mid-thirties, he's long since given up hope that he'll meet a compatible alpha, let alone his destined mate. He's fulfilled by his career, his poetry, his cat, and his friends.

When Jason Sabel, a much younger alpha, imprints on Vale in a shocking and public way, longings are ignited that can't be ignored. Fighting their strong sexual urges, Jason and Vale must agree to contract with each other before they can consummate their passion.

But for Vale, being with Jason means giving up his independence and placing his future in the hands of an untested alpha—as well as facing the scars of his own tumultuous past. He isn't sure it's worth it. But Jason isn't giving up his destined mate without a fight.

This is a gay romance novel, 118,000 words, with a strong happy ending, as well as a well-crafted, **non-shifter** omegaverse, with alphas, betas, omegas, male pregnancy, heat, and **knotting**. Content warning for pregnancy loss and aftermath.

Other Books by Leta Blake

Contemporary

Will & Patrick Wake Up Married
Will & Patrick's Endless Honeymoon
Cowboy Seeks Husband
The Difference Between
Bring on Forever
Stay Lucky

Sports

The River Leith

The Training Season Series
Training Season
Training Complex

Musicians

Smoky Mountain Dreams
Vespertine

New Adult

Punching the V-Card

Winter Holidays

The Home for the Holidays Series
Mr. Frosty Pants
Mr. Naughty List
Mr. Jingle Bells

Fantasy

Any Given Lifetime

Re-imagined Fairy Tales

Flight
Levity

Paranormal & Shifters

Angel Undone
Omega Mine

Horror

Raise Up Heart

Omegaverse

Heat of Love Series
Slow Heat
Alpha Heat
Slow Birth
Bitter Heat

For Sale Series
Heat for Sale

Coming of Age

'90s Coming of Age Series
Pictures of You
You Are Not Me

Audiobooks

Leta Blake at Audible

Discover more about the author online

Leta Blake
letablake.com

About the Author

Author of the bestselling book *Smoky Mountain Dreams* and the fan favorite Omegaverse series *Heat of Love*, Leta Blake's educational and professional background is in psychology and finance, respectively. However, her passion has always been for writing. She enjoys crafting romance stories and exploring the psyches of imaginary people. At home in the Southern U.S., Leta works hard at achieving balance between her writing and her family life.